Copyright © 2020 by Gavin Aung Than
Original interior design by Gavin Aung Than and
Benjamin Fairclough © Penguin Random House Australia Pty Ltd.

All rights reserved. Published in the United States by Random House Children's Books,
a division of Penguin Random House LLC, New York. Originally published by Puffin Books,
an imprint of Penguin Random House Australia Pty Ltd., Sydney, in 2020.

Random House and the colophon are registered trademarks of Penguin Random House LLC.
RH Graphic with the book design is a trademark of Penguin Random House LLC.

Visit us on the Web! rhcbooks.com

Educators and librarians, for a variety of teaching tools,
visit us at RHTeachersLibrarians.com

Library of Congress Cataloging-in-Publication Data is available upon request.
ISBN 978-0-593-17516-3 (trade pbk.)
ISBN 978-0-593-17513-2 (hardcover)
ISBN 978-0-593-17515-6 (ebook)

The artist used Adobe Photoshop to create the illustrations for this book.
The text of this book is set in 11-point Sugary Pancake.
This edition's cover and interior design by Sylvia Bi and colorization by Sarah Stern

MANUFACTURED IN CHINA
10 9 8 7 6 5 4 3 2 1
First American Edition

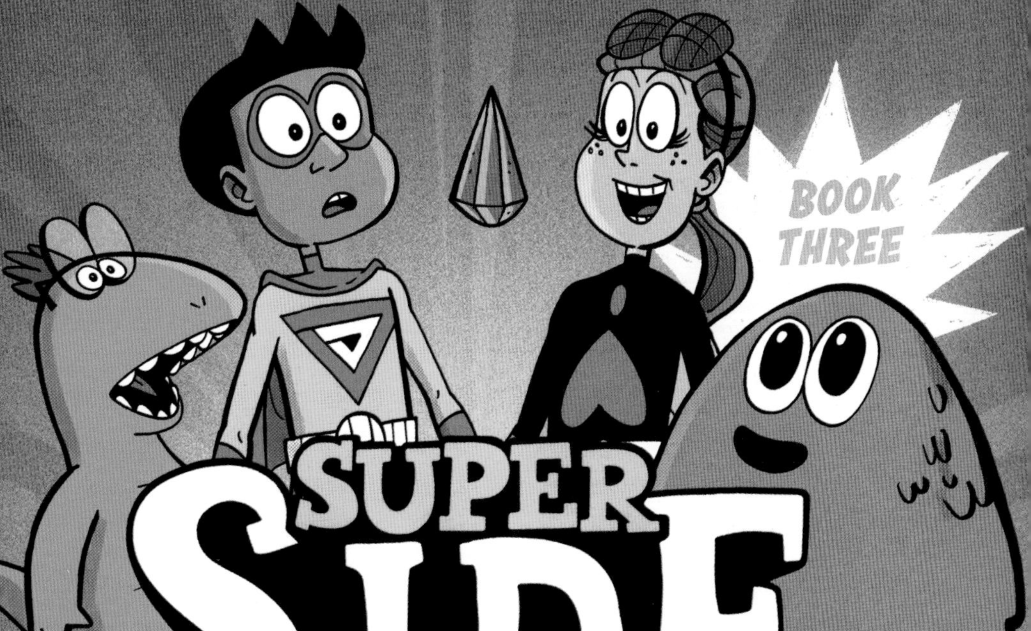
BOOK THREE

SUPER SIDEKICKS

TRIAL OF HEROES

Gavin Aung Than

Color by Sarah Stern

Random House New York

PREVIOUSLY . . .

Four superhero sidekicks were sick of being bullied by their selfish grown-up partners, so they decided to form their own team. They are the . . .

SUPER SIDEKICKS!

JUNIOR JUSTICE

Born leader. Expert martial artist. Brilliant detective. Assisted by Ada, the world's most advanced belt buckle.

FLYGIRL

Acrobatic flyer. Bug whisperer. Cricket lover (the sport and the insect). Uses dangerous bug balls to subdue enemies.

DINOMITE

Dinosaur shape-shifter. Physics professor. Poetry connoisseur. Would rather be reading a book.

GOO

Limitless stretch factor. Untapped power potential. Still has nightmares about his past as a bad guy.

THE GROWN-UPS

Captain Perfect, the world's most beloved (and obnoxious) superhero; Rampagin' Rita, simple yet scary strong; and Blast Radius, who hasn't met a problem he couldn't solve by blowing it up.

Chapter 1

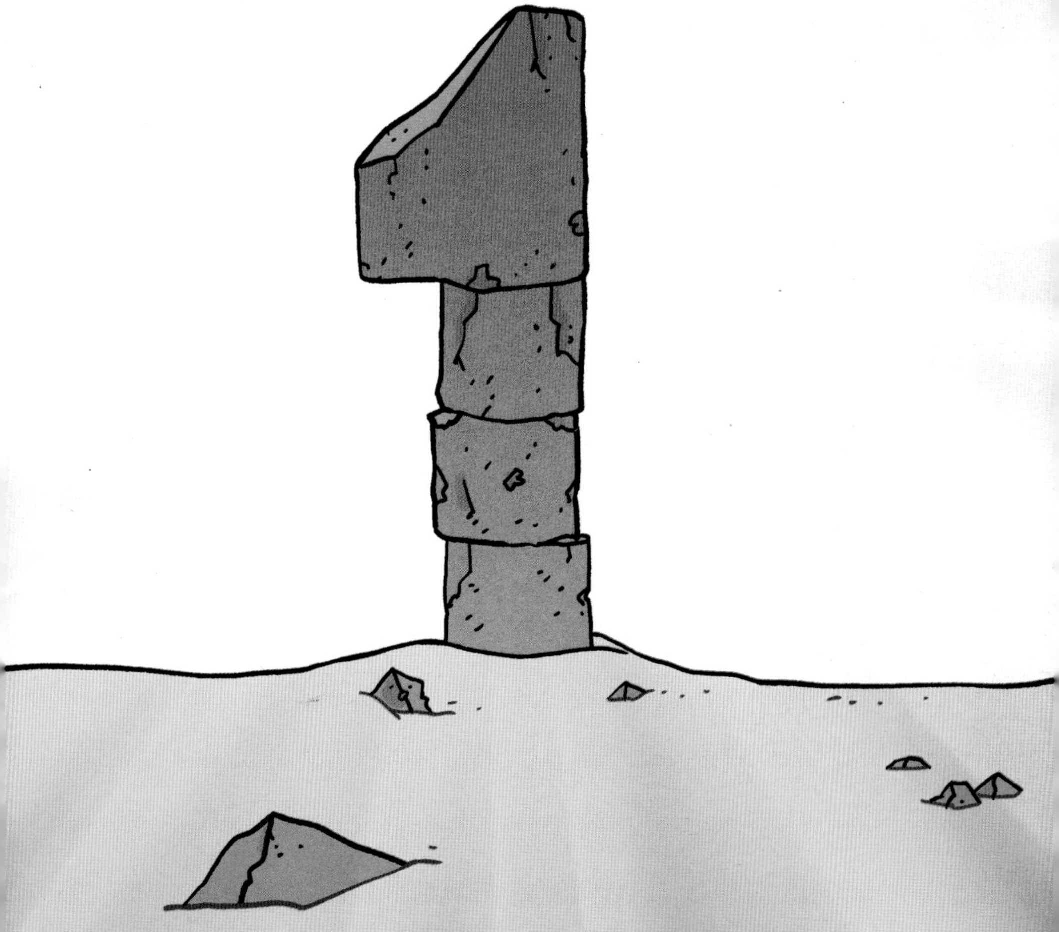

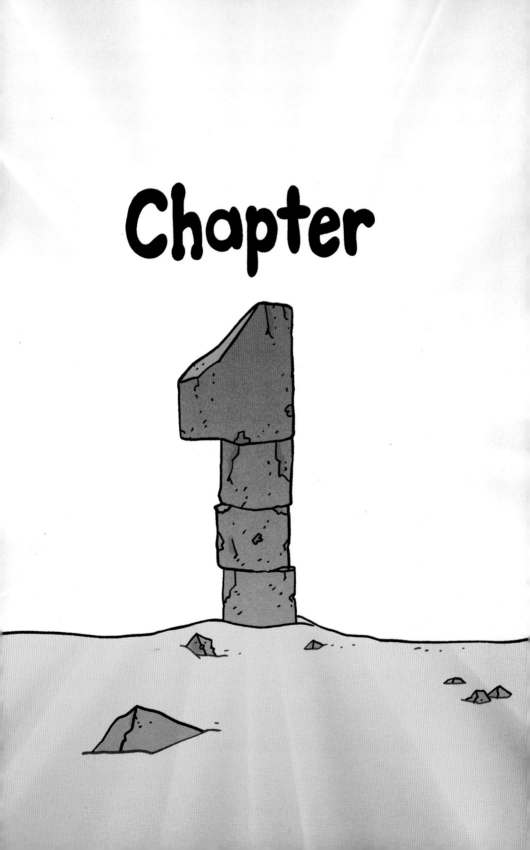

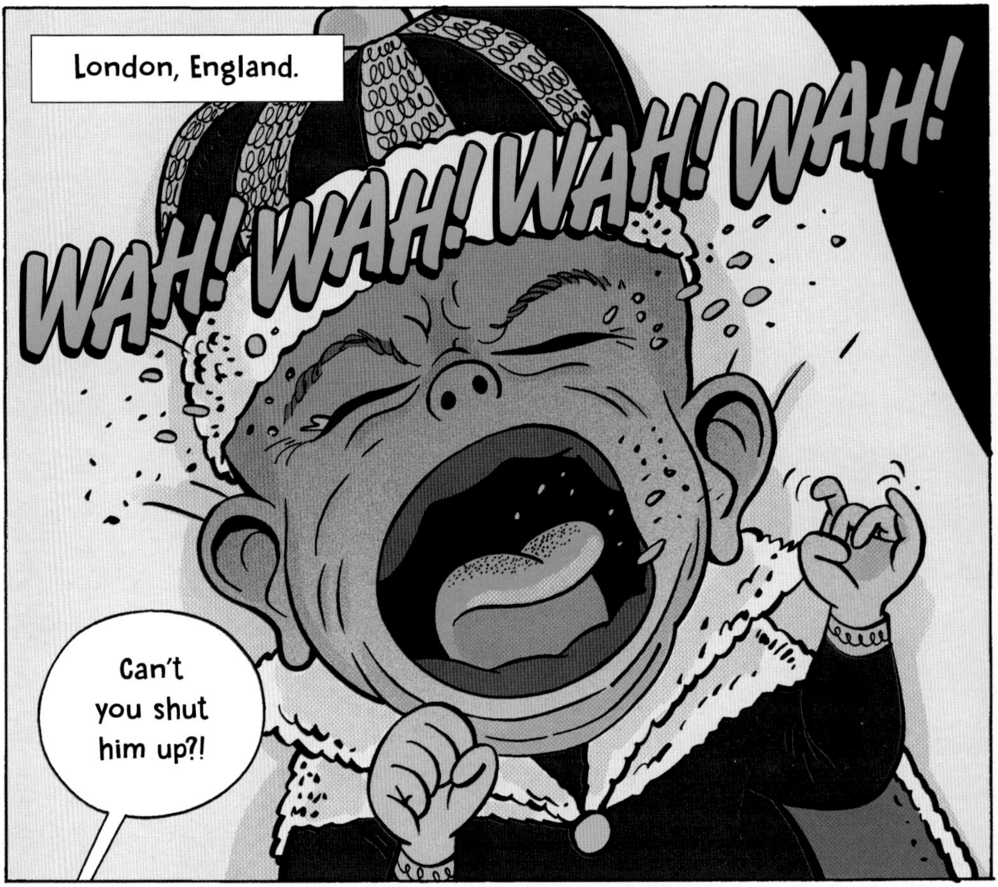
London, England.
WAH! WAH! WAH! WAH!
Can't you shut him up?!

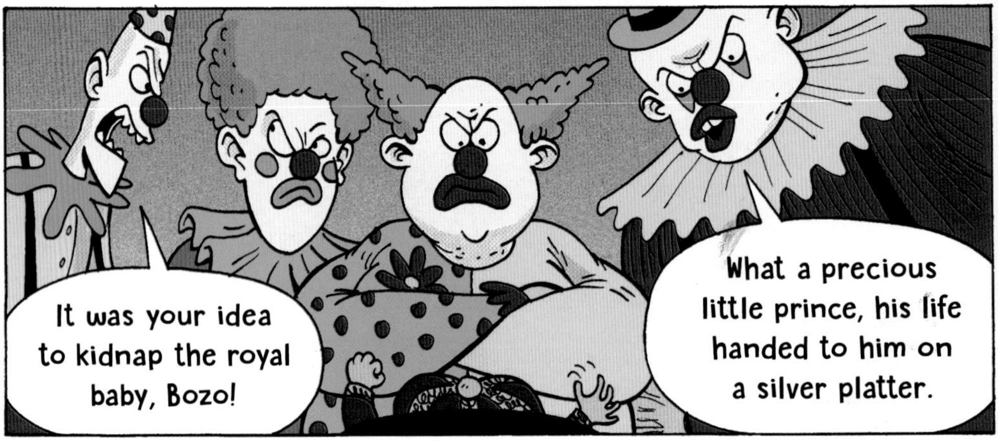
It was your idea to kidnap the royal baby, Bozo!
What a precious little prince, his life handed to him on a silver platter.

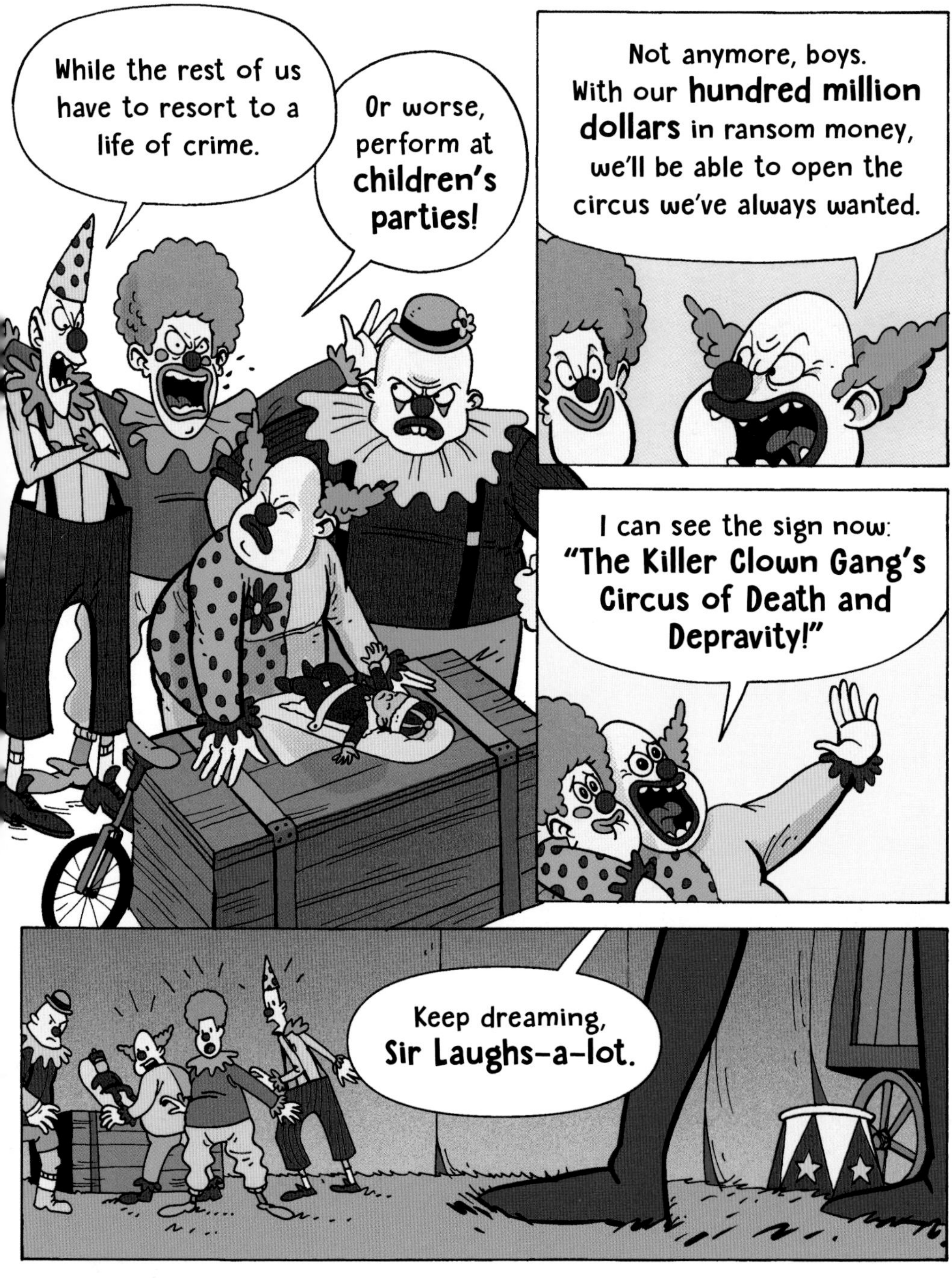
While the rest of us have to resort to a life of crime.
Or worse, perform at children's parties!
Not anymore, boys. With our hundred million dollars in ransom money, we'll be able to open the circus we've always wanted.
I can see the sign now: "The Killer Clown Gang's Circus of Death and Depravity!"
Keep dreaming, Sir Laughs-a-lot.

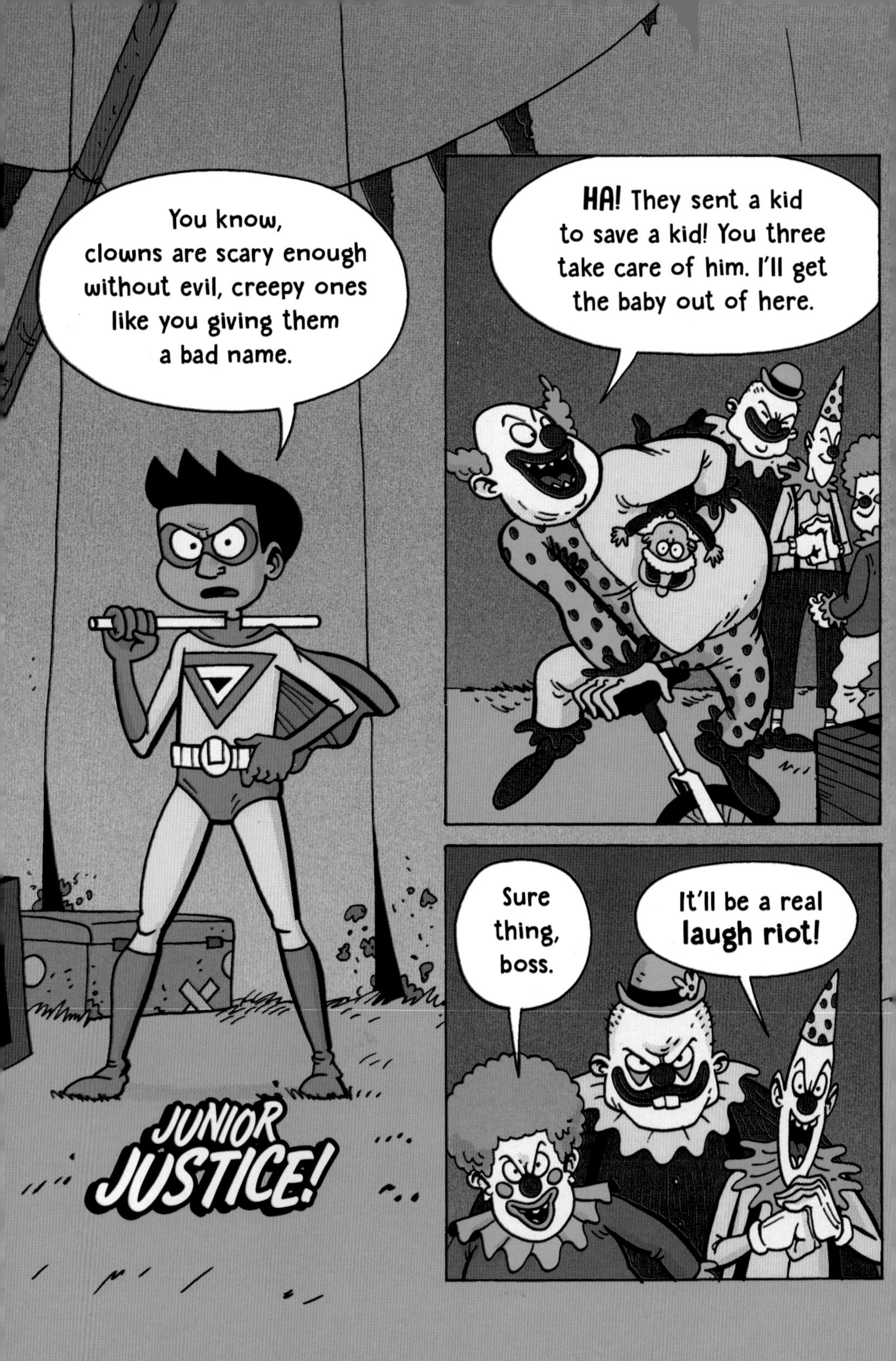

You know, clowns are scary enough without evil, creepy ones like you giving them a bad name.
JUNIOR JUSTICE!
HA! They sent a kid to save a kid! You three take care of him. I'll get the baby out of here.
Sure thing, boss.
It'll be a real laugh riot!

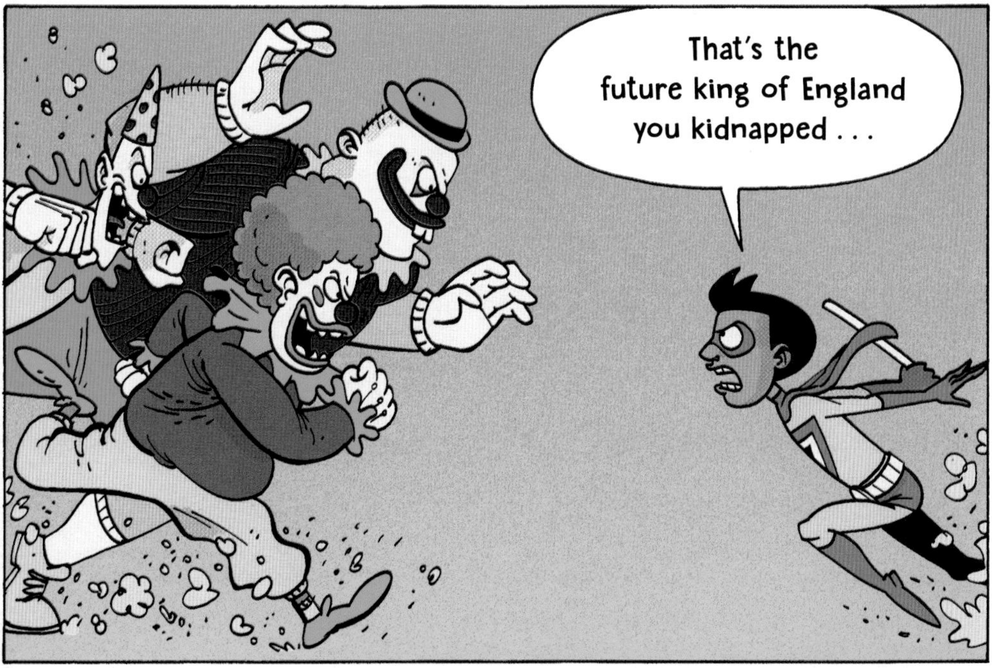
That's the future king of England you kidnapped . . .

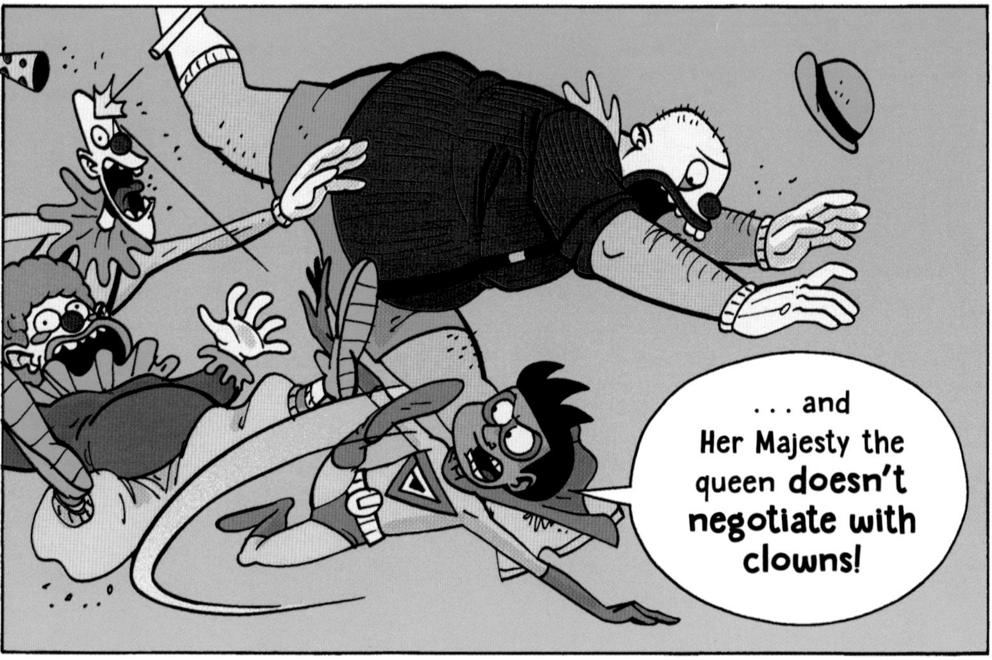
. . . and Her Majesty the queen doesn't negotiate with clowns!

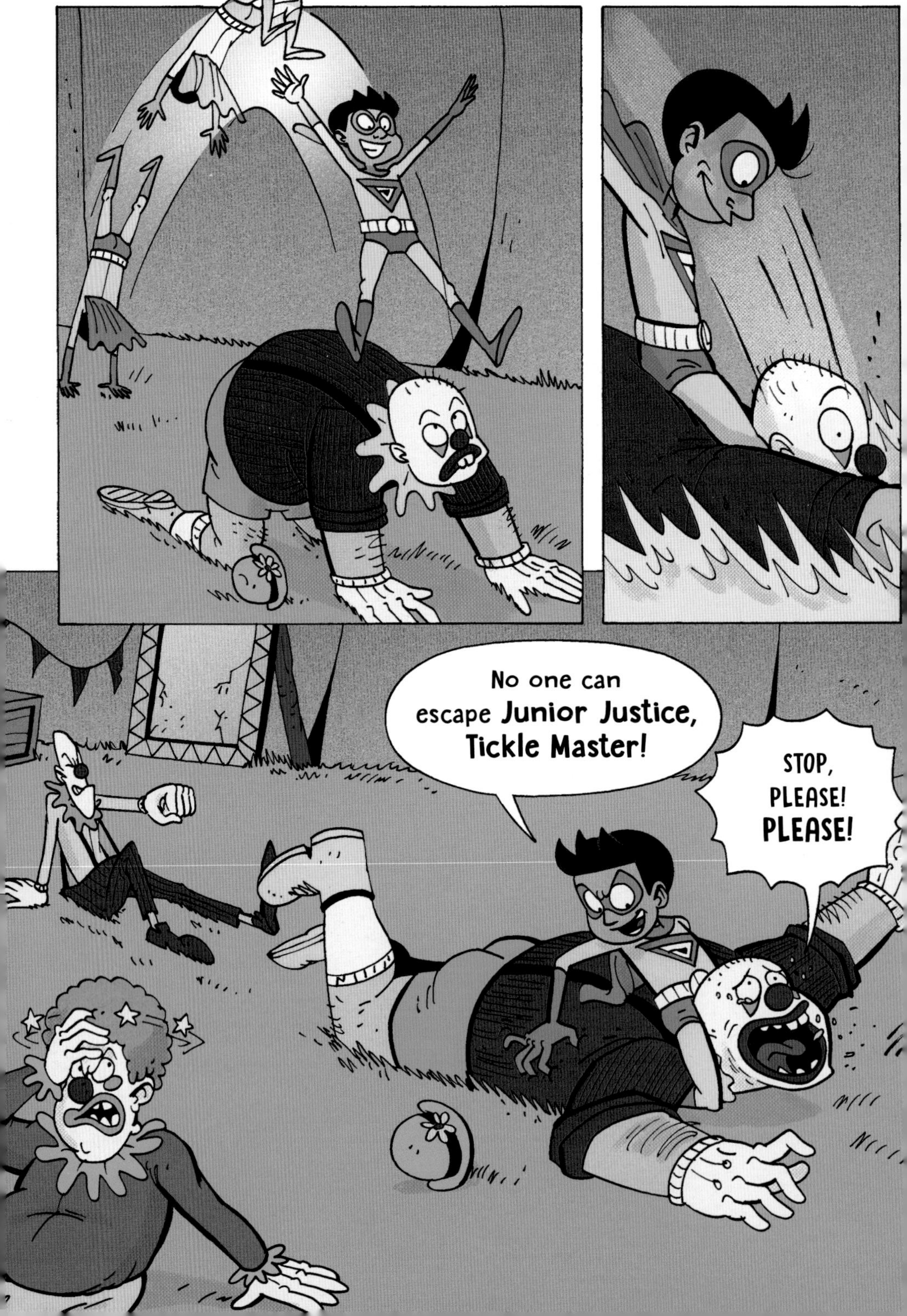
No one can escape Junior Justice, Tickle Master!
STOP, PLEASE! PLEASE!

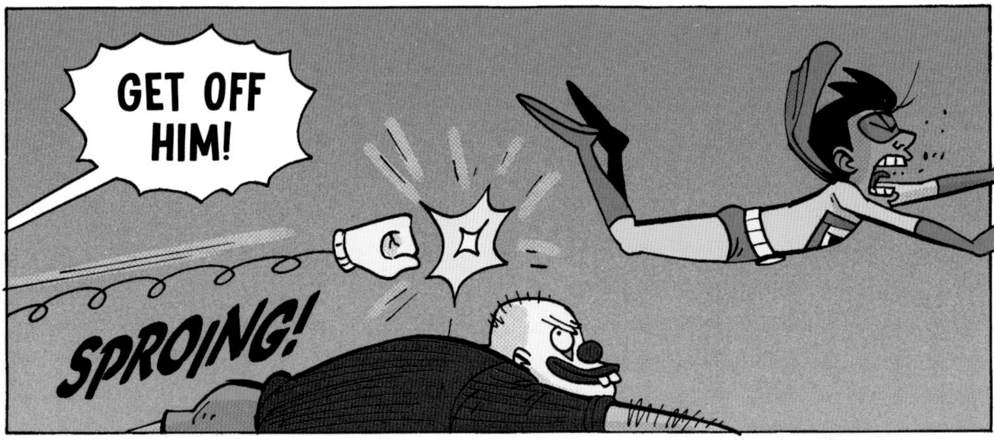
GET OFF HIM!
SPROING!

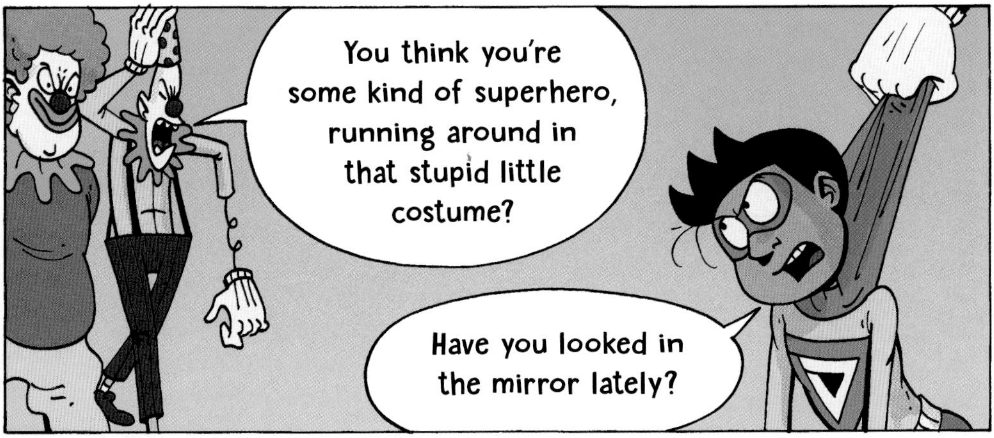
You think you're some kind of superhero, running around in that stupid little costume?
Have you looked in the mirror lately?

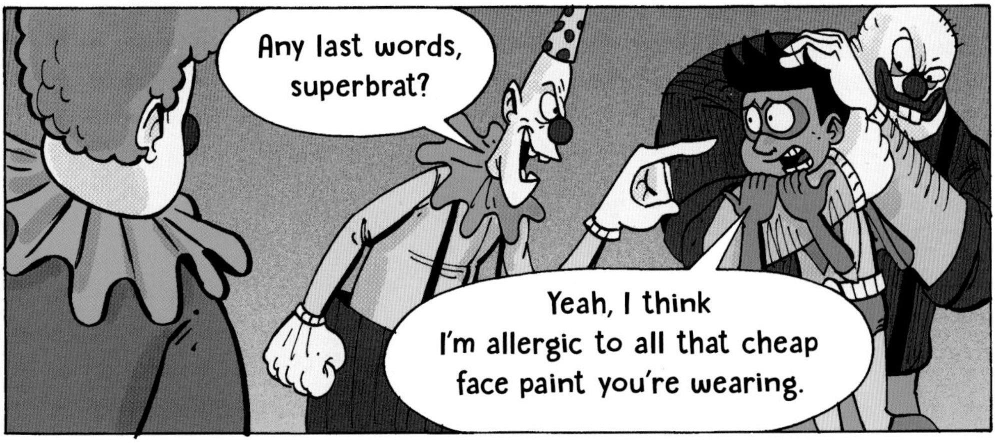
Any last words, superbrat?
Yeah, I think I'm allergic to all that cheap face paint you're wearing.

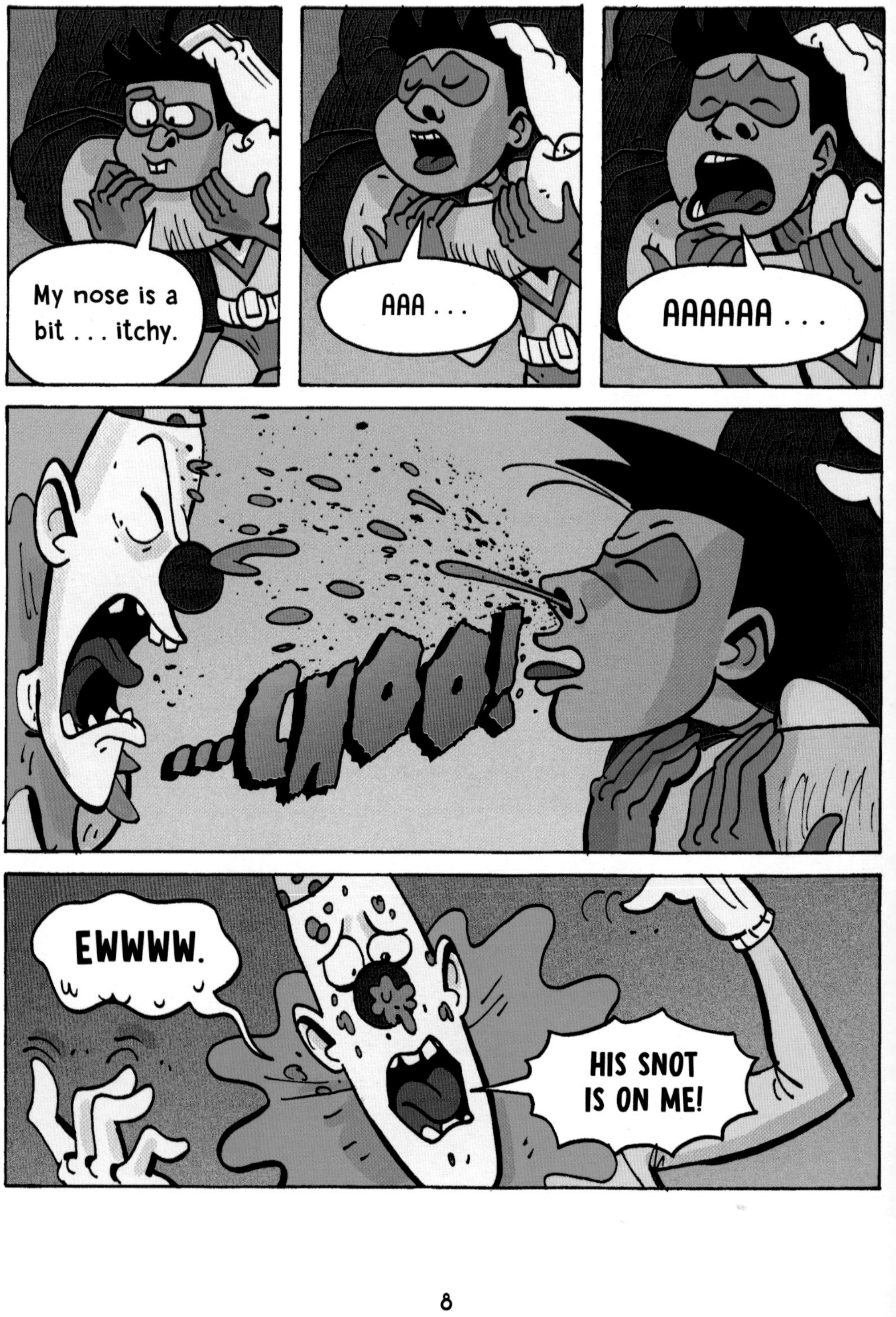

My nose is a bit . . . itchy.
AAA . . .
AAAAAA . . .
CHOO!
EWWWW.
HIS SNOT IS ON ME!

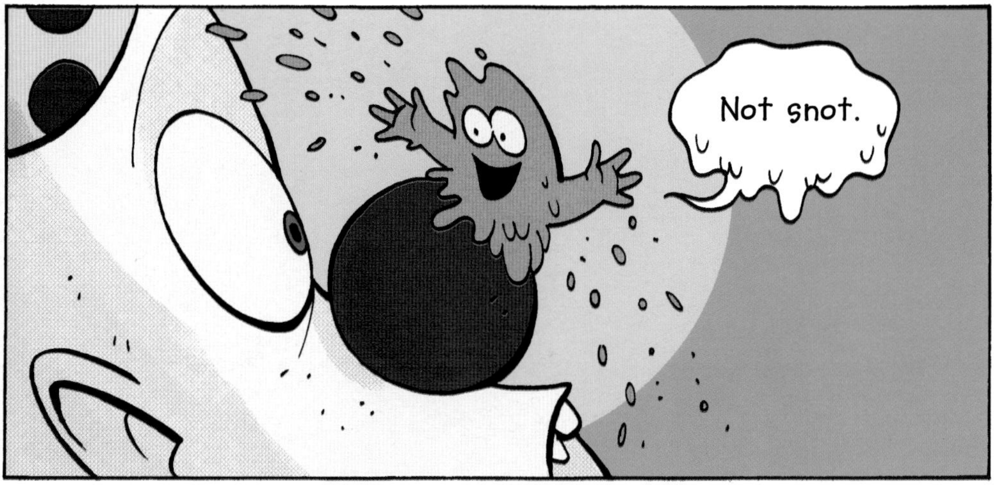
Not snot.

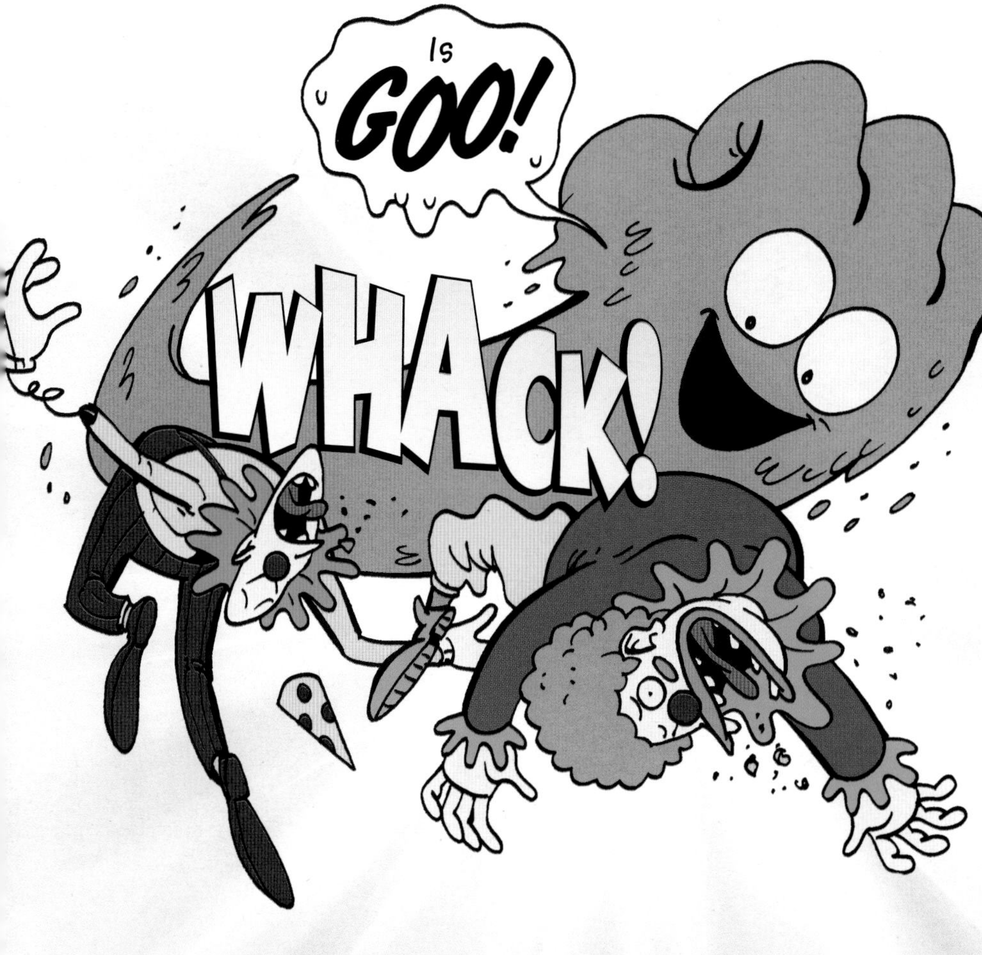
Is GOO!
WHACK!

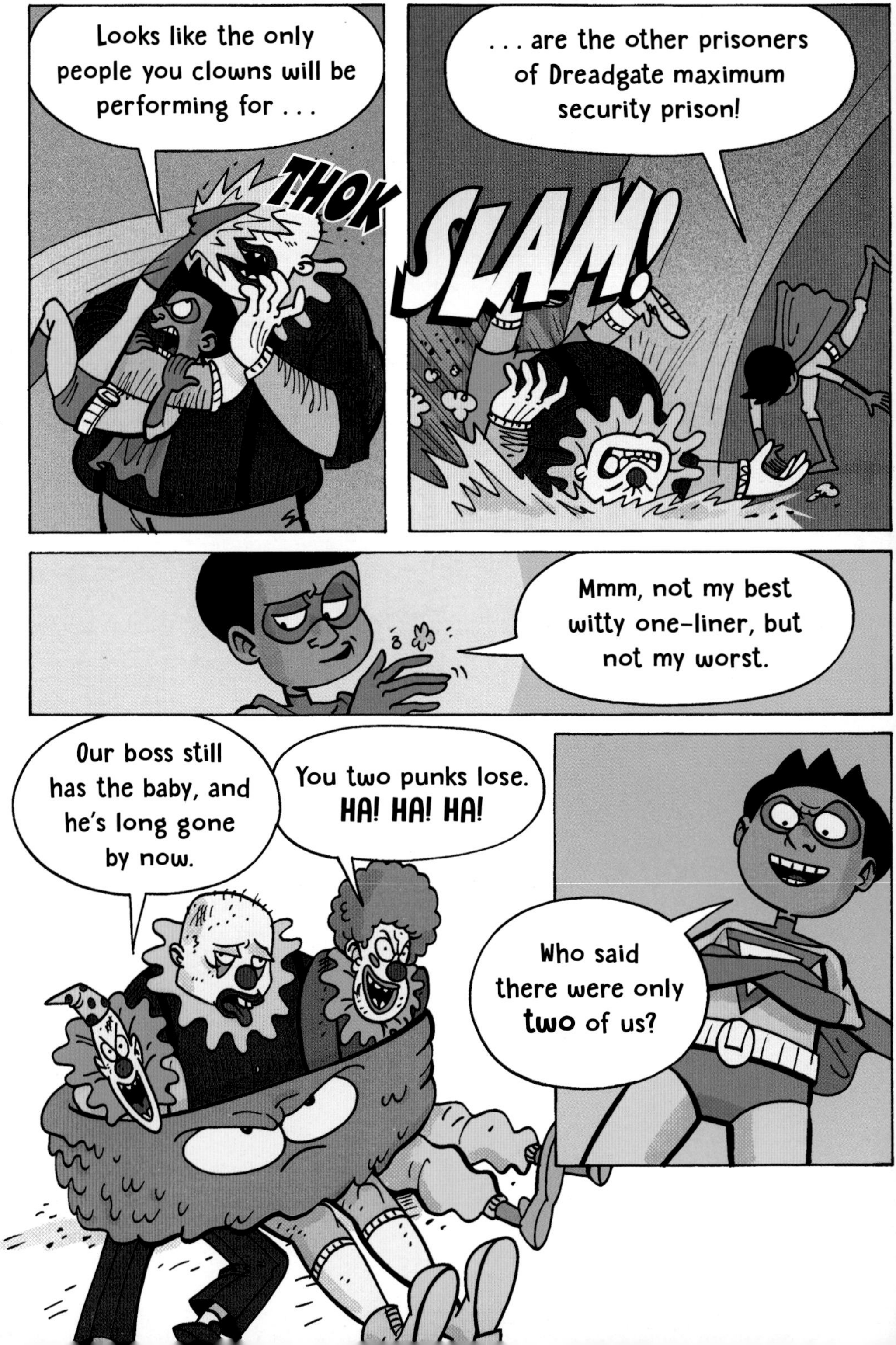

Looks like the only people you clowns will be performing for . . .
THOK
SLAM!
. . . are the other prisoners of Dreadgate maximum security prison!
Mmm, not my best witty one-liner, but not my worst.
Our boss still has the baby, and he's long gone by now.
You two punks lose. HA! HA! HA!
Who said there were only two of us?

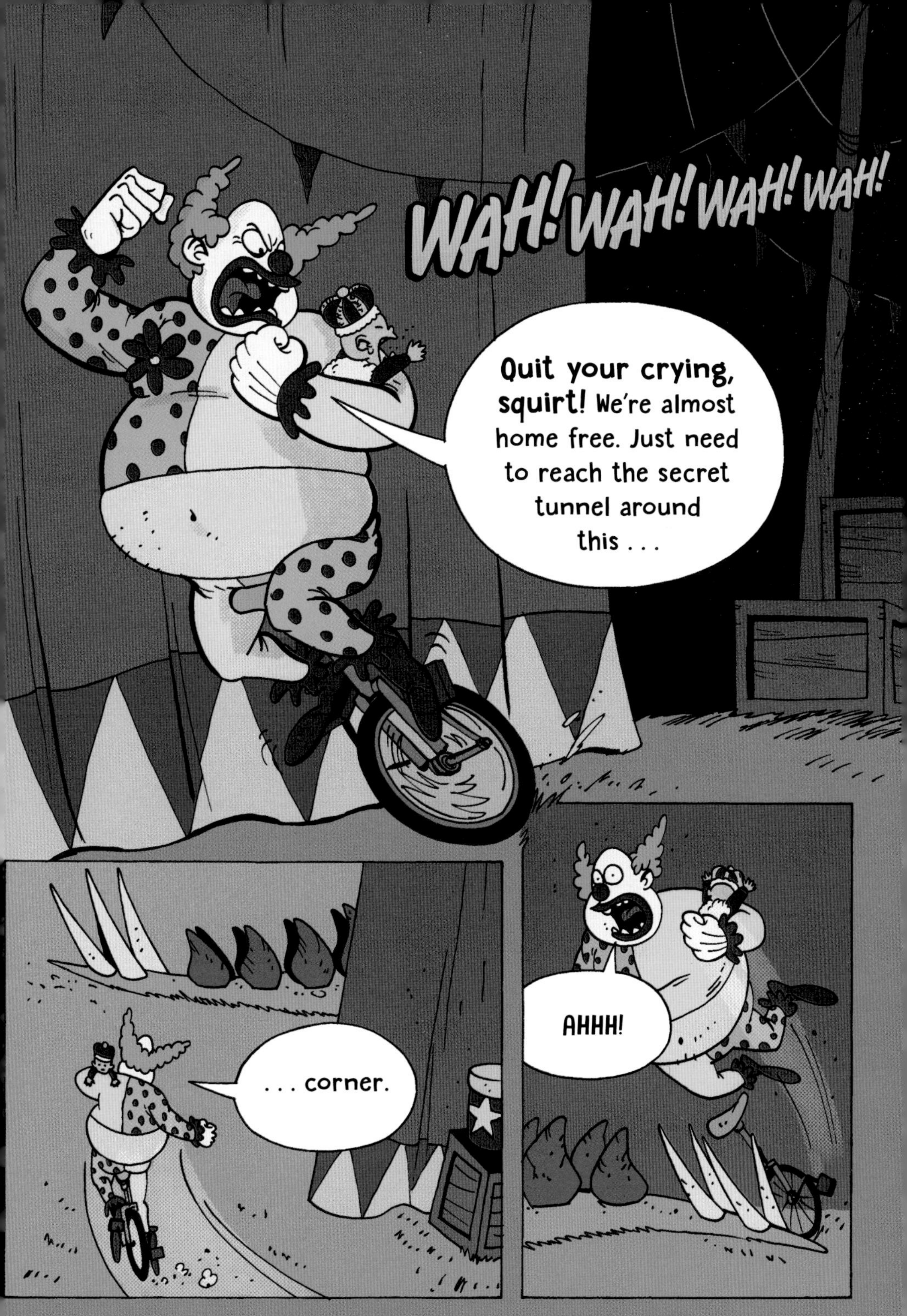
WAH! WAH! WAH! WAH!
Quit your crying, squirt! We're almost home free. Just need to reach the secret tunnel around this . . .
. . . corner.
AHHH!

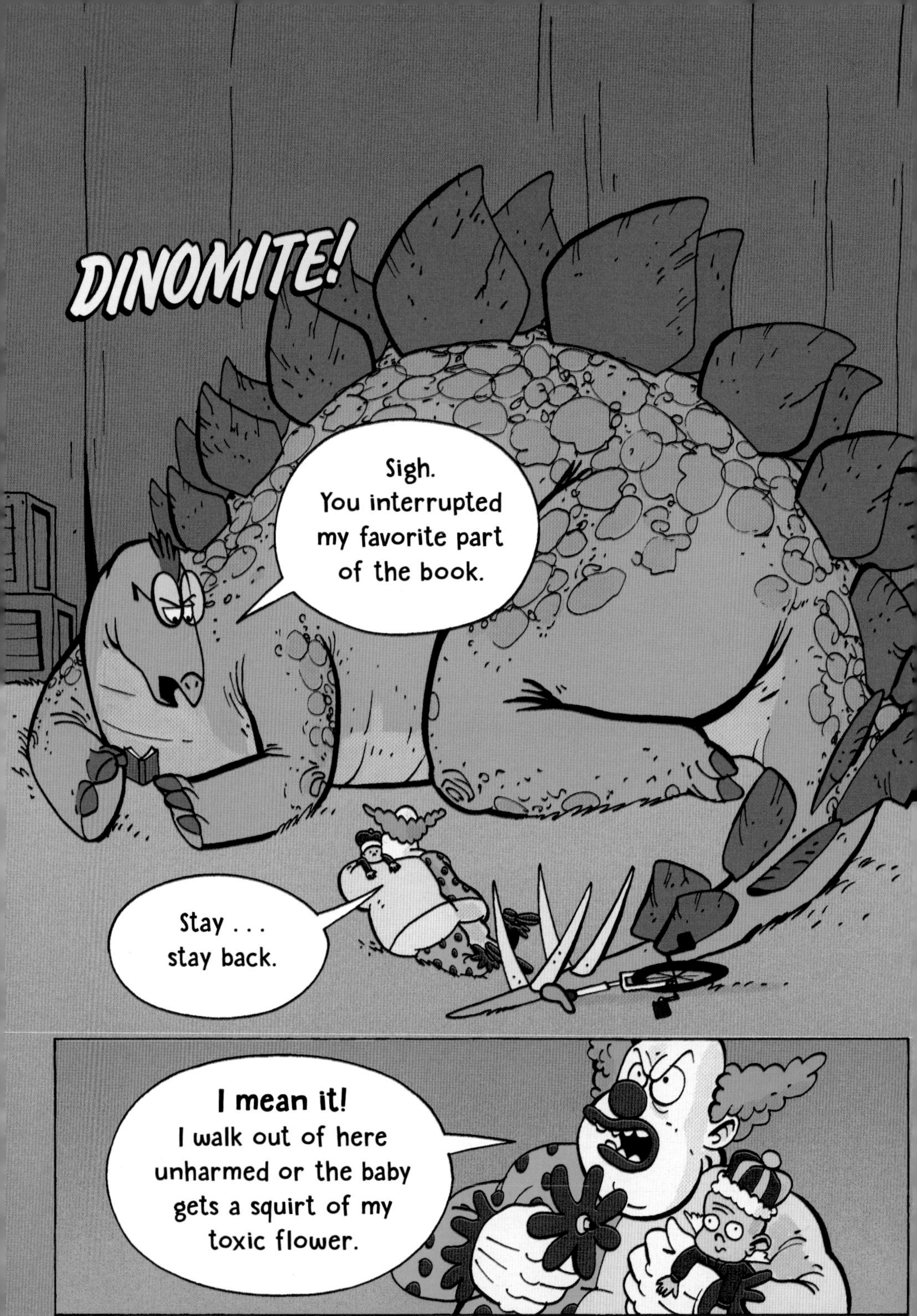
DINOMITE!
Sigh. You interrupted my favorite part of the book.
Stay . . . stay back.
I mean it! I walk out of here unharmed or the baby gets a squirt of my toxic flower.

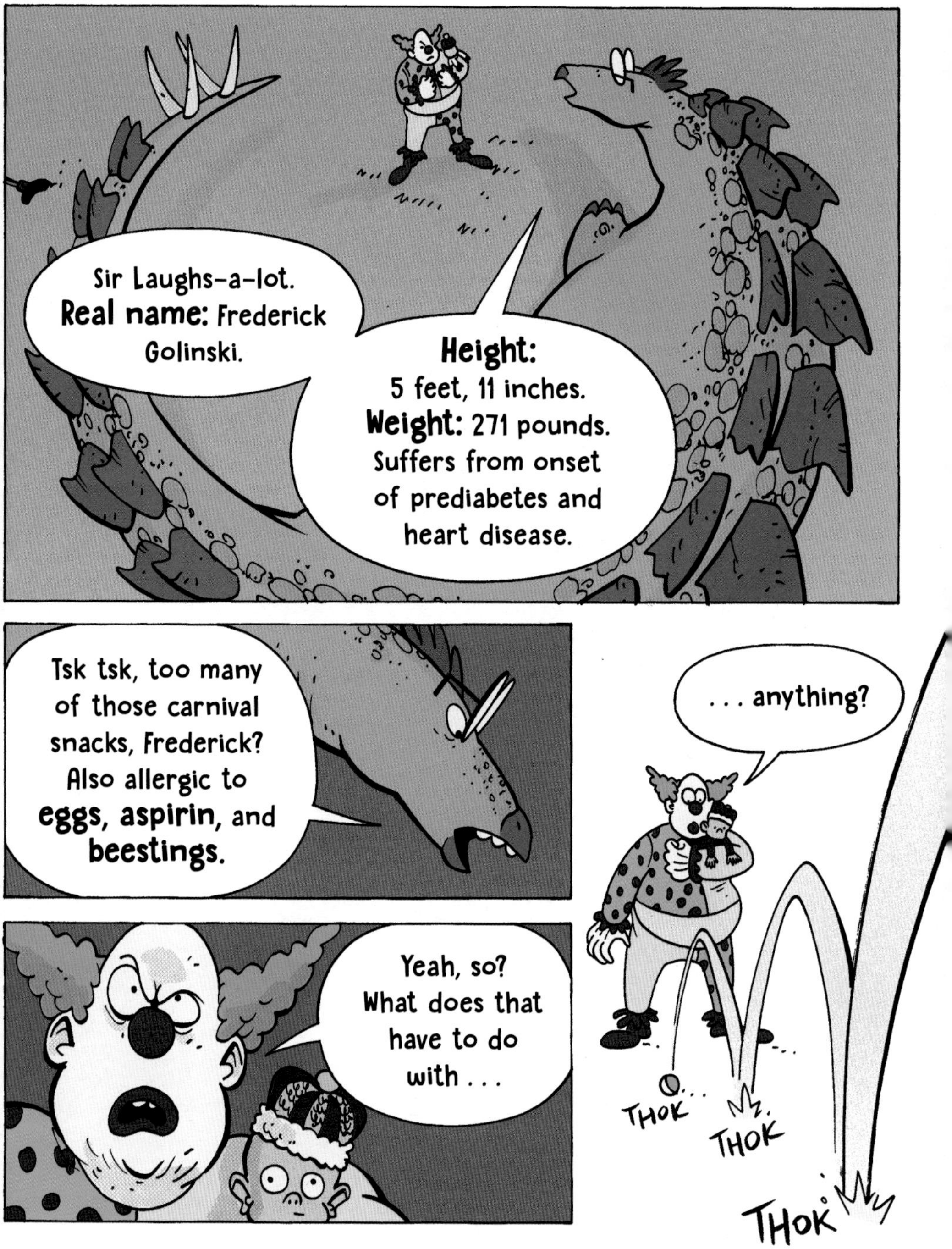
Sir Laughs-a-lot. **Real name:** Frederick Golinski.
Height: 5 feet, 11 inches. **Weight:** 271 pounds. Suffers from onset of prediabetes and heart disease.
Tsk tsk, too many of those carnival snacks, Frederick? Also allergic to **eggs, aspirin**, and **beestings.**
Yeah, so? What does that have to do with . . .
. . . anything?
THOK
THOK
THOK

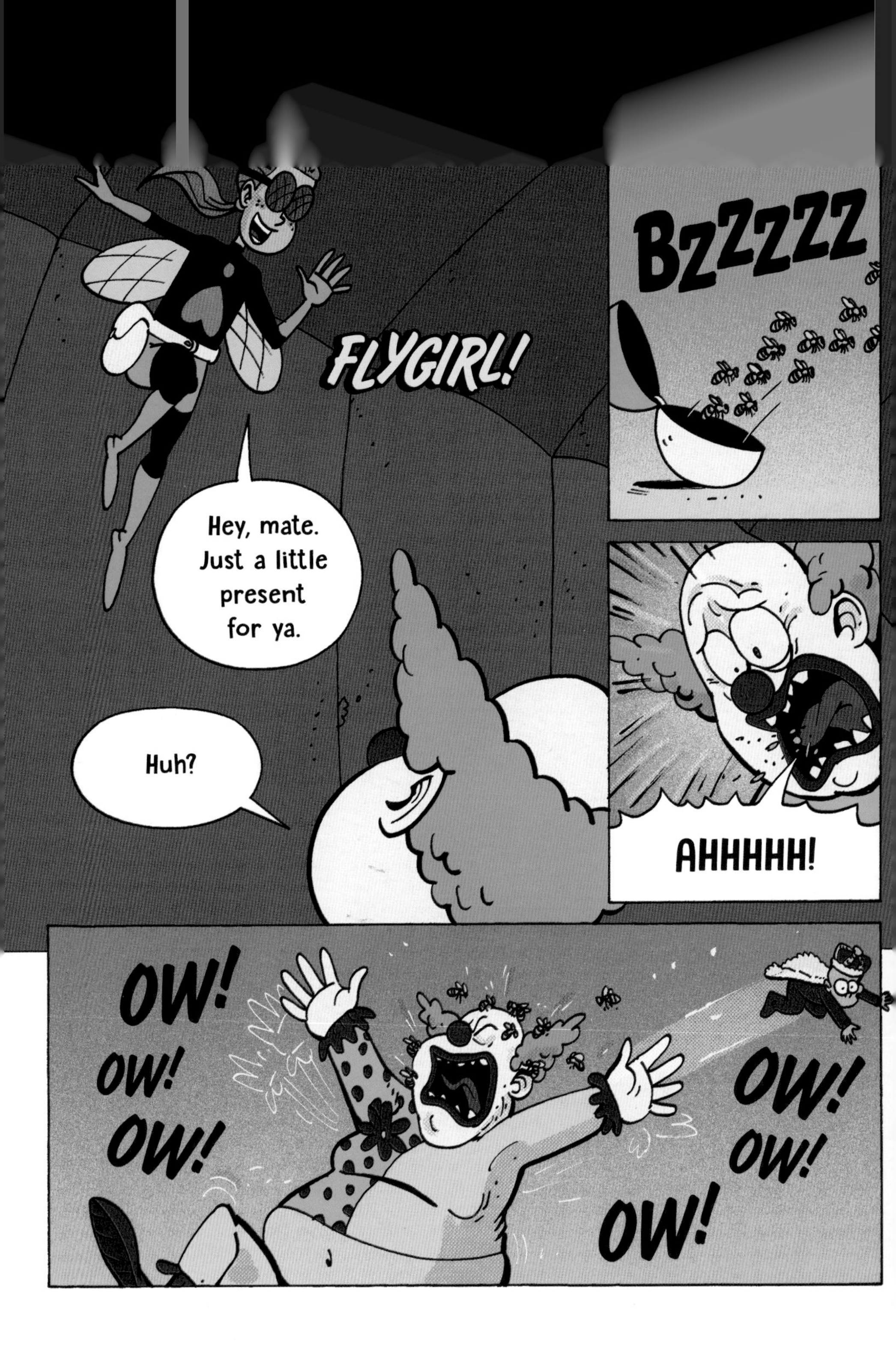
FLYGIRL!
Hey, mate. Just a little present for ya.
Huh?
BzZZZZ
AHHHHH!
OW! OW! OW!
OW! OW!
OW!

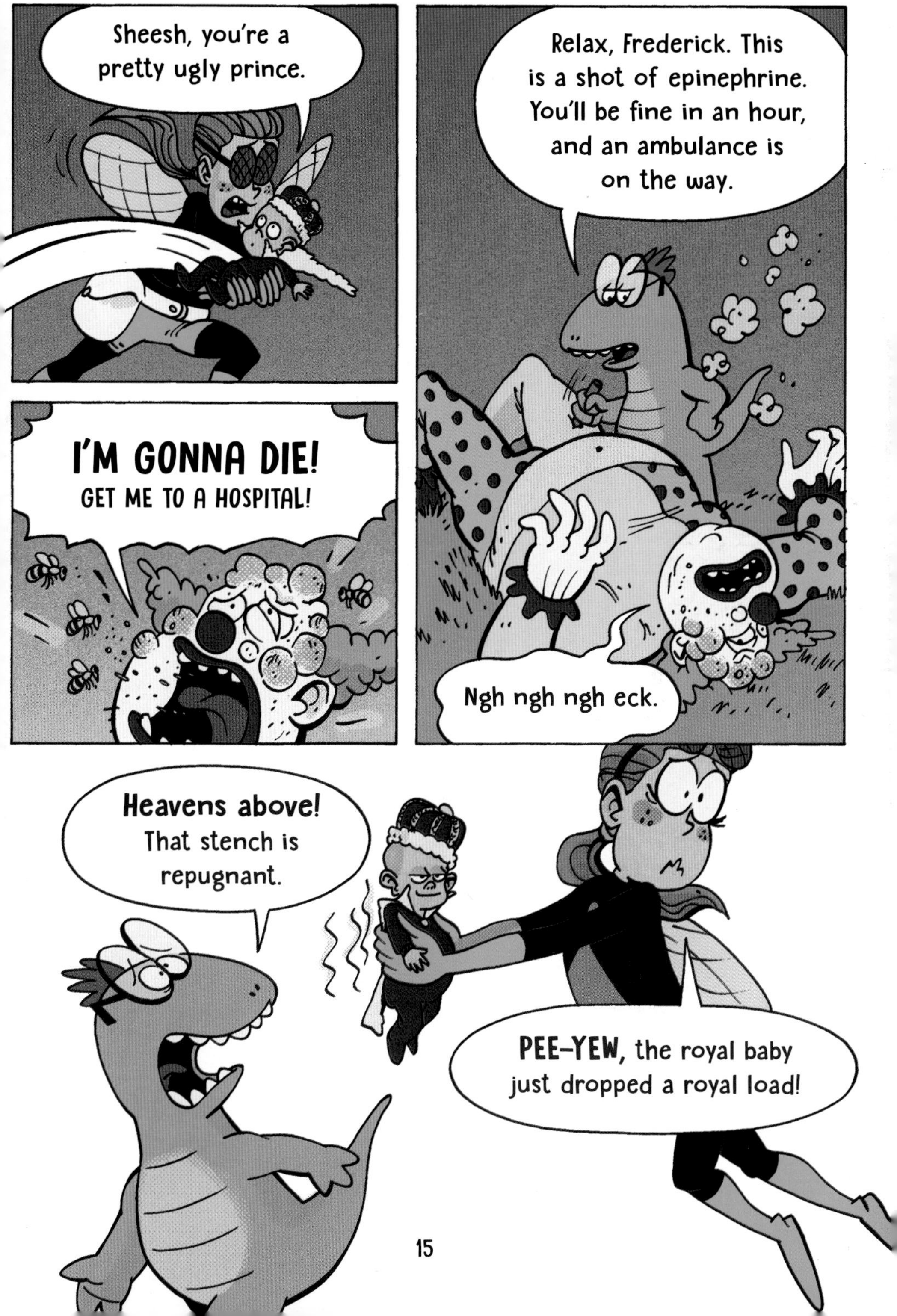
Sheesh, you're a pretty ugly prince.
Relax, Frederick. This is a shot of epinephrine. You'll be fine in an hour, and an ambulance is on the way.
I'M GONNA DIE! GET ME TO A HOSPITAL!
Ngh ngh ngh eck.
Heavens above! That stench is repugnant.
PEE-YEW, the royal baby just dropped a royal load!

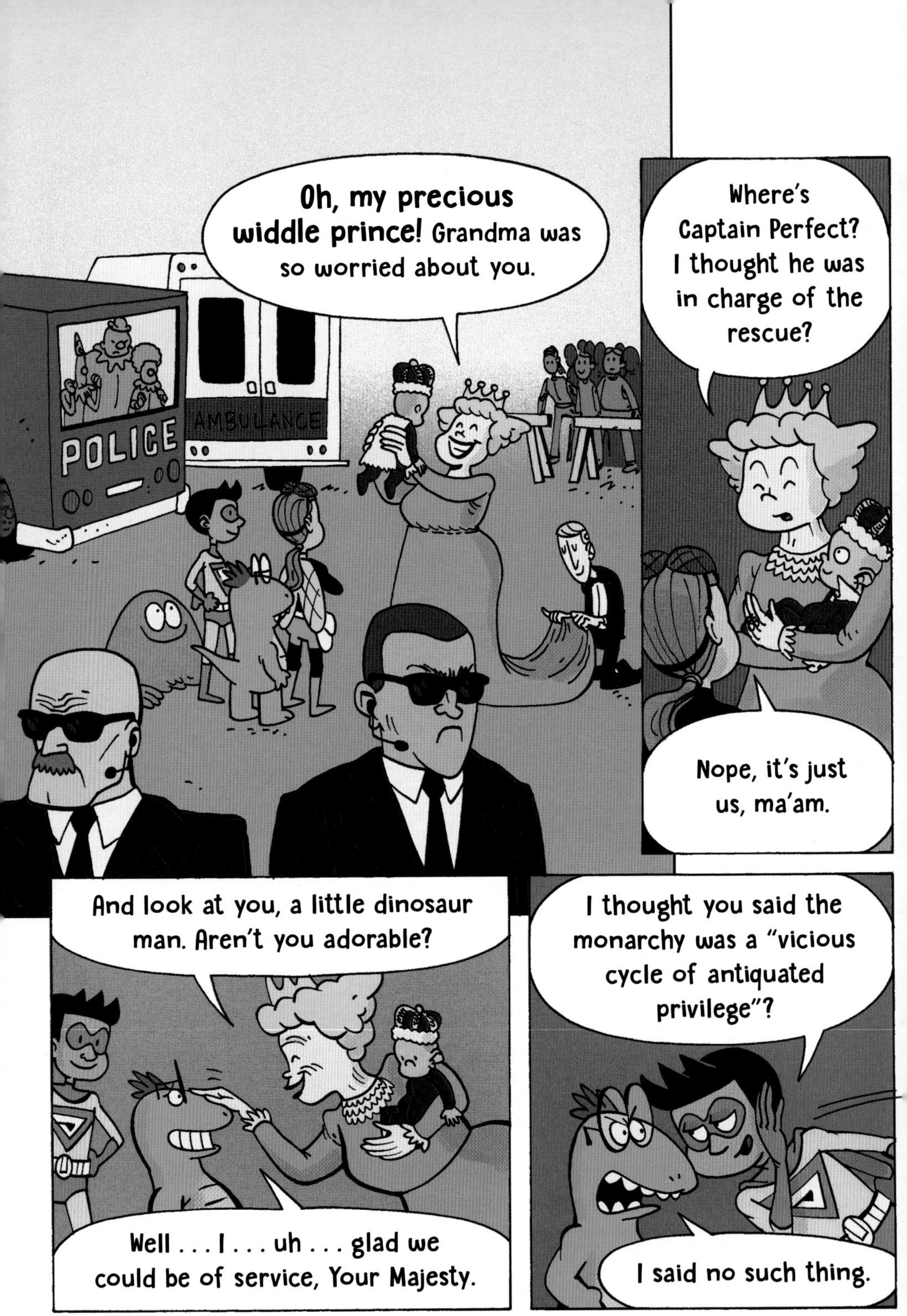
Oh, my precious widdle prince! Grandma was so worried about you.
POLICE
AMBULANCE
Where's Captain Perfect? I thought he was in charge of the rescue?
Nope, it's just us, ma'am.
And look at you, a little dinosaur man. Aren't you adorable?
Well . . . I . . . uh . . . glad we could be of service, Your Majesty.
I thought you said the monarchy was a "vicious cycle of antiquated privilege"?
I said no such thing.

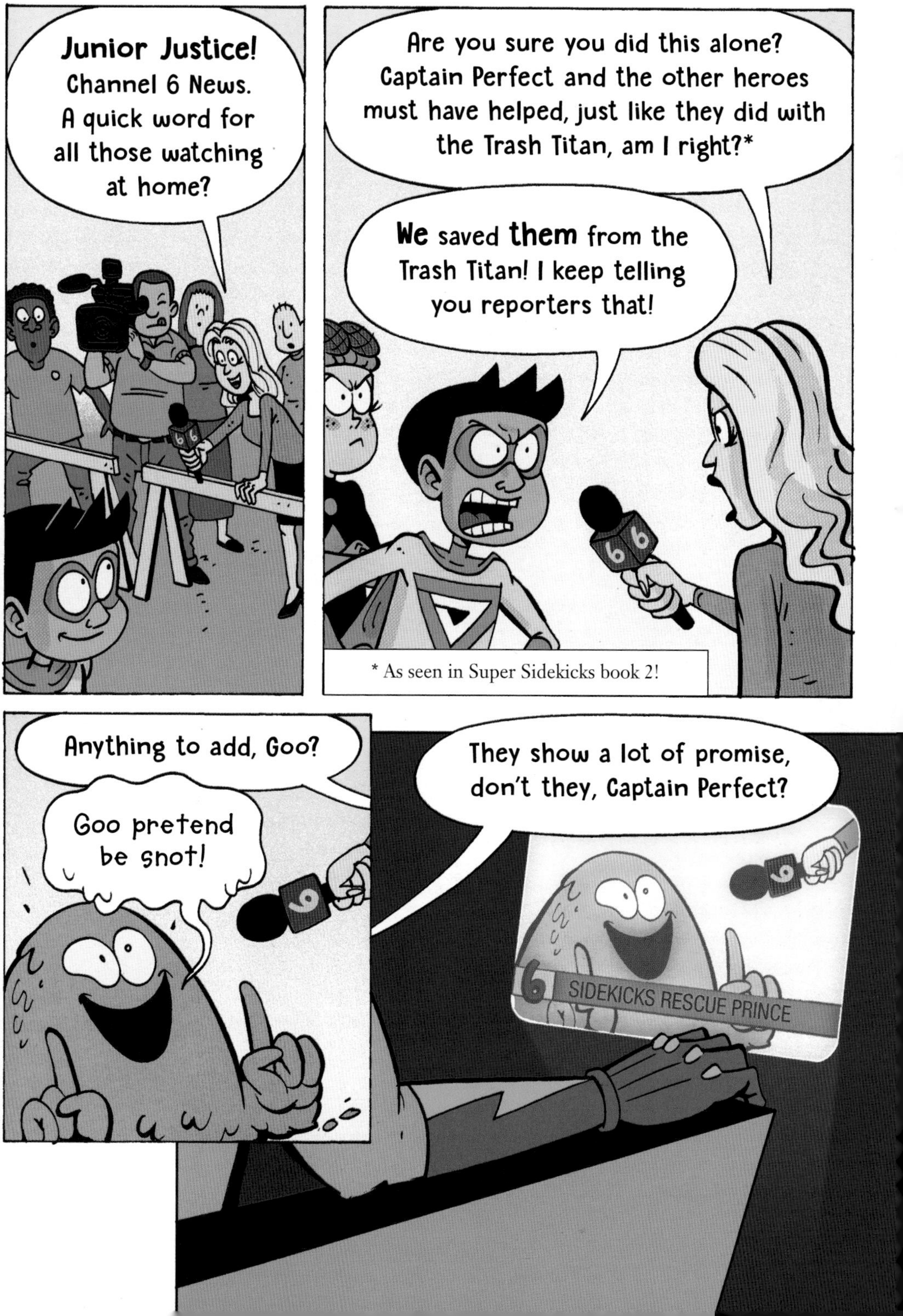
Junior Justice! Channel 6 News. A quick word for all those watching at home?
Are you sure you did this alone? Captain Perfect and the other heroes must have helped, just like they did with the Trash Titan, am I right?*
We saved them from the Trash Titan! I keep telling you reporters that!
* As seen in Super Sidekicks book 2!
Anything to add, Goo?
Goo pretend be snot!
They show a lot of promise, don't they, Captain Perfect?
6
SIDEKICKS RESCUE PRINCE

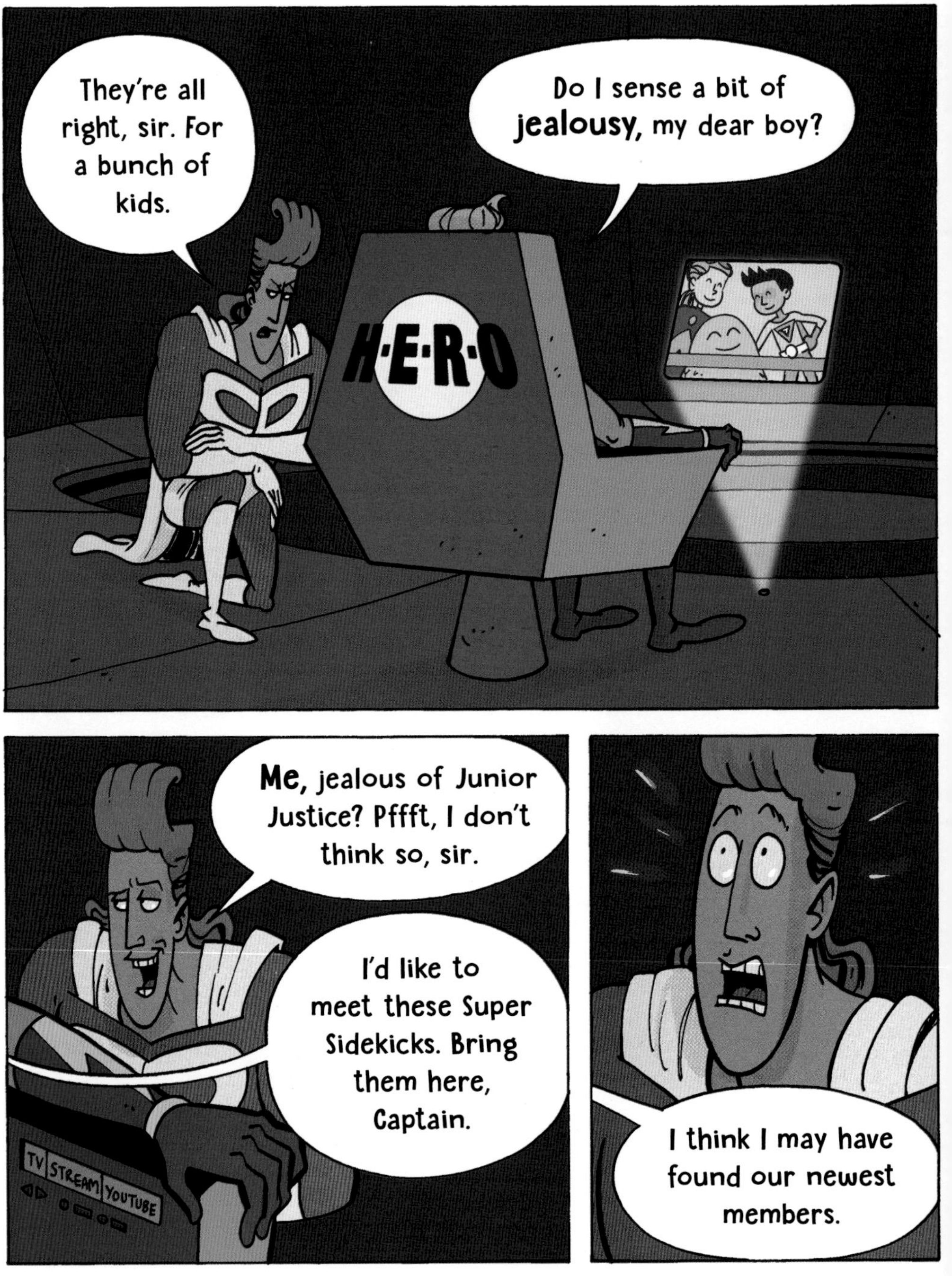
They're all right, sir. For a bunch of kids.
Do I sense a bit of jealousy, my dear boy?
H·E·R·O
Me, jealous of Junior Justice? Pffft, I don't think so, sir.
I'd like to meet these Super Sidekicks. Bring them here, Captain.
TV STREAM YOUTUBE
I think I may have found our newest members.

Chapter

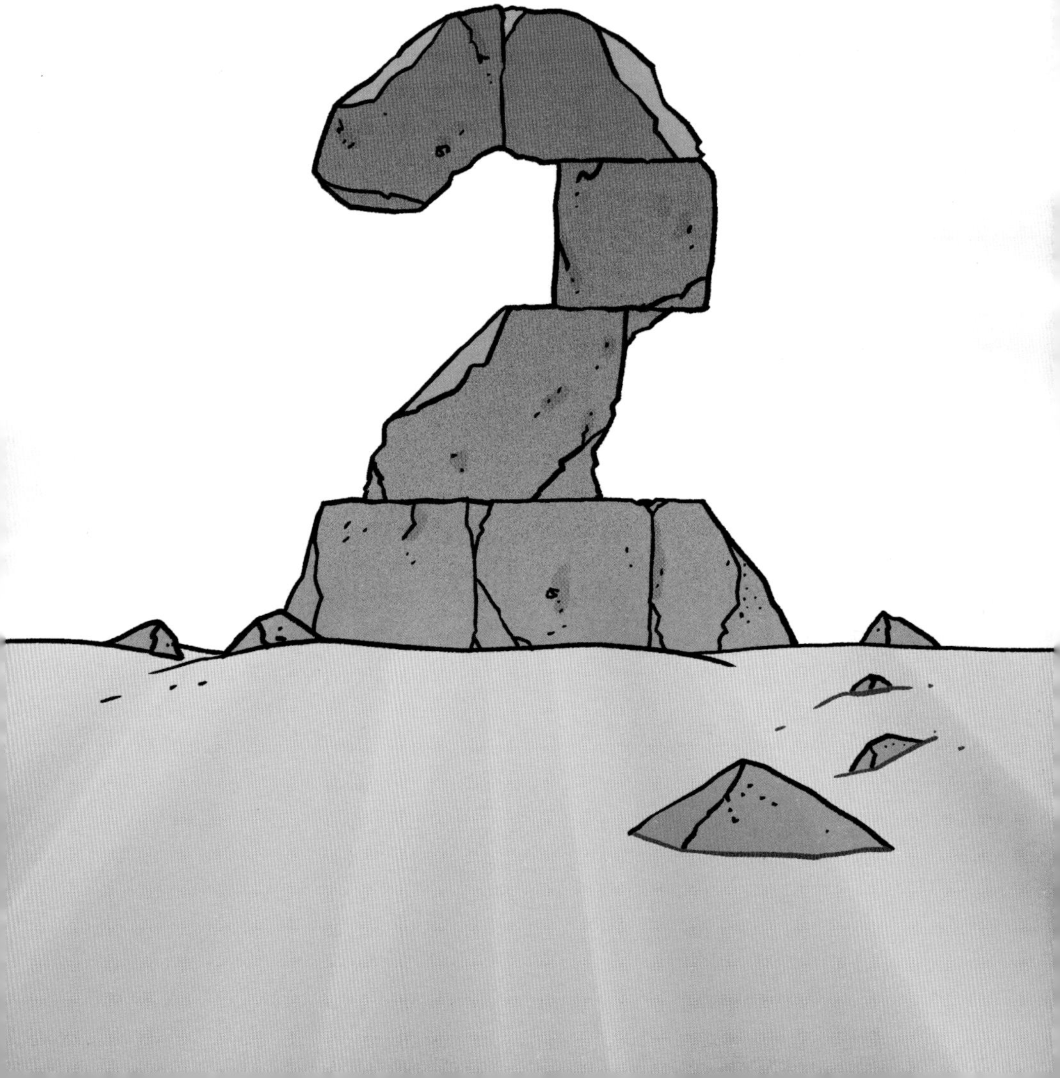

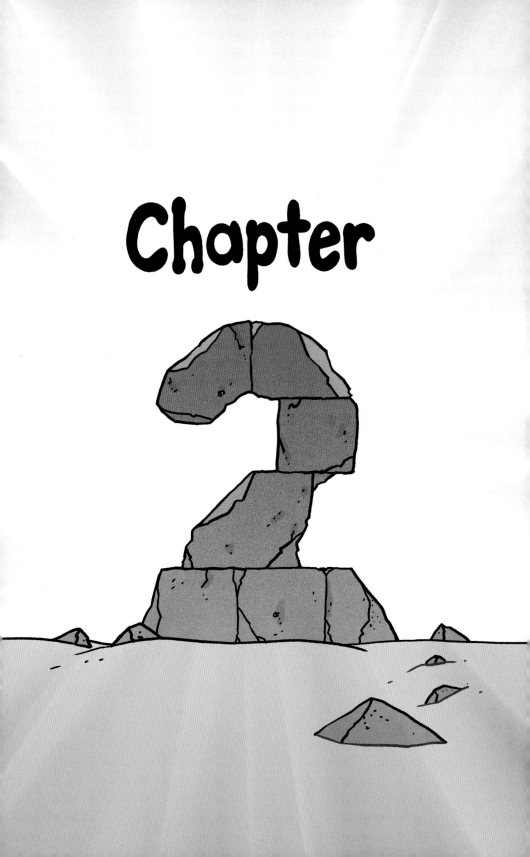

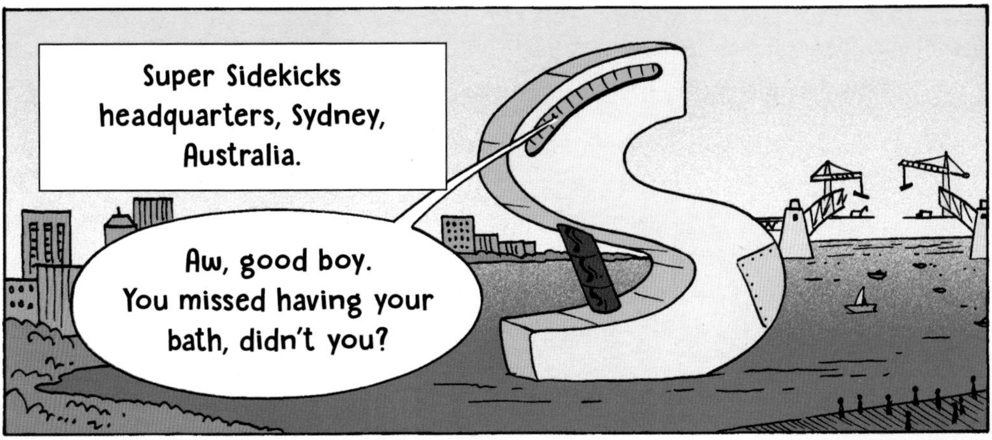
Super Sidekicks headquarters, Sydney, Australia.
Aw, good boy. You missed having your bath, didn't you?

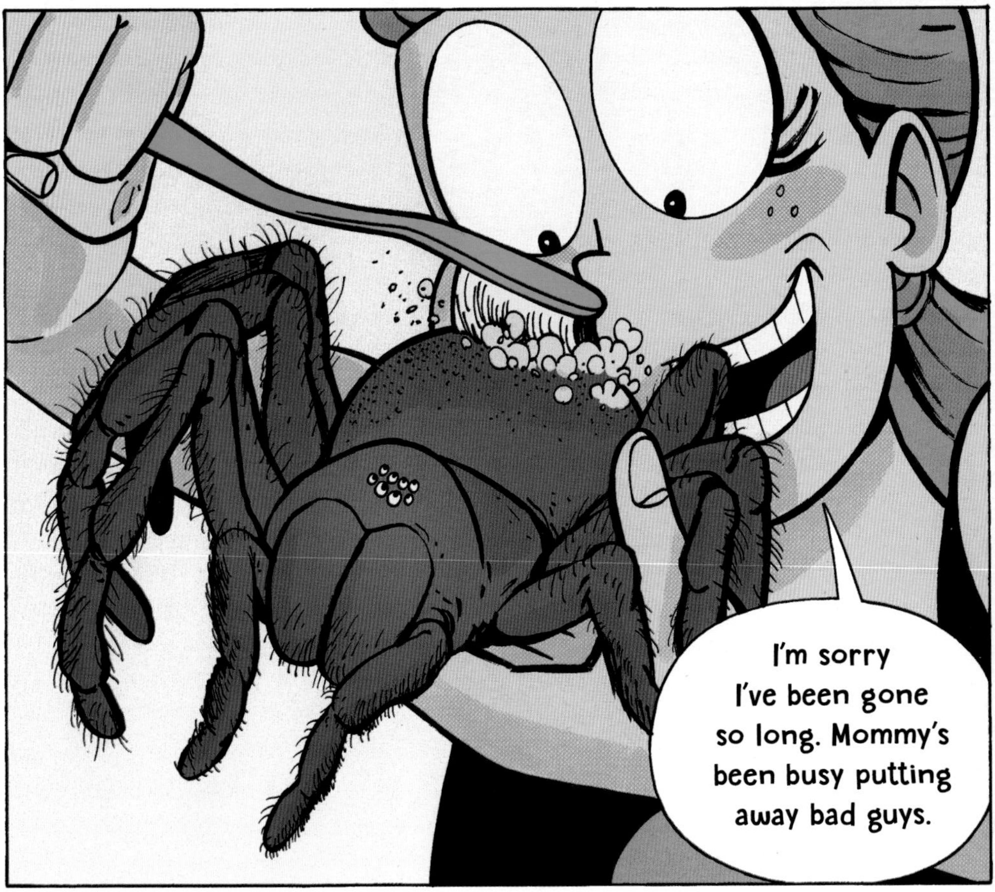
I'm sorry I've been gone so long. Mommy's been busy putting away bad guys.

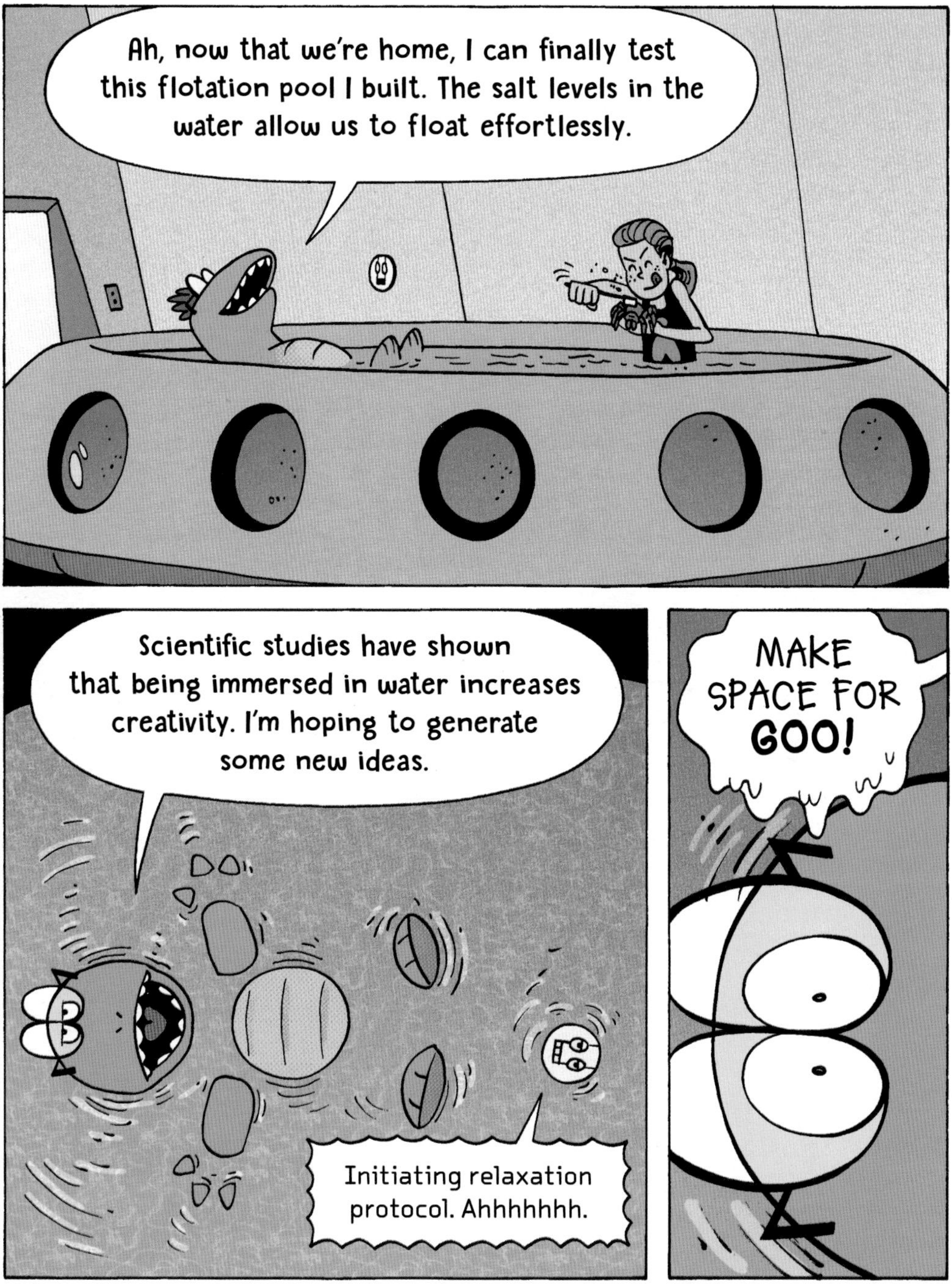
Ah, now that we're home, I can finally test this flotation pool I built. The salt levels in the water allow us to float effortlessly.
Scientific studies have shown that being immersed in water increases creativity. I'm hoping to generate some new ideas.
Initiating relaxation protocol. Ahhhhhhh.
MAKE SPACE FOR GOO!

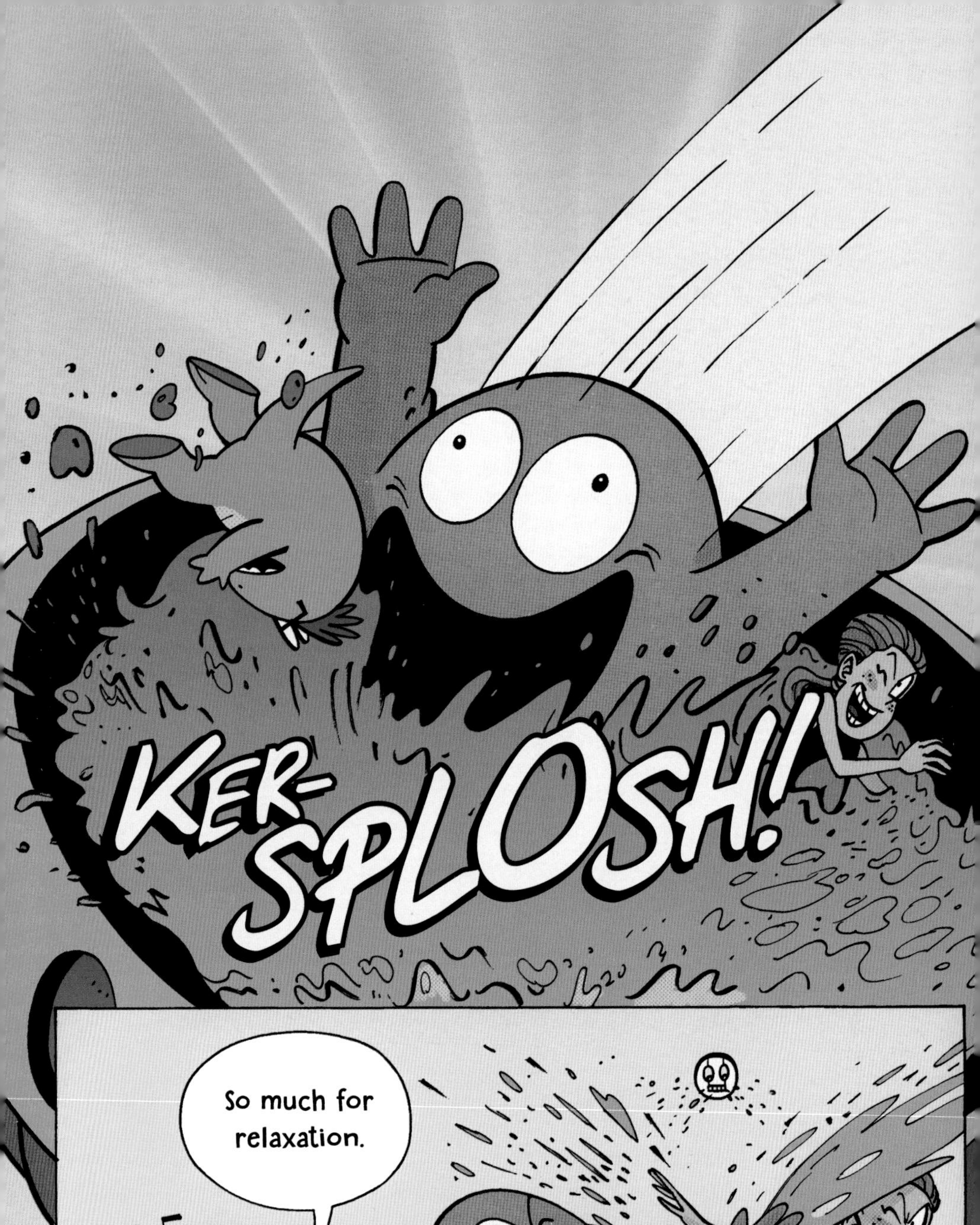
KER-
SPLOSH!
So much for relaxation.

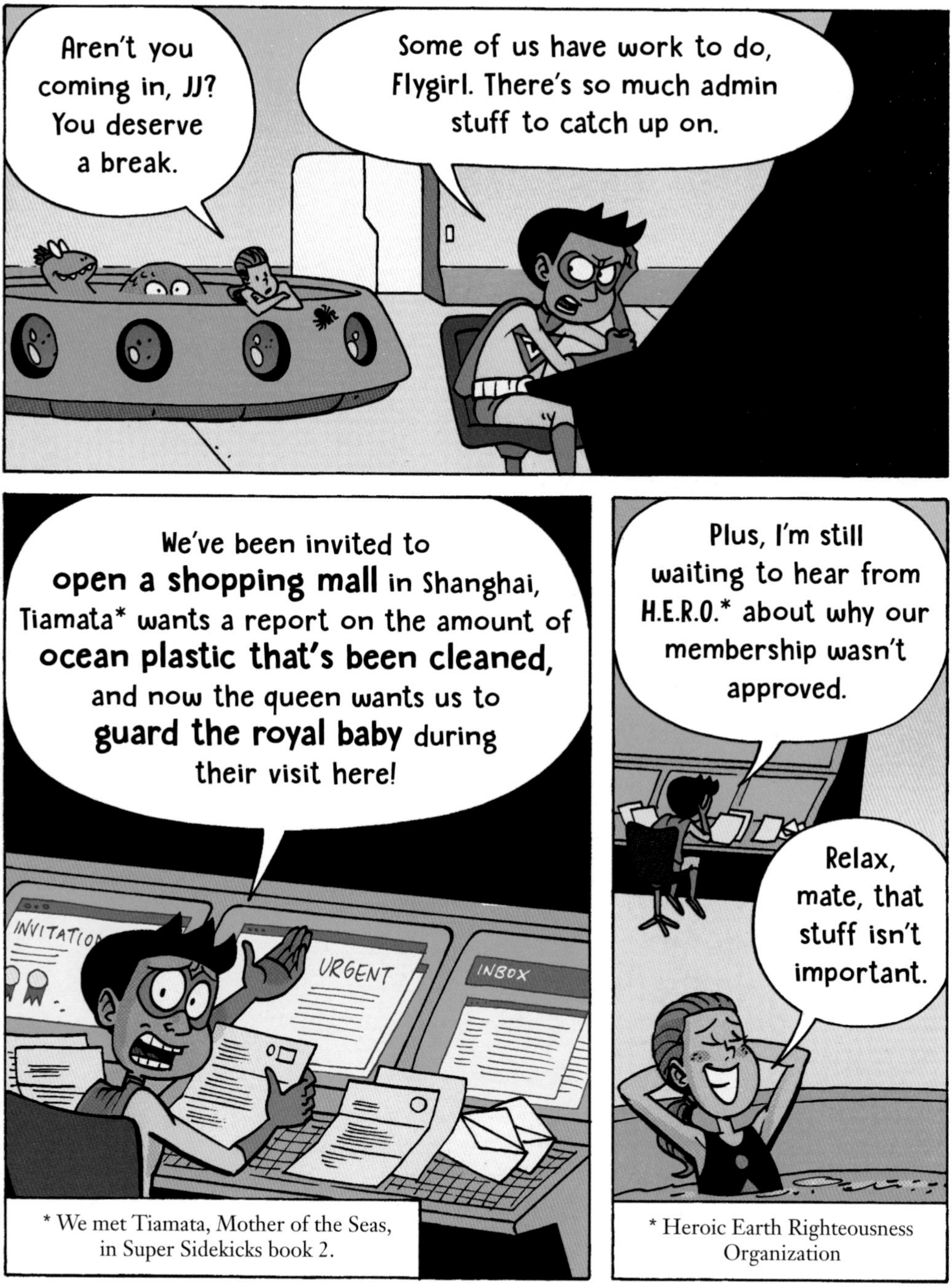
Aren't you coming in, JJ? You deserve a break.
Some of us have work to do, Flygirl. There's so much admin stuff to catch up on.
We've been invited to **open a shopping mall** in Shanghai, Tiamata* wants a report on the amount of **ocean plastic that's been cleaned,** and now the queen wants us to **guard the royal baby** during their visit here!
URGENT
INBOX
Plus, I'm still waiting to hear from H.E.R.O.* about why our membership wasn't approved.
Relax, mate, that stuff isn't important.

* We met Tiamata, Mother of the Seas, in Super Sidekicks book 2.

* Heroic Earth Righteousness Organization

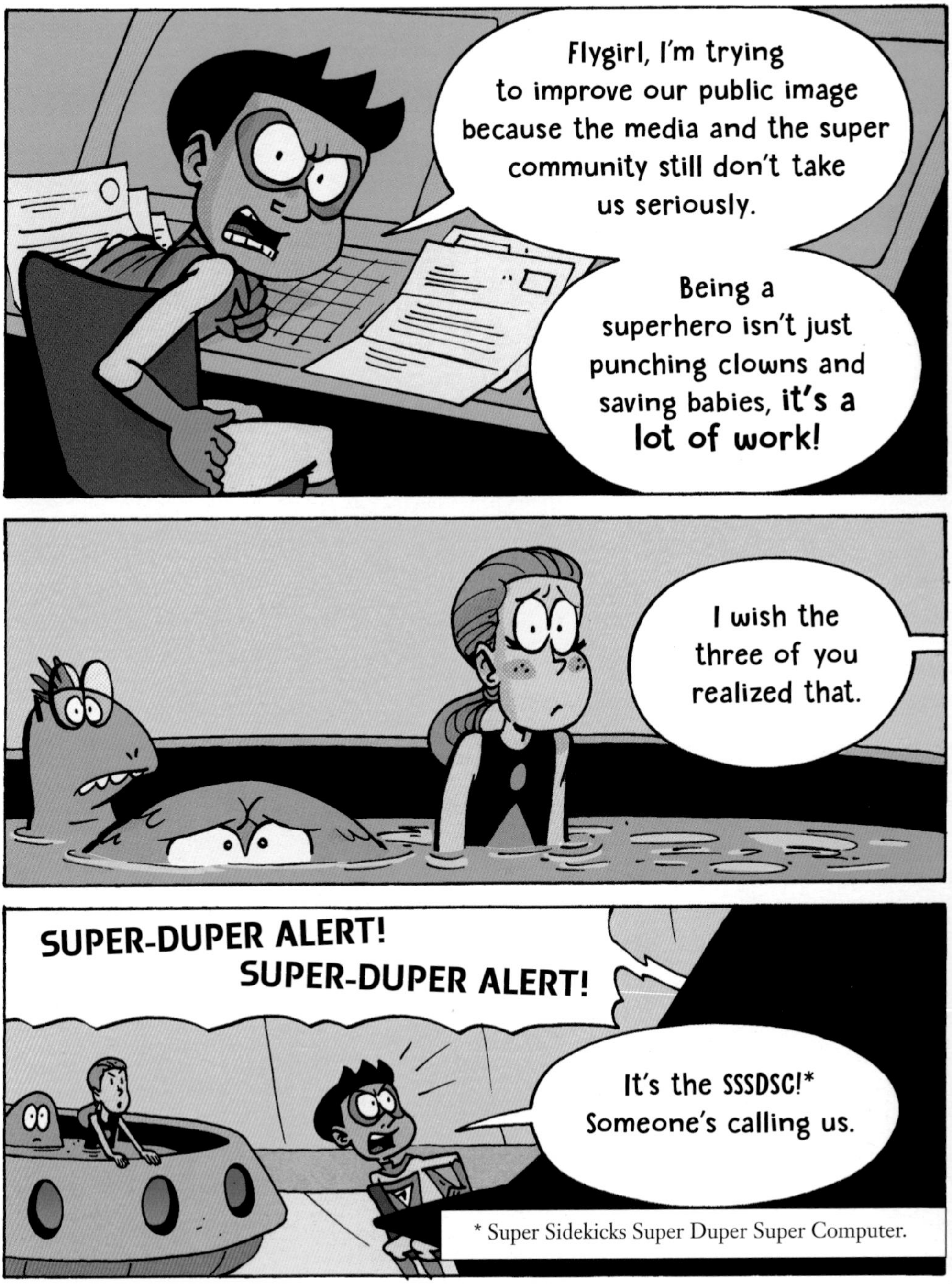
Flygirl, I'm trying to improve our public image because the media and the super community still don't take us seriously.
Being a superhero isn't just punching clowns and saving babies, it's a lot of work!
I wish the three of you realized that.
SUPER-DUPER ALERT! SUPER-DUPER ALERT!
It's the SSSDSC!* Someone's calling us.
* Super Sidekicks Super Duper Super Computer.

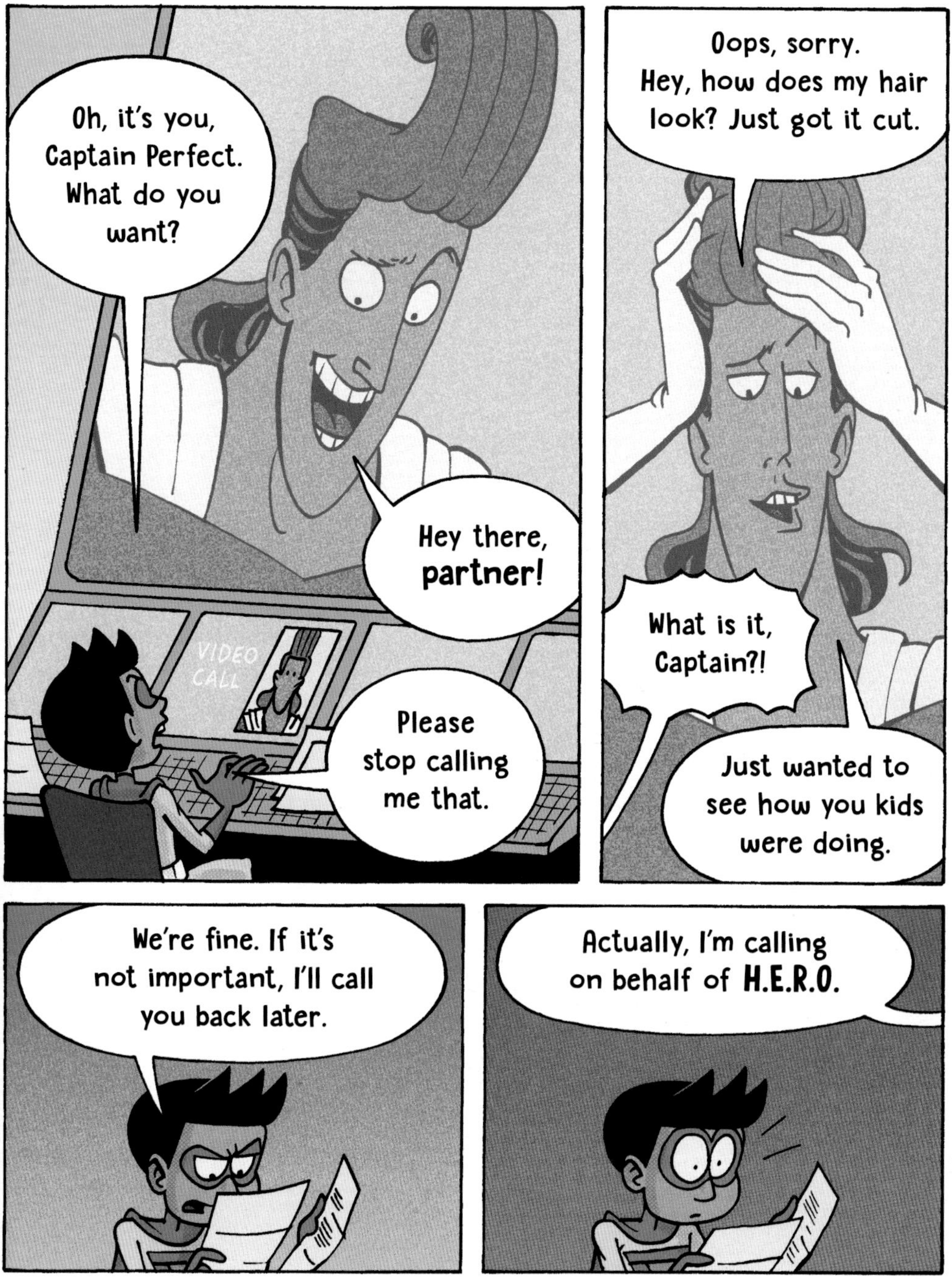
Oh, it's you, Captain Perfect. What do you want?
Hey there, partner!
VIDEO CALL
Please stop calling me that.
Oops, sorry. Hey, how does my hair look? Just got it cut.
What is it, Captain?!
Just wanted to see how you kids were doing.
We're fine. If it's not important, I'll call you back later.
Actually, I'm calling on behalf of H.E.R.O.

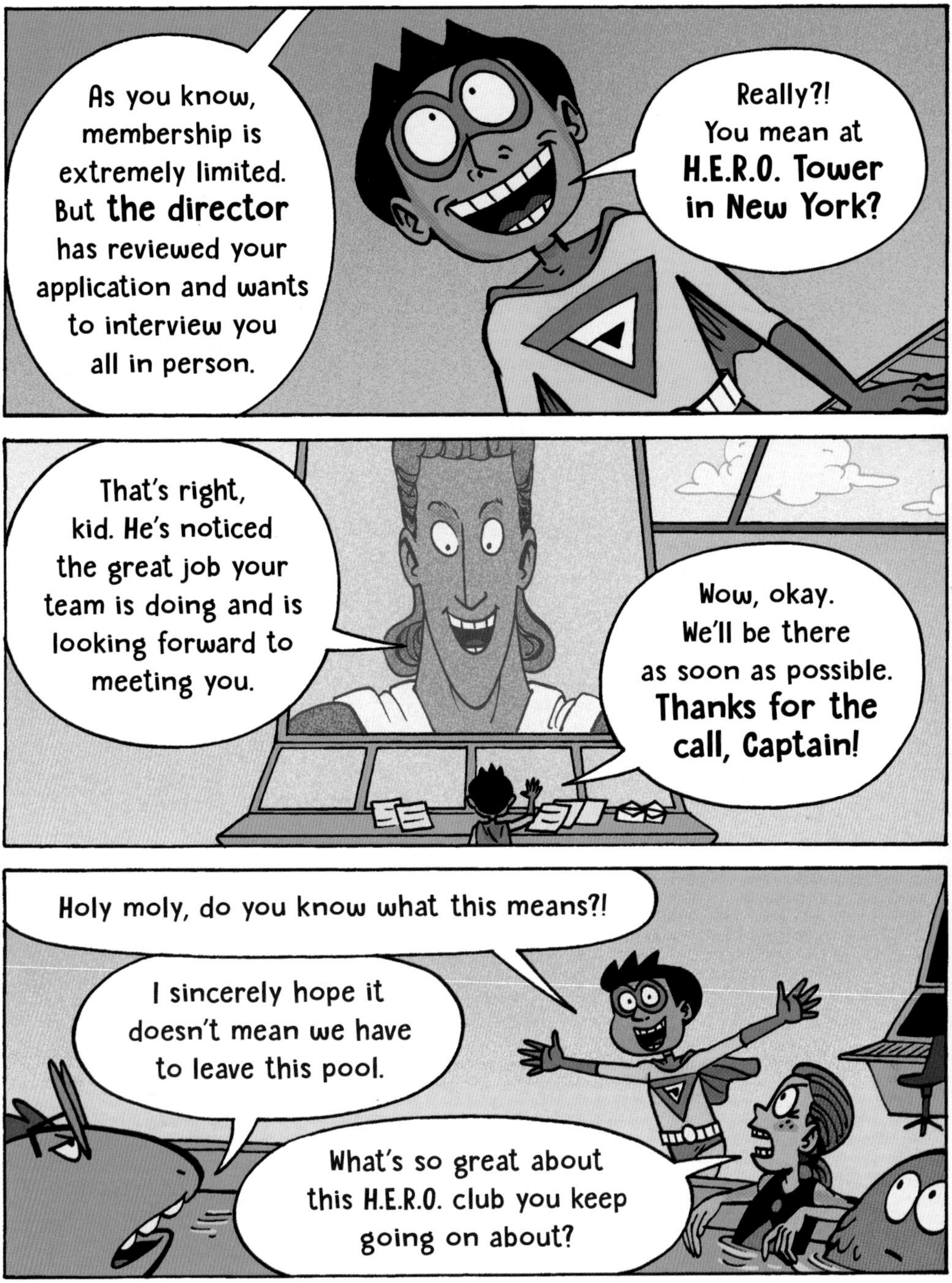
As you know, membership is extremely limited. But the director has reviewed your application and wants to interview you all in person.
Really?! You mean at H.E.R.O. Tower in New York?
That's right, kid. He's noticed the great job your team is doing and is looking forward to meeting you.
Wow, okay. We'll be there as soon as possible. Thanks for the call, Captain!
Holy moly, do you know what this means?!
I sincerely hope it doesn't mean we have to leave this pool.
What's so great about this H.E.R.O. club you keep going on about?

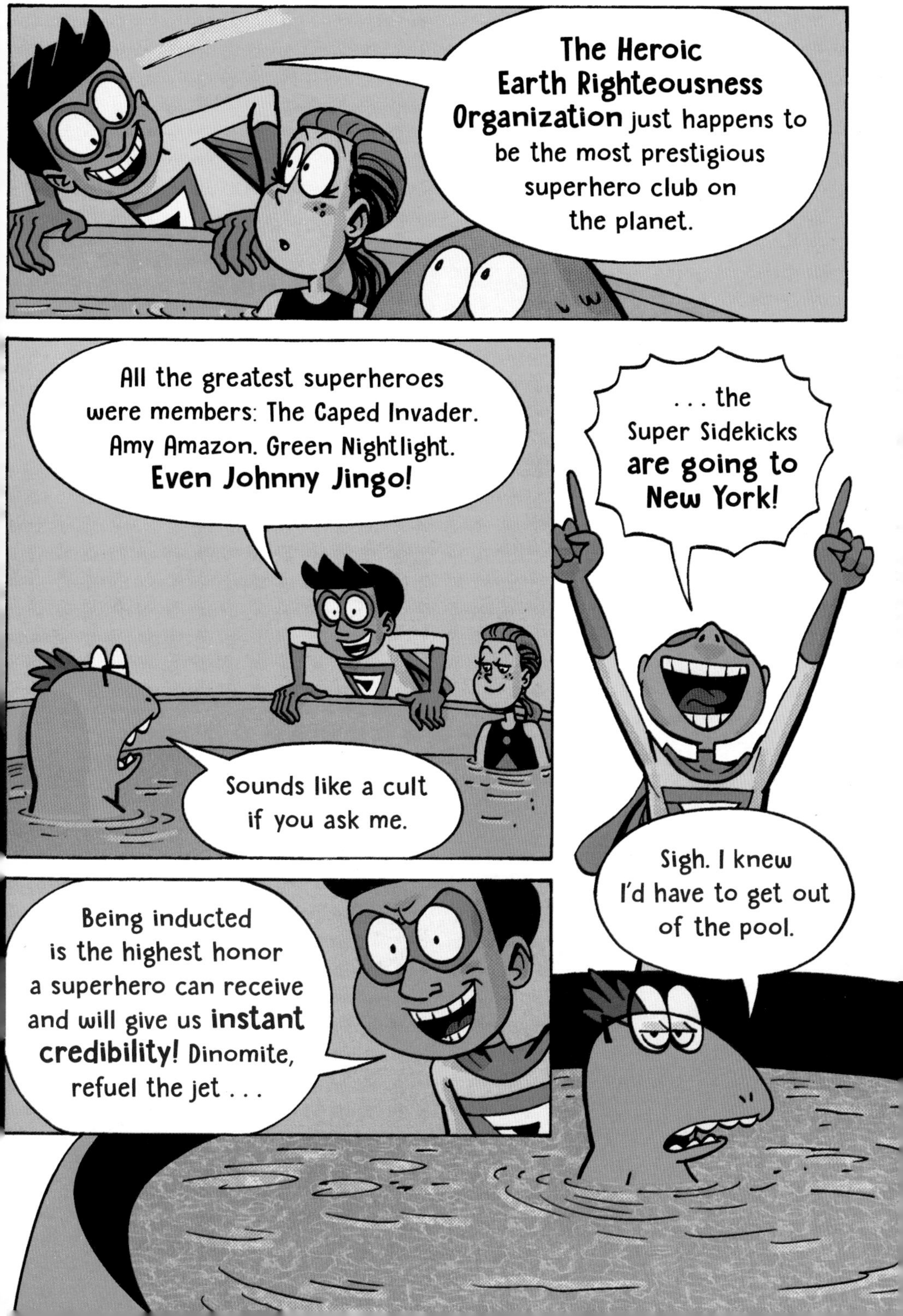
The Heroic Earth Righteousness Organization just happens to be the most prestigious superhero club on the planet.
All the greatest superheroes were members: The Caped Invader. Amy Amazon. Green Nightlight. Even Johnny Jingo!
Sounds like a cult if you ask me.
Being inducted is the highest honor a superhero can receive and will give us instant credibility! Dinomite, refuel the jet . . .
. . . the Super Sidekicks are going to New York!
Sigh. I knew I'd have to get out of the pool.

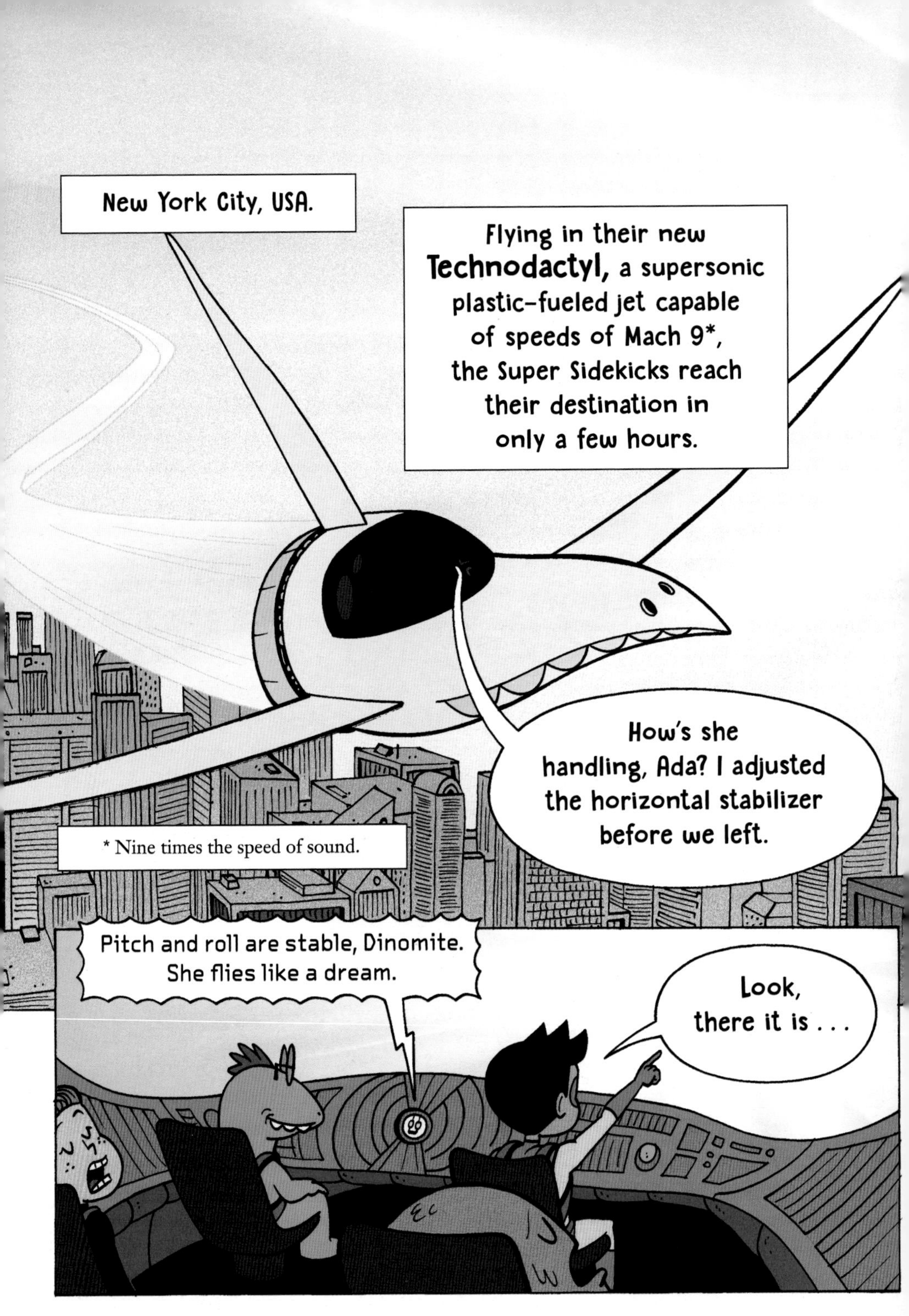

New York City, USA.
Flying in their new Technodactyl, a supersonic plastic-fueled jet capable of speeds of Mach 9*, the Super Sidekicks reach their destination in only a few hours.
How's she handling, Ada? I adjusted the horizontal stabilizer before we left.
* Nine times the speed of sound.
Pitch and roll are stable, Dinomite. She flies like a dream.
Look, there it is . . .

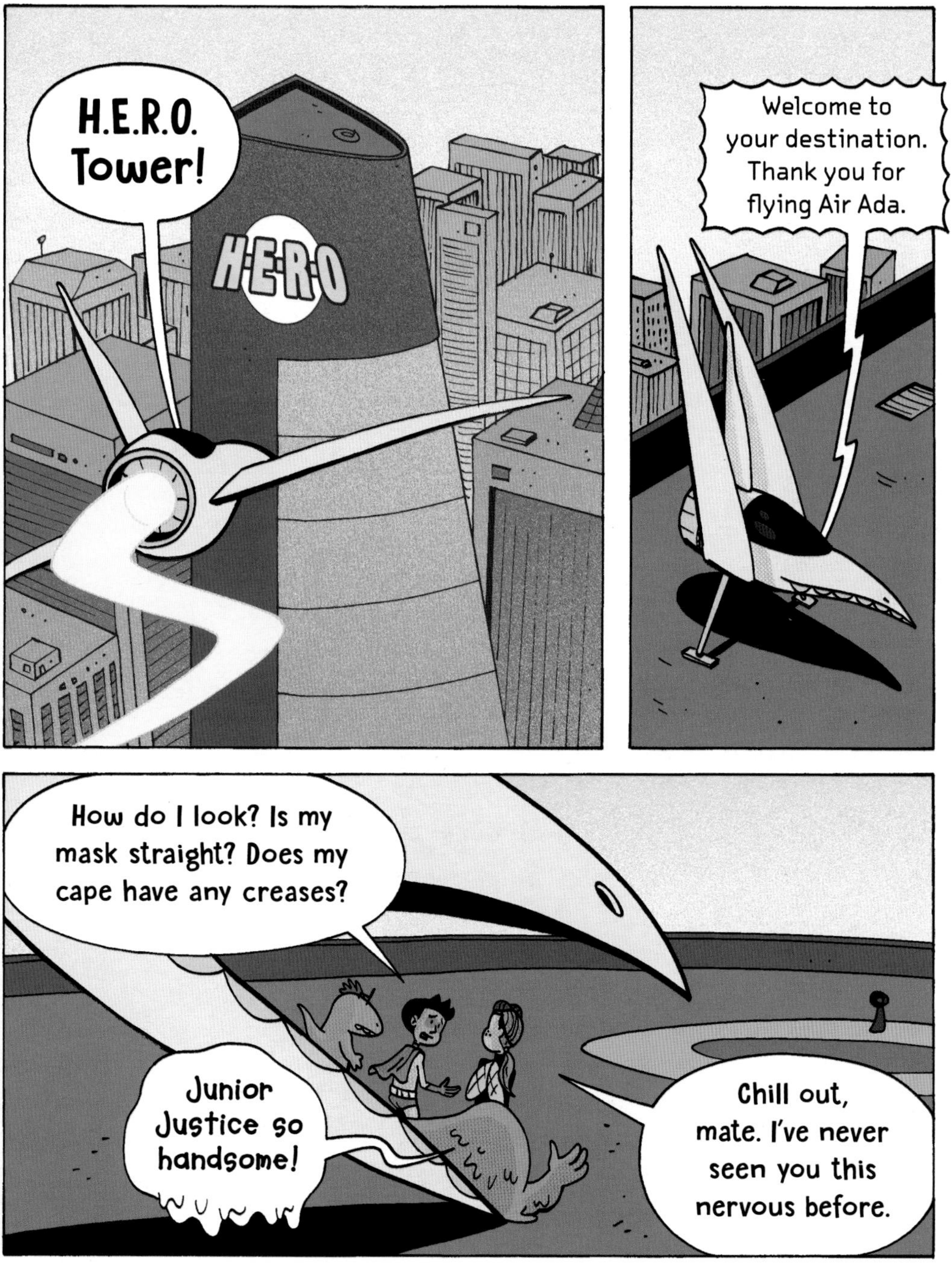
H.E.R.O. Tower!
H·E·R·O
Welcome to your destination. Thank you for flying Air Ada.
How do I look? Is my mask straight? Does my cape have any creases?
Junior Justice so handsome!
Chill out, mate. I've never seen you this nervous before.

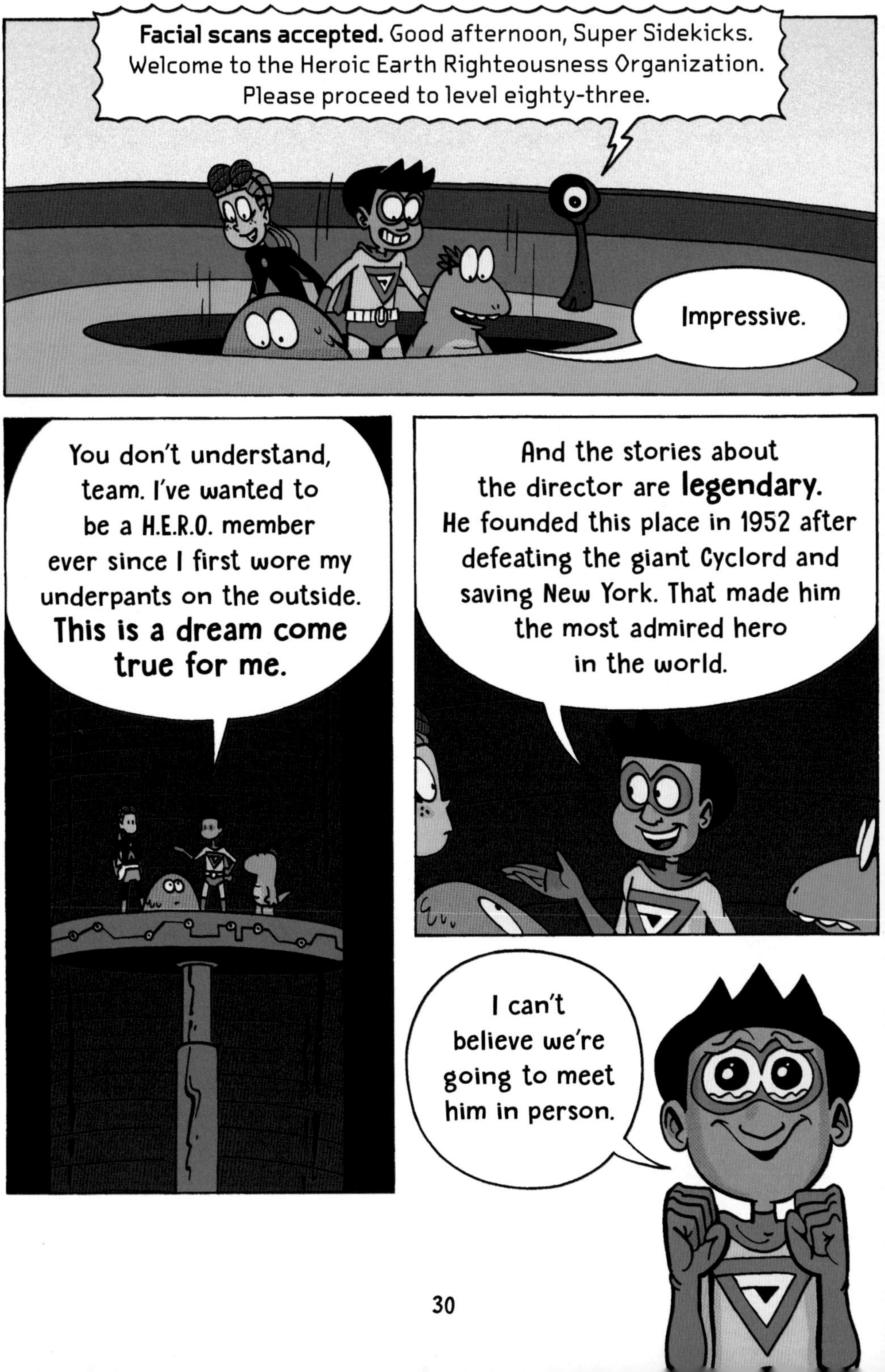
Facial scans accepted. Good afternoon, Super Sidekicks. Welcome to the Heroic Earth Righteousness Organization. Please proceed to level eighty-three.
Impressive.
You don't understand, team. I've wanted to be a H.E.R.O. member ever since I first wore my underpants on the outside. **This is a dream come true for me.**
And the stories about the director are **legendary.** He founded this place in 1952 after defeating the giant Cyclord and saving New York. That made him the most admired hero in the world.
I can't believe we're going to meet him in person.

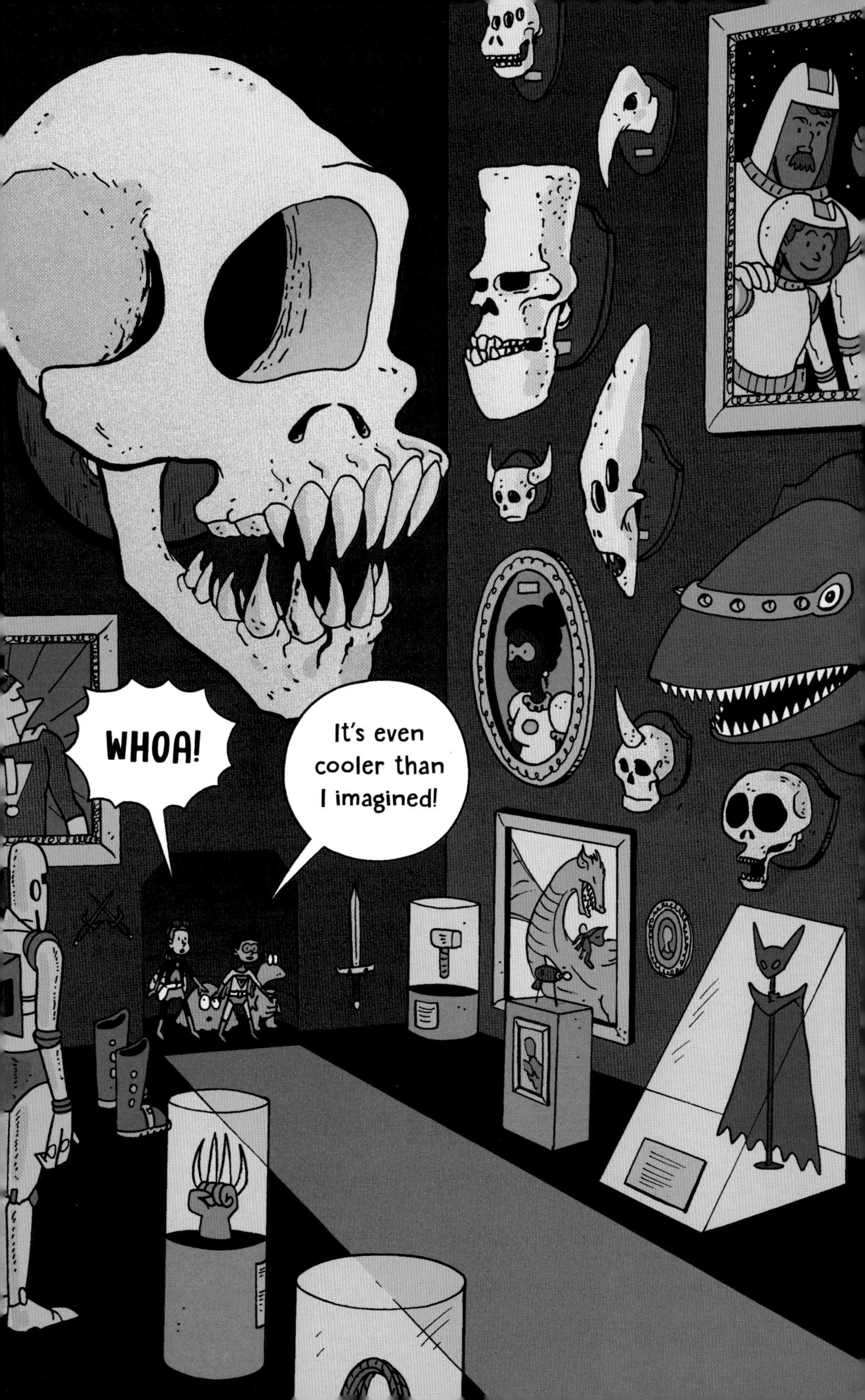
WHOA!
It's even cooler than I imagined!

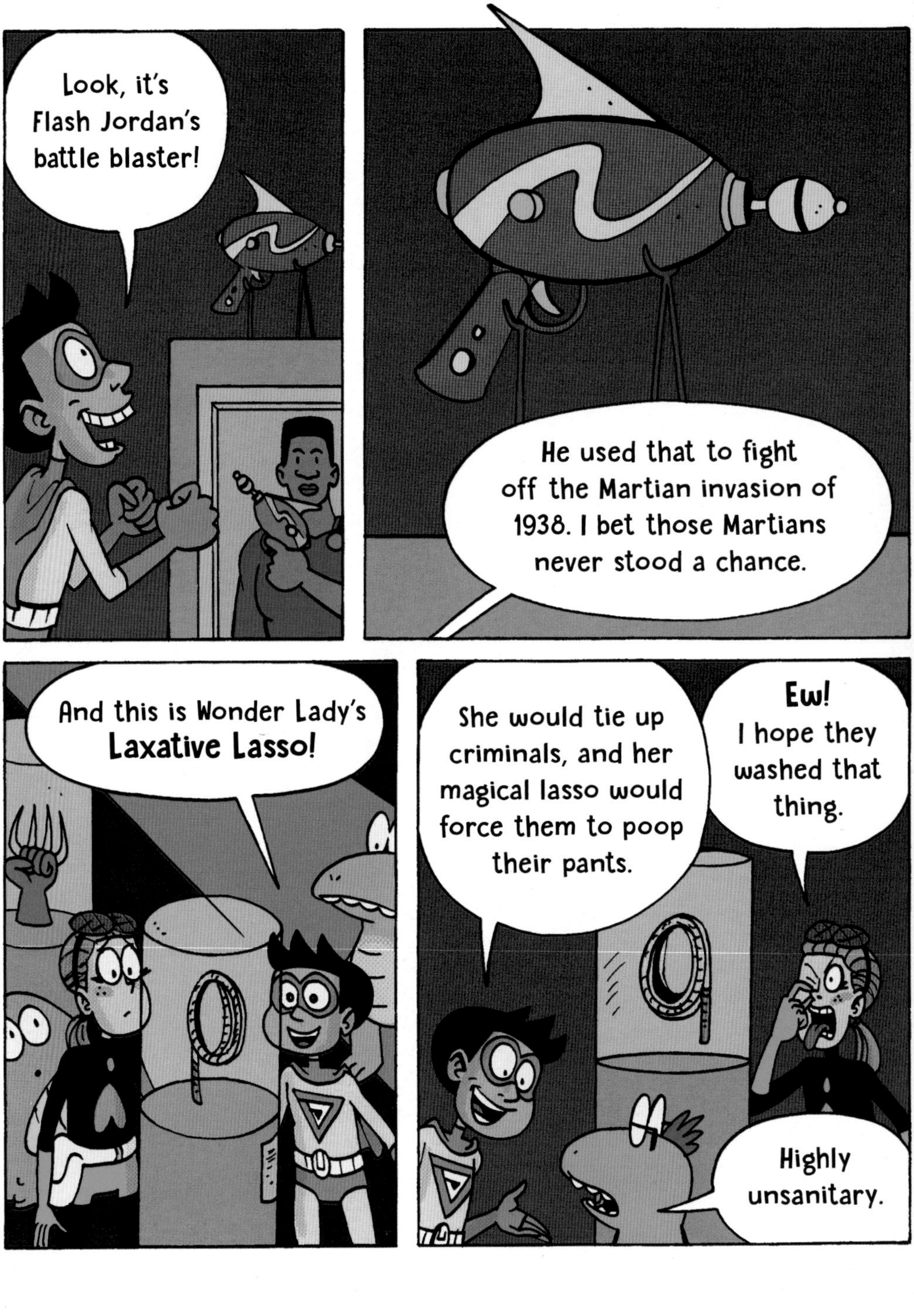
Look, it's Flash Jordan's battle blaster!
He used that to fight off the Martian invasion of 1938. I bet those Martians never stood a chance.
And this is Wonder Lady's **Laxative Lasso!**
She would tie up criminals, and her magical lasso would force them to poop their pants.
Ew! I hope they washed that thing.
Highly unsanitary.

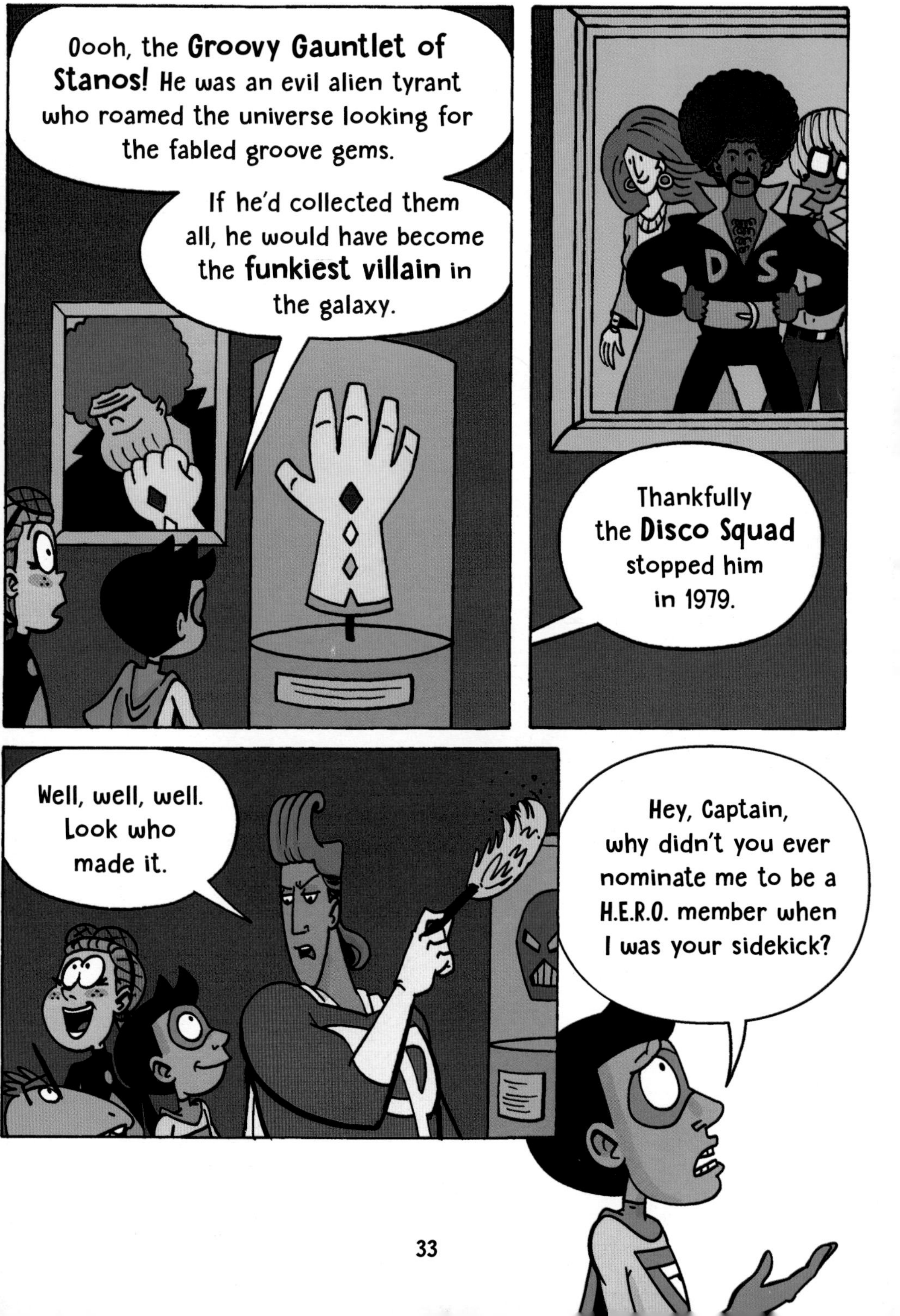
Oooh, the Groovy Gauntlet of Stanos! He was an evil alien tyrant who roamed the universe looking for the fabled groove gems.
If he'd collected them all, he would have become the funkiest villain in the galaxy.
Thankfully the Disco Squad stopped him in 1979.
Well, well, well. Look who made it.
Hey, Captain, why didn't you ever nominate me to be a H.E.R.O. member when I was your sidekick?

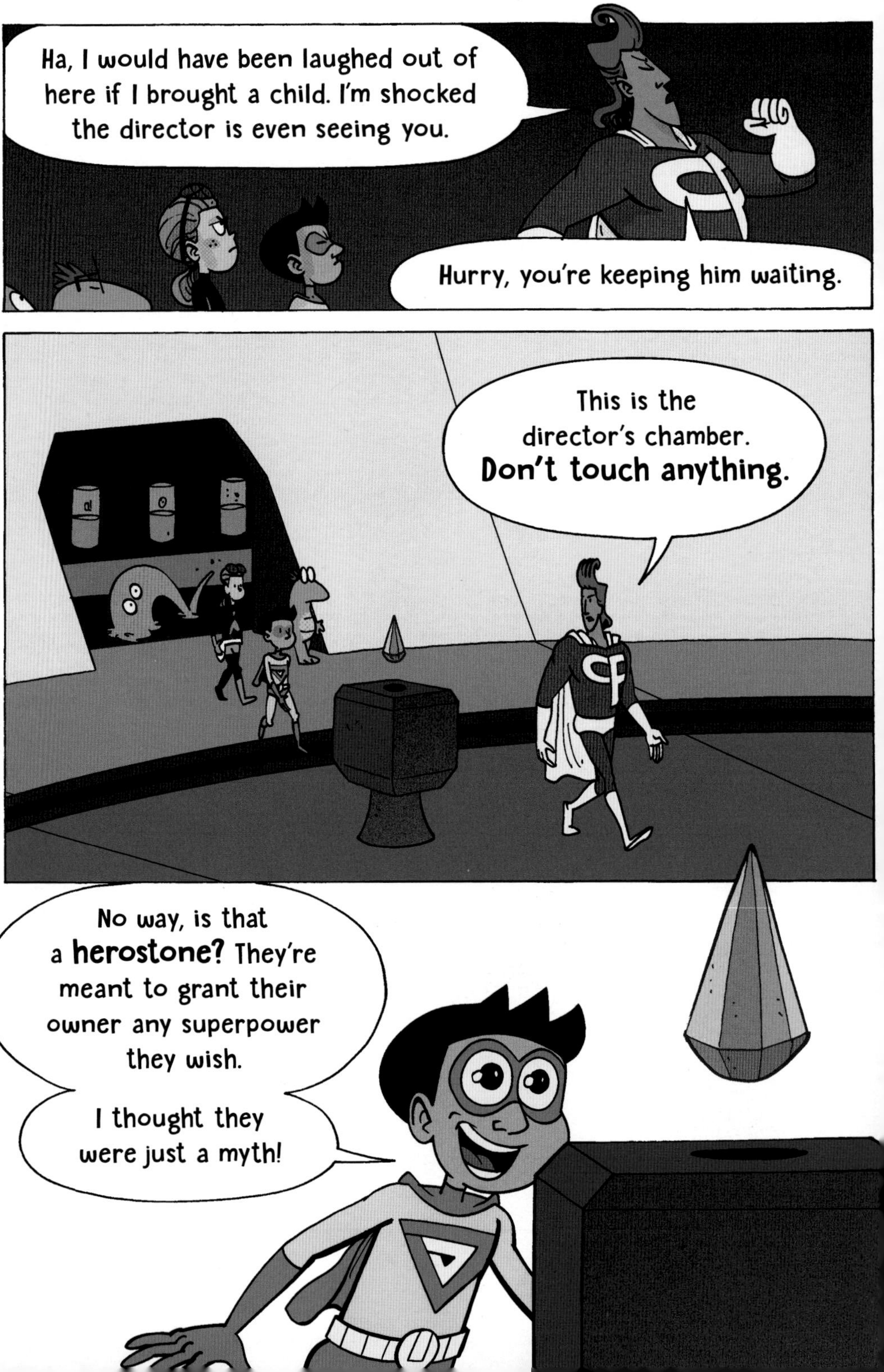
Ha, I would have been laughed out of here if I brought a child. I'm shocked the director is even seeing you.
Hurry, you're keeping him waiting.
This is the director's chamber. Don't touch anything.
No way, is that a herostone? They're meant to grant their owner any superpower they wish.
I thought they were just a myth!

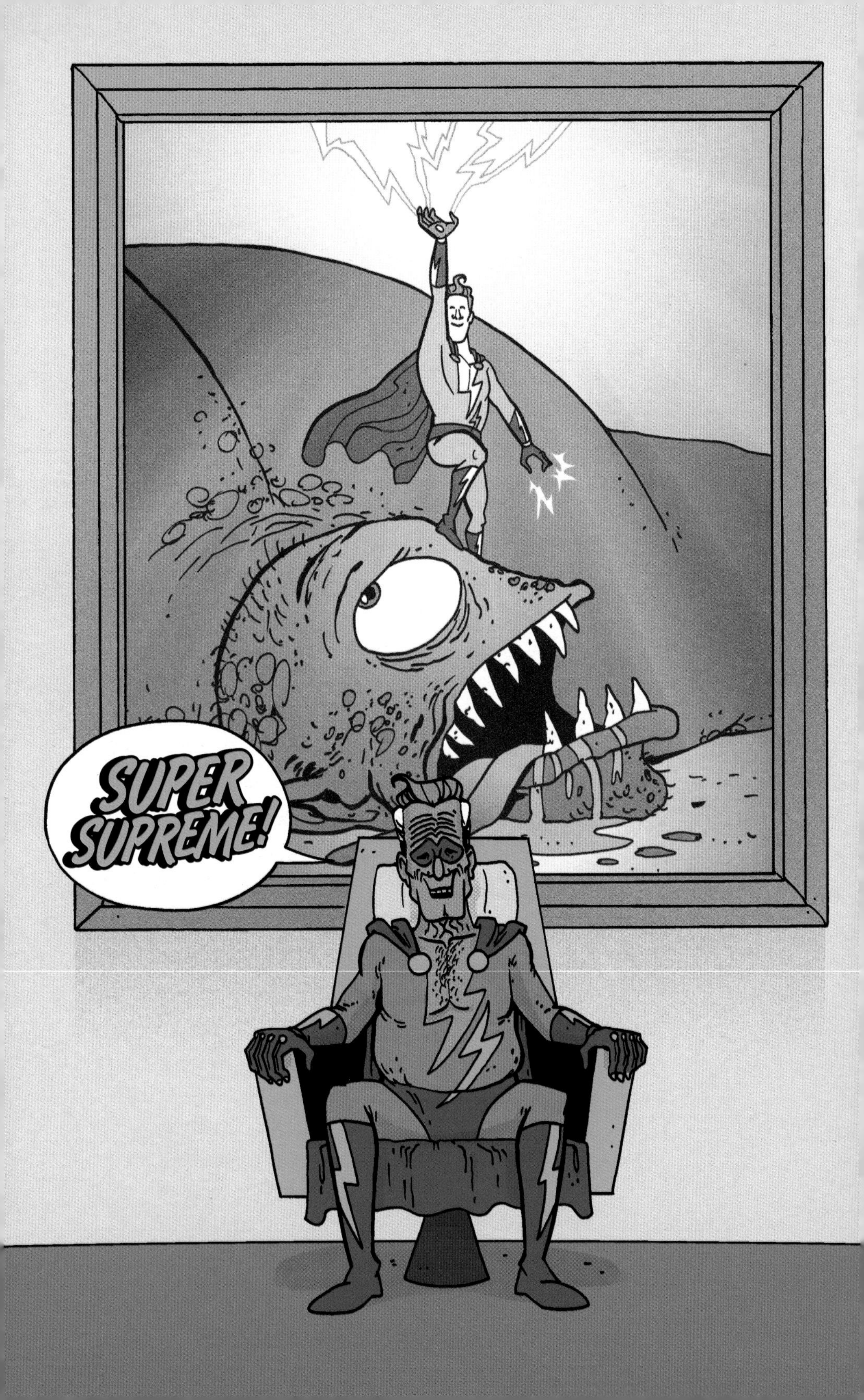
SUPER SUPREME!

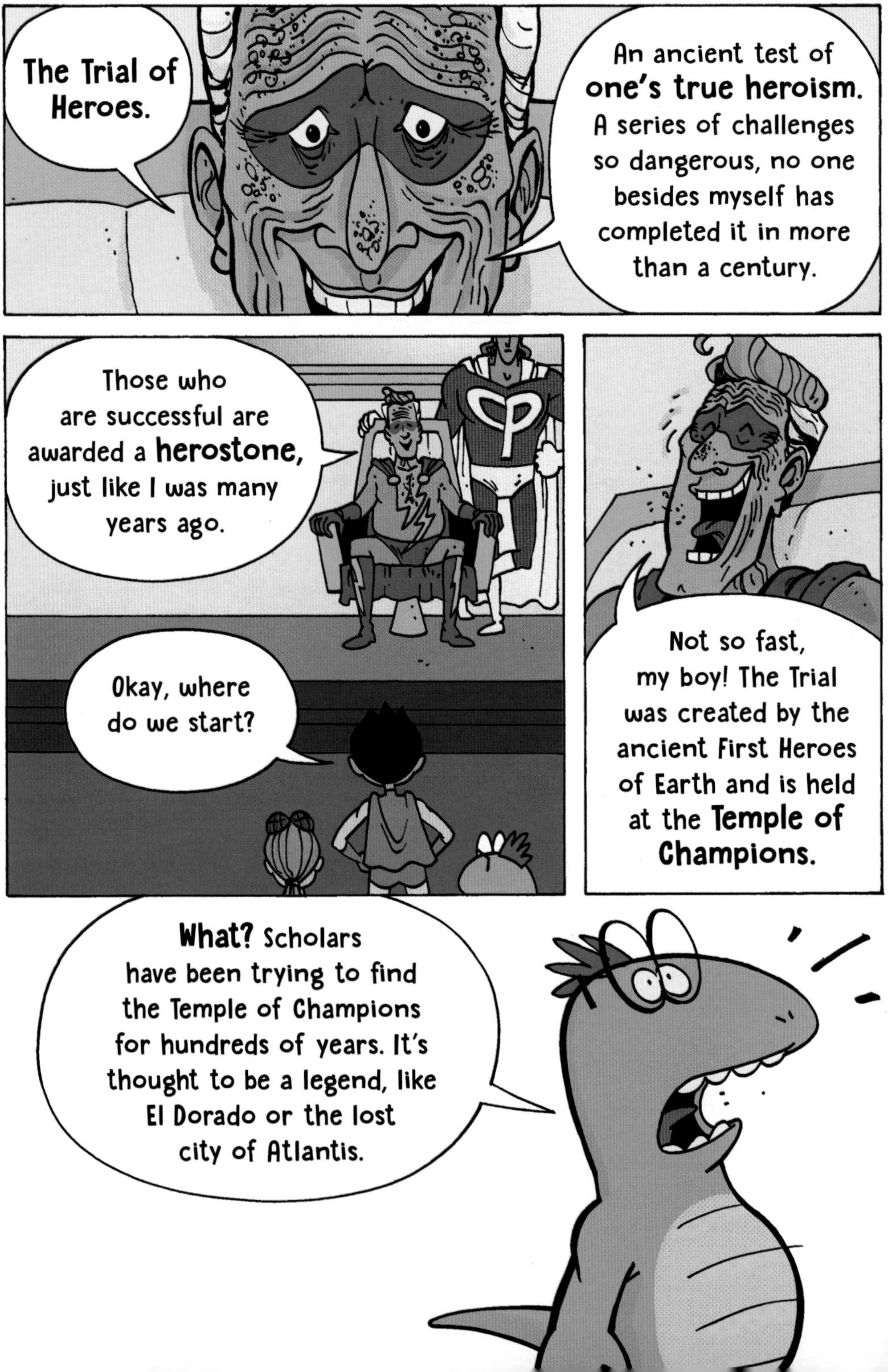
The Trial of Heroes.
An ancient test of one's true heroism. A series of challenges so dangerous, no one besides myself has completed it in more than a century.
Those who are successful are awarded a herostone, just like I was many years ago.
Okay, where do we start?
Not so fast, my boy! The Trial was created by the ancient First Heroes of Earth and is held at the Temple of Champions.
What? Scholars have been trying to find the Temple of Champions for hundreds of years. It's thought to be a legend, like El Dorado or the lost city of Atlantis.

41

43

44

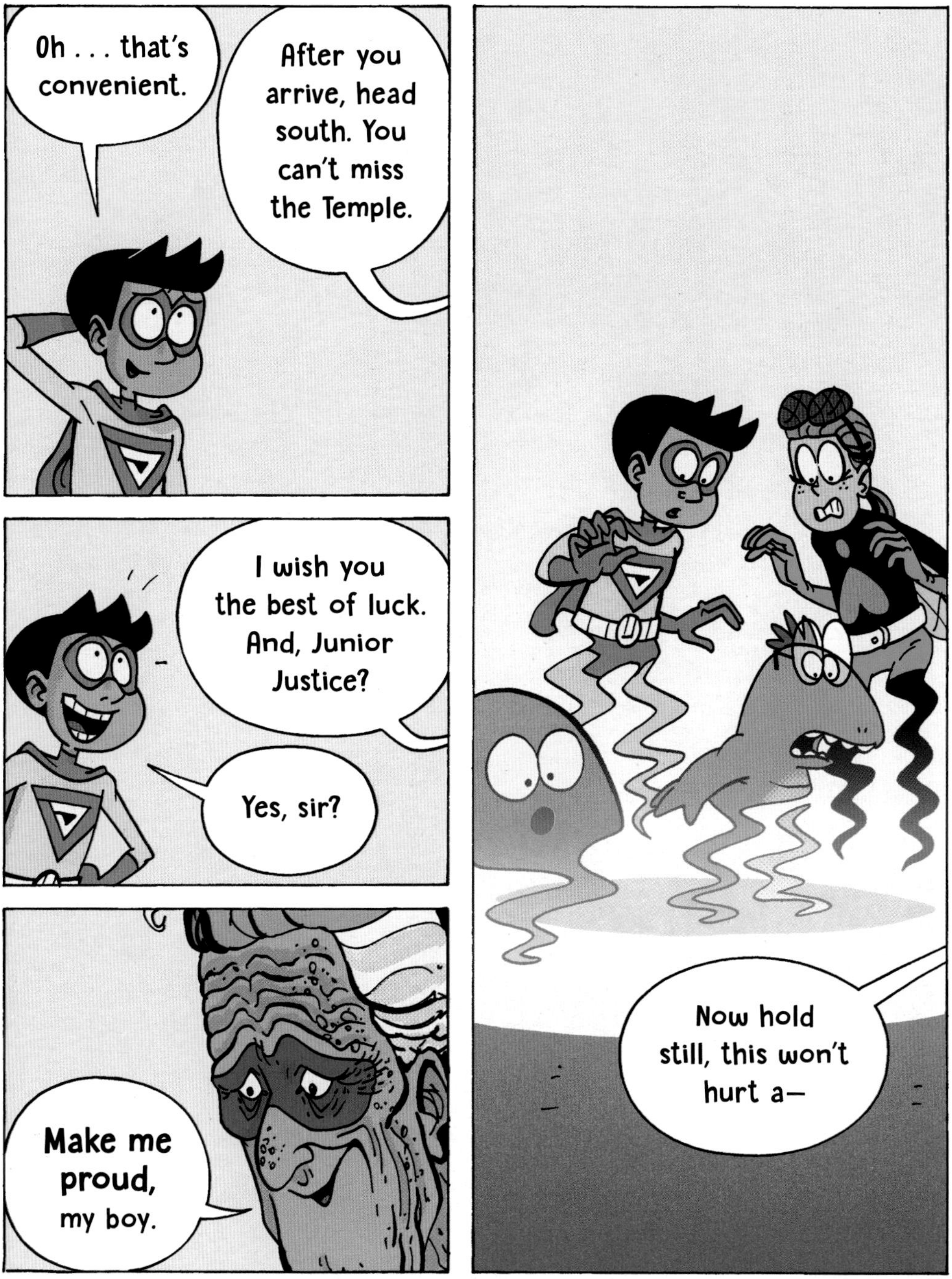
Oh . . . that's convenient.
After you arrive, head south. You can't miss the Temple.
I wish you the best of luck. And, Junior Justice?
Yes, sir?
Make me proud, my boy.
Now hold still, this won't hurt a—

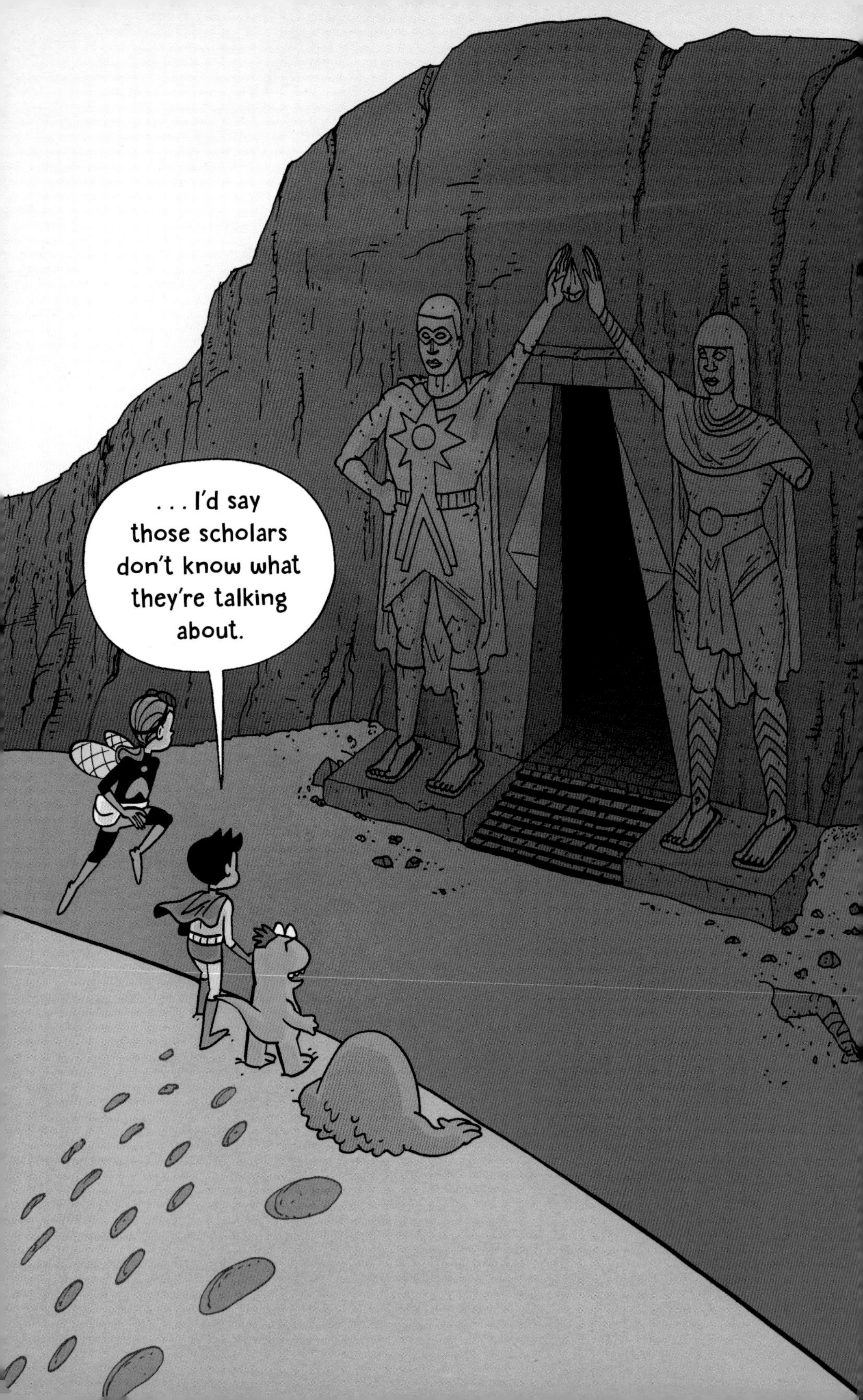
. . . I'd say those scholars don't know what they're talking about.

Chapter

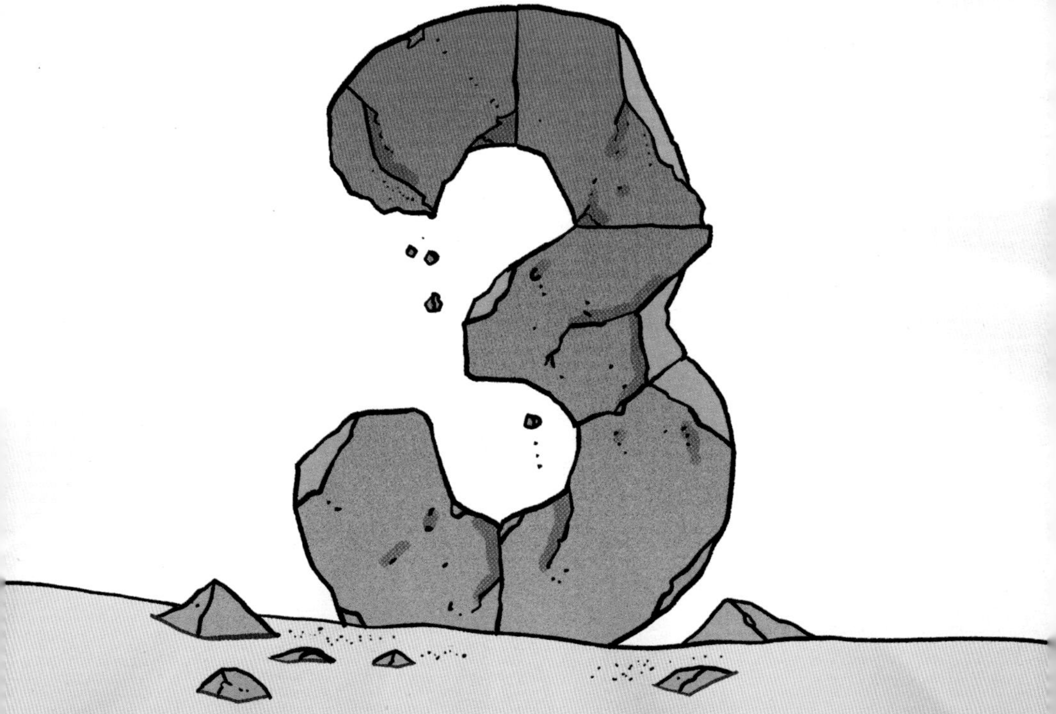
3

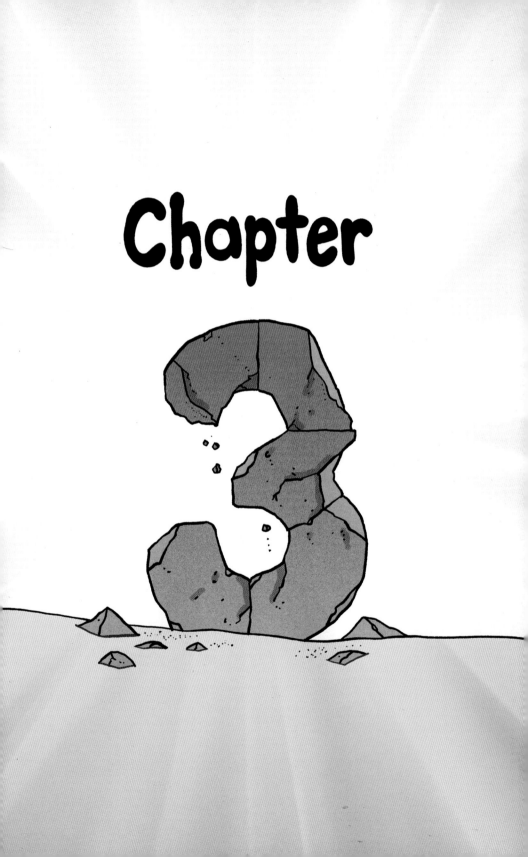

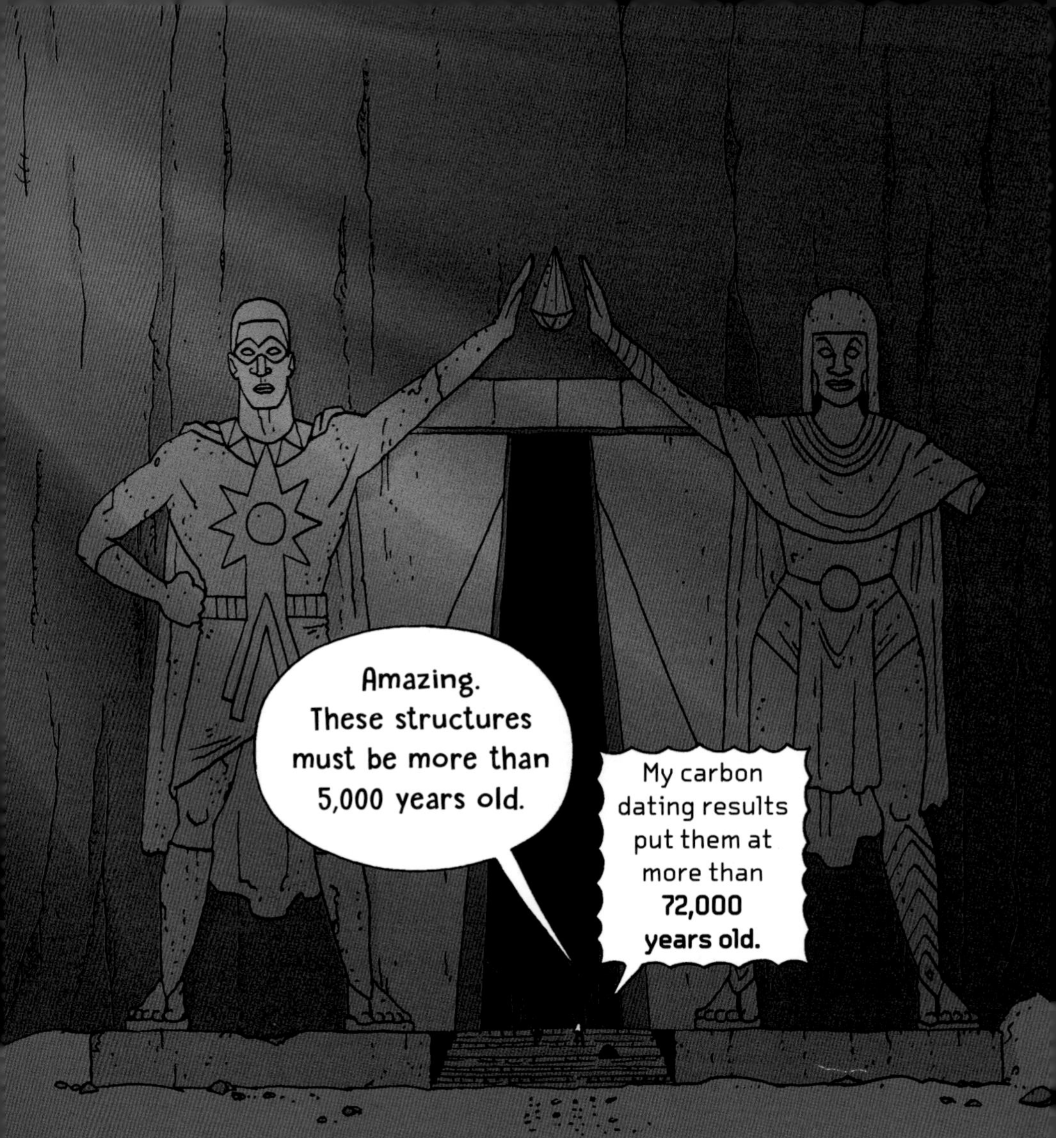
Amazing. These structures must be more than 5,000 years old.
My carbon dating results put them at more than **72,000 years old.**

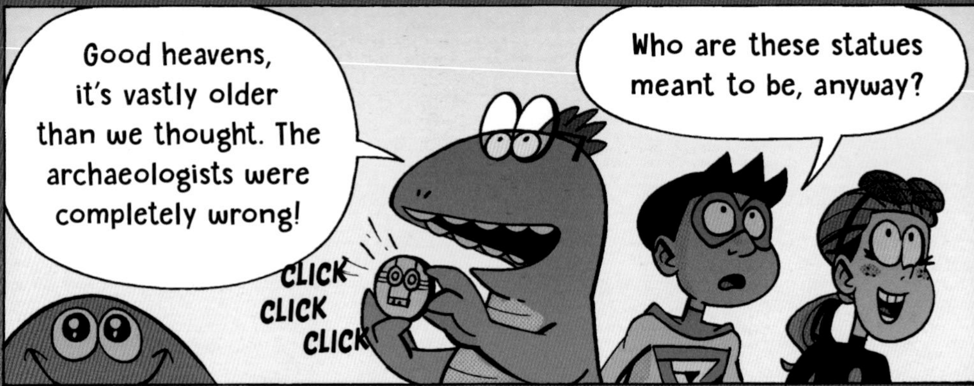
Good heavens, it's vastly older than we thought. The archaeologists were completely wrong!
CLICK CLICK CLICK
Who are these statues meant to be, anyway?

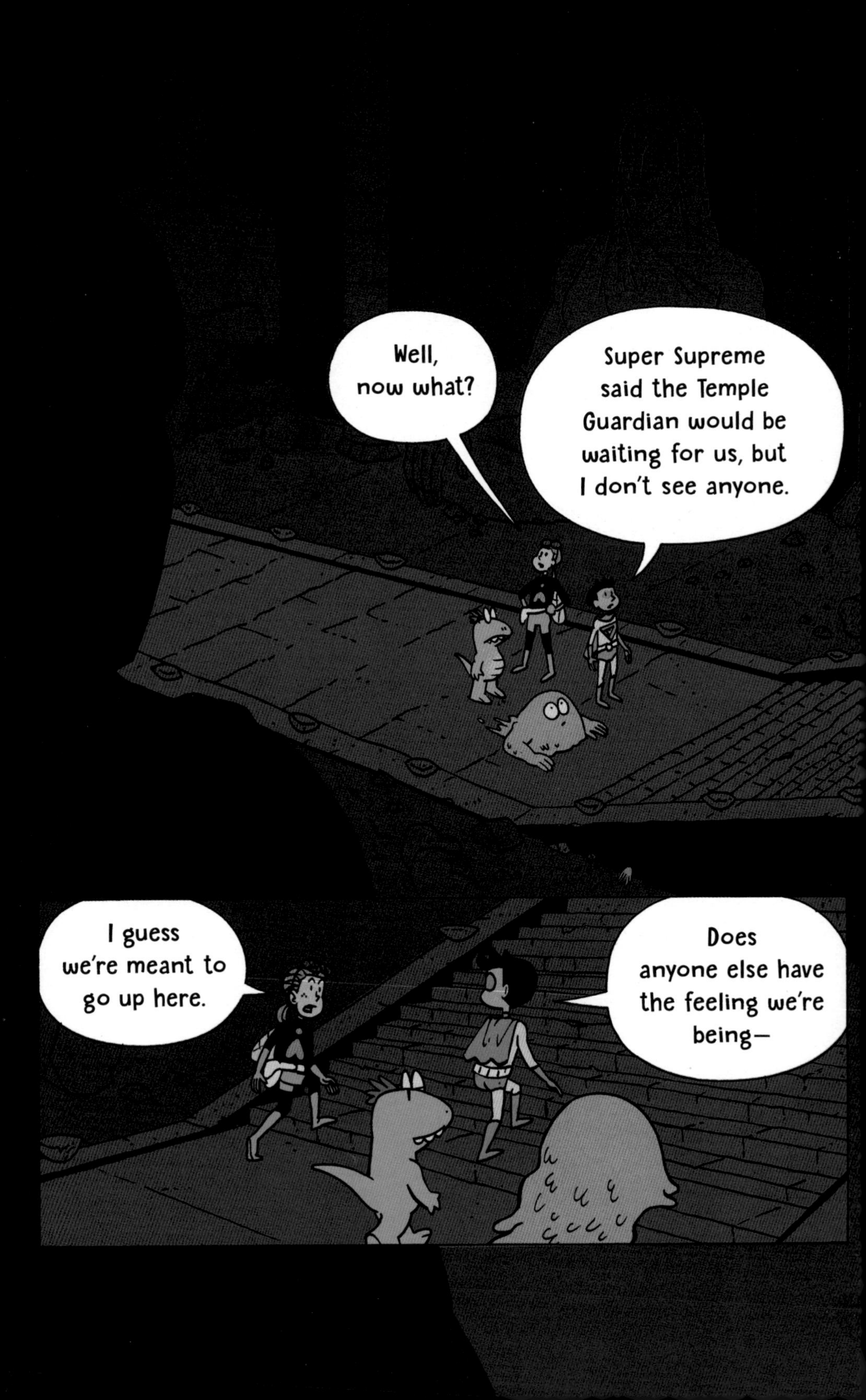
Well, now what?
Super Supreme said the Temple Guardian would be waiting for us, but I don't see anyone.
I guess we're meant to go up here.
Does anyone else have the feeling we're being—

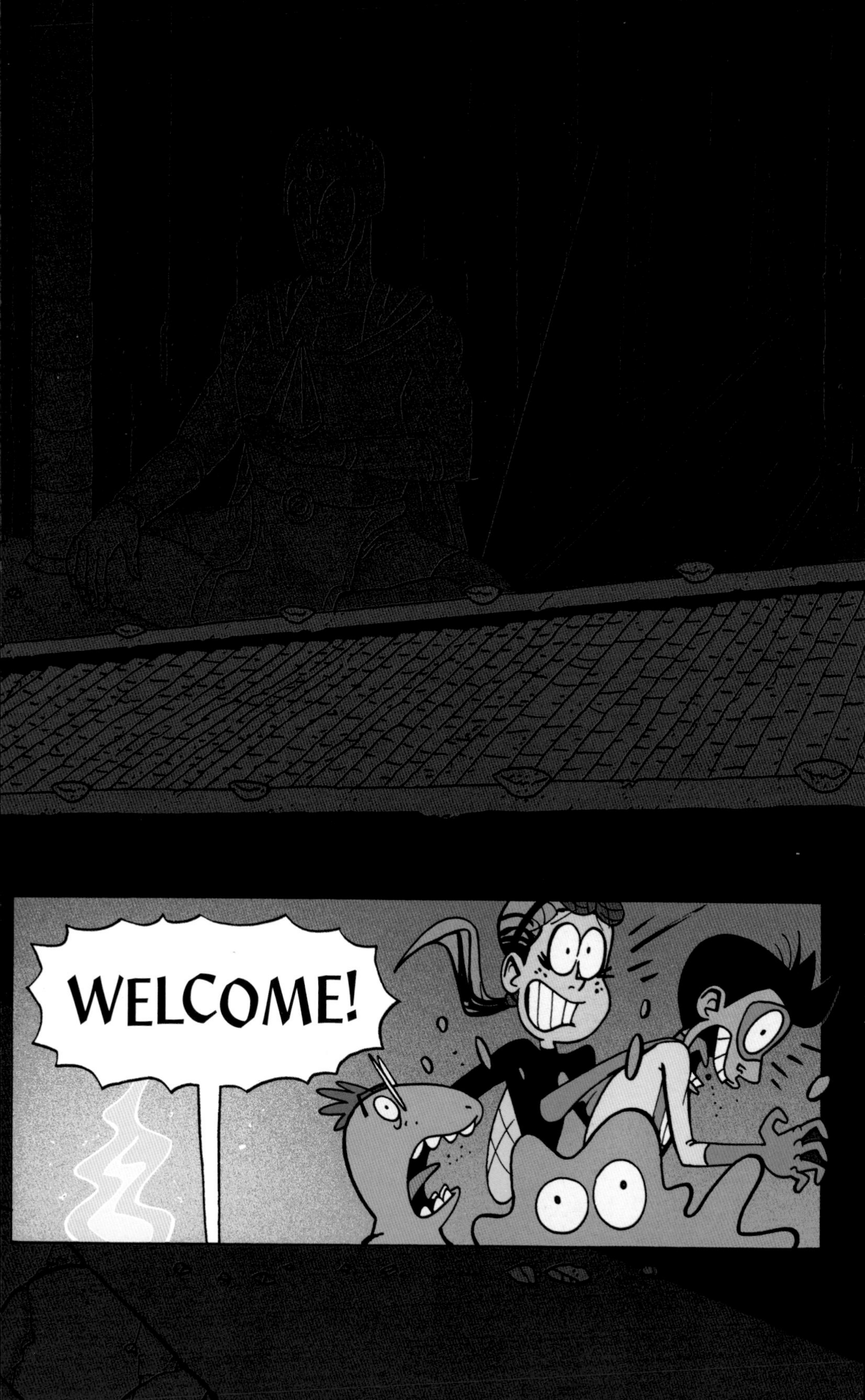
WELCOME!

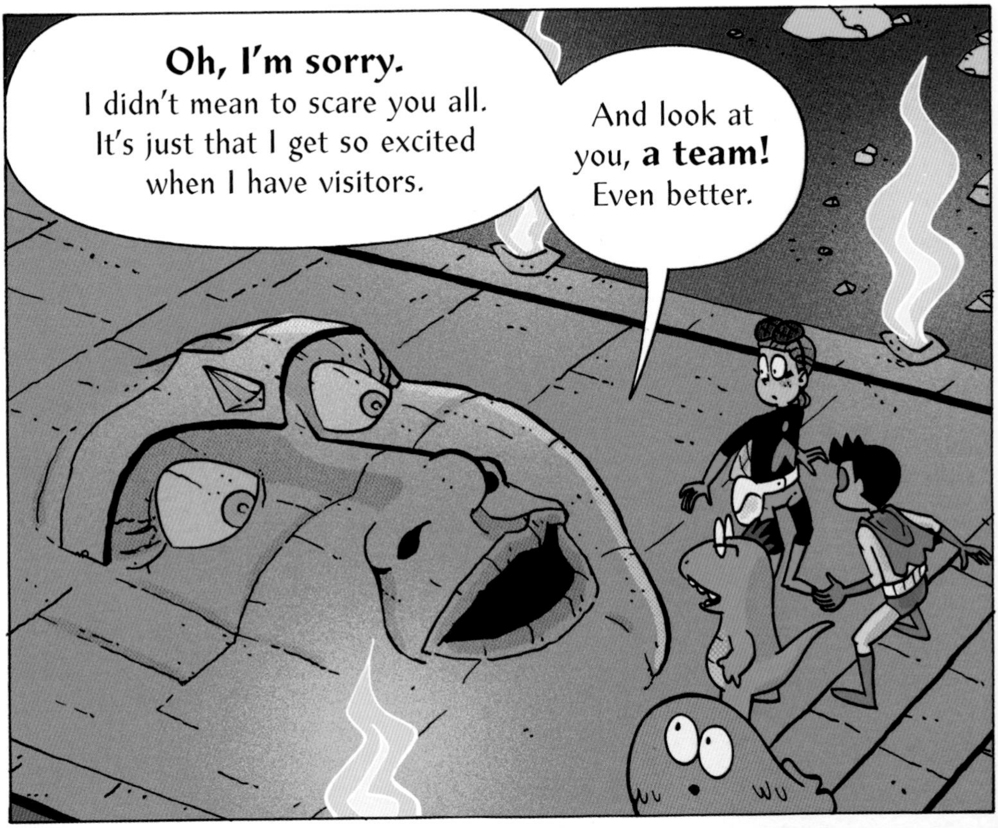
Oh, I'm sorry.
I didn't mean to scare you all. It's just that I get so excited when I have visitors.
And look at you, **a team!** Even better.

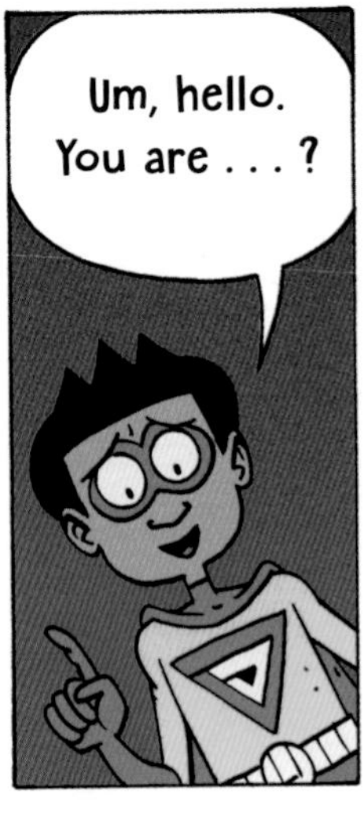
Um, hello. You are . . . ?

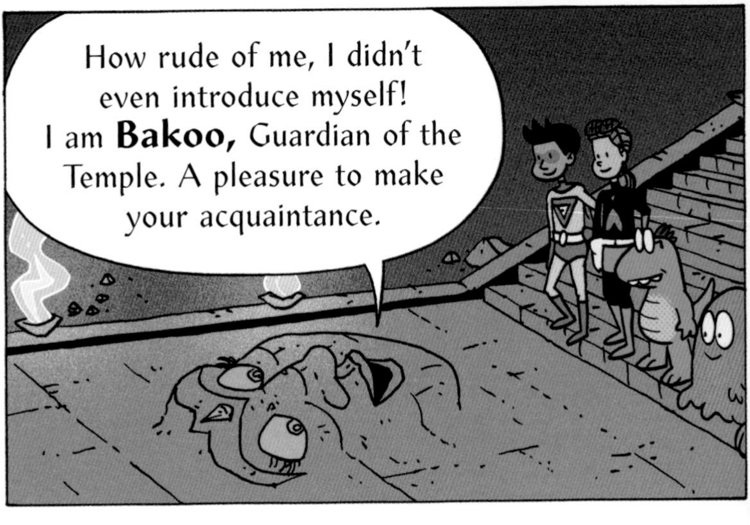
How rude of me, I didn't even introduce myself! I am **Bakoo,** Guardian of the Temple. A pleasure to make your acquaintance.

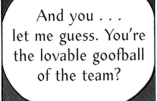
And you . . . let me guess. You're the lovable goofball of the team?

I'll have you know I've been shortlisted for the Nobel Prize!

No, Goo lovable goofball!

My mistake. I wish I'd known you were coming. This place is an **absolute mess.** Here, let me clean up a bit.

Yes, guarding this temple is a thankless task, but someone has to do it!

SWEEP SWEEP

SWEEP

You see, my people celebrated the ideals of **heroism and justice above all.** But, in a society where **everyone** had incredible powers, we needed a way to test who was a real hero and who wasn't. Thus we built this temple, and the **Trial of Heroes** was born.
That is why you're here, isn't it? **For the Trial?**
You bet. We plan to complete it!
Ha ha ha! If I had a gold coin for every time I've heard that . . . ! I've met many like you, Junior Justice. Confident and full of bravado! Such a shame that you'll most likely be **dead** by the day's end.

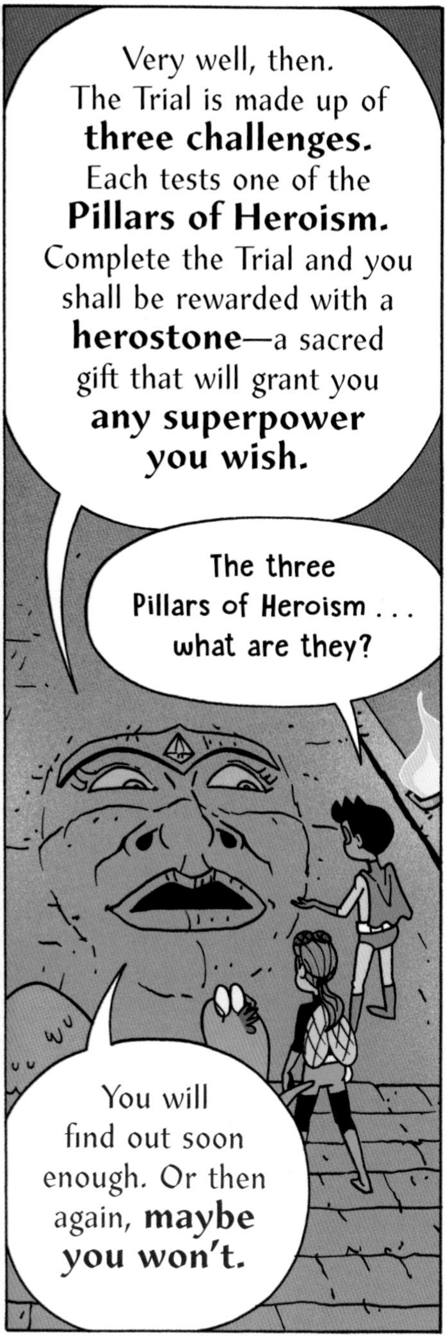
Very well, then. The Trial is made up of **three challenges.** Each tests one of the **Pillars of Heroism.** Complete the Trial and you shall be rewarded with a **herostone**—a sacred gift that will grant you **any superpower you wish.**
The three Pillars of Heroism . . . what are they?
You will find out soon enough. Or then again, **maybe you won't.**

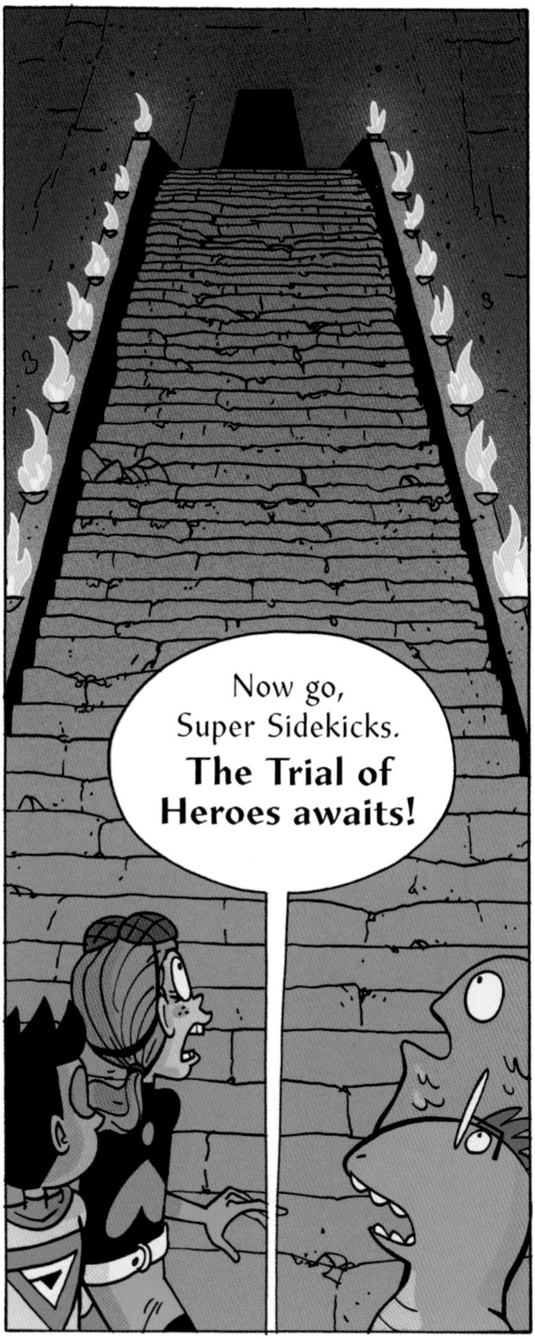
Now go, Super Sidekicks. **The Trial of Heroes awaits!**

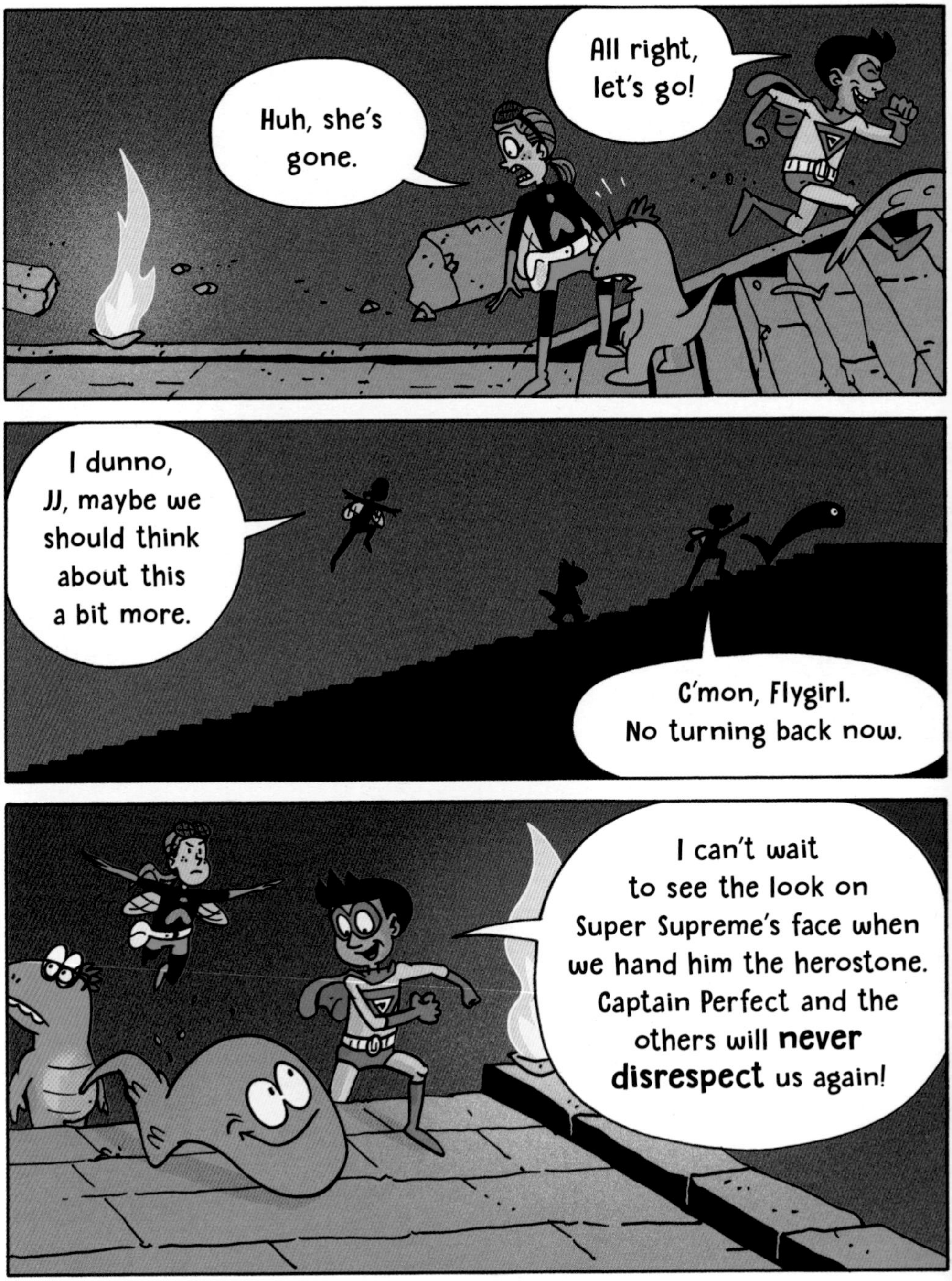
Huh, she's gone.
All right, let's go!
I dunno, JJ, maybe we should think about this a bit more.
C'mon, Flygirl. No turning back now.
I can't wait to see the look on Super Supreme's face when we hand him the herostone. Captain Perfect and the others will **never disrespect** us again!

Look, there's some kind of inscription on the wall.
Challenge one is the courage pit, An ocean fire of highest stakes. Are you worthy or will you quit? For powers not a hero makes.
Mmm, it's a poem. Basic rhyme scheme. Nowhere near as stirring as my own—
SLAM!
That can't be good.

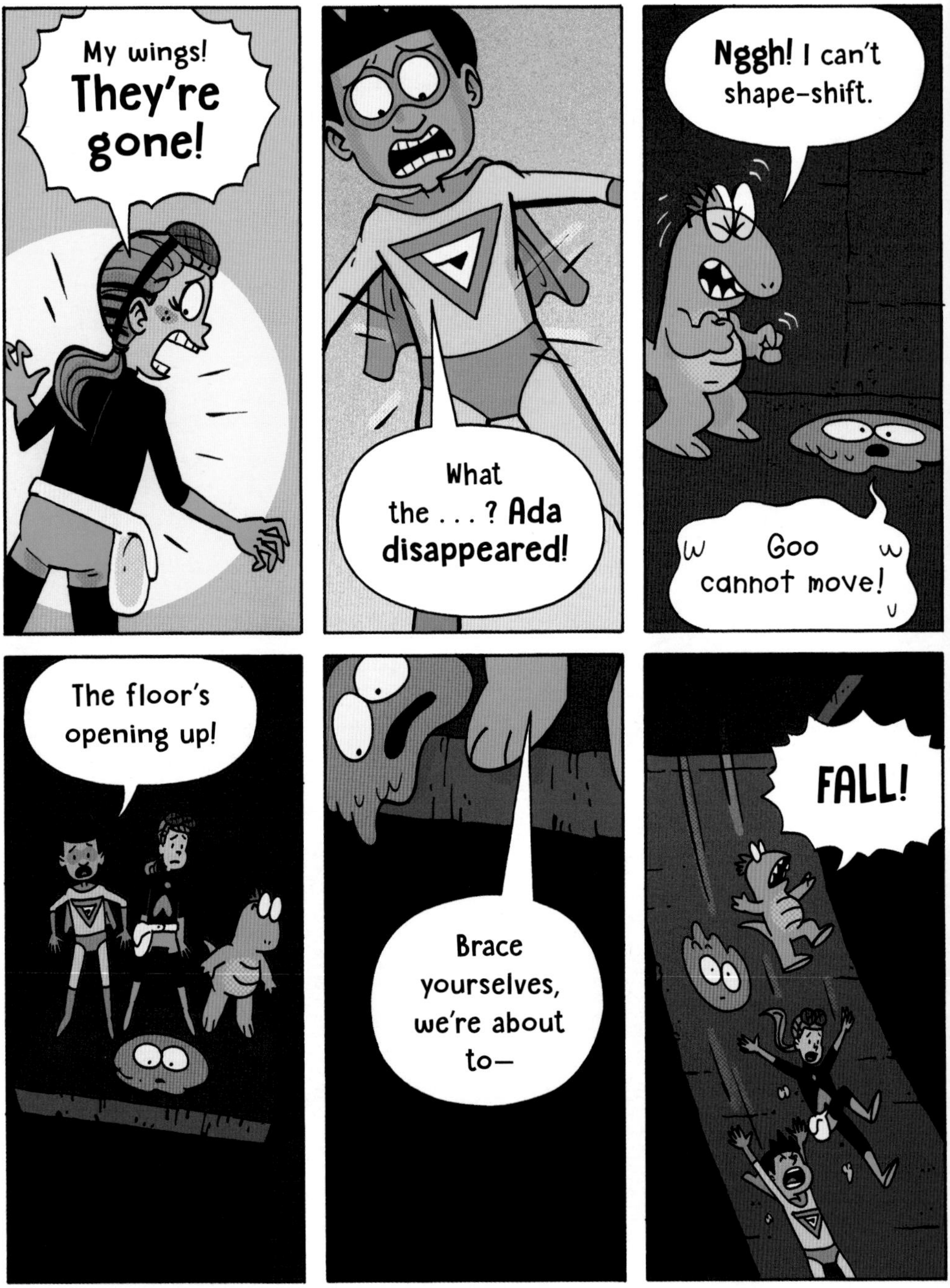
My wings! They're gone!
What the . . . ? Ada disappeared!
Nggh! I can't shape-shift.
Goo cannot move!
The floor's opening up!
Brace yourselves, we're about to—
FALL!

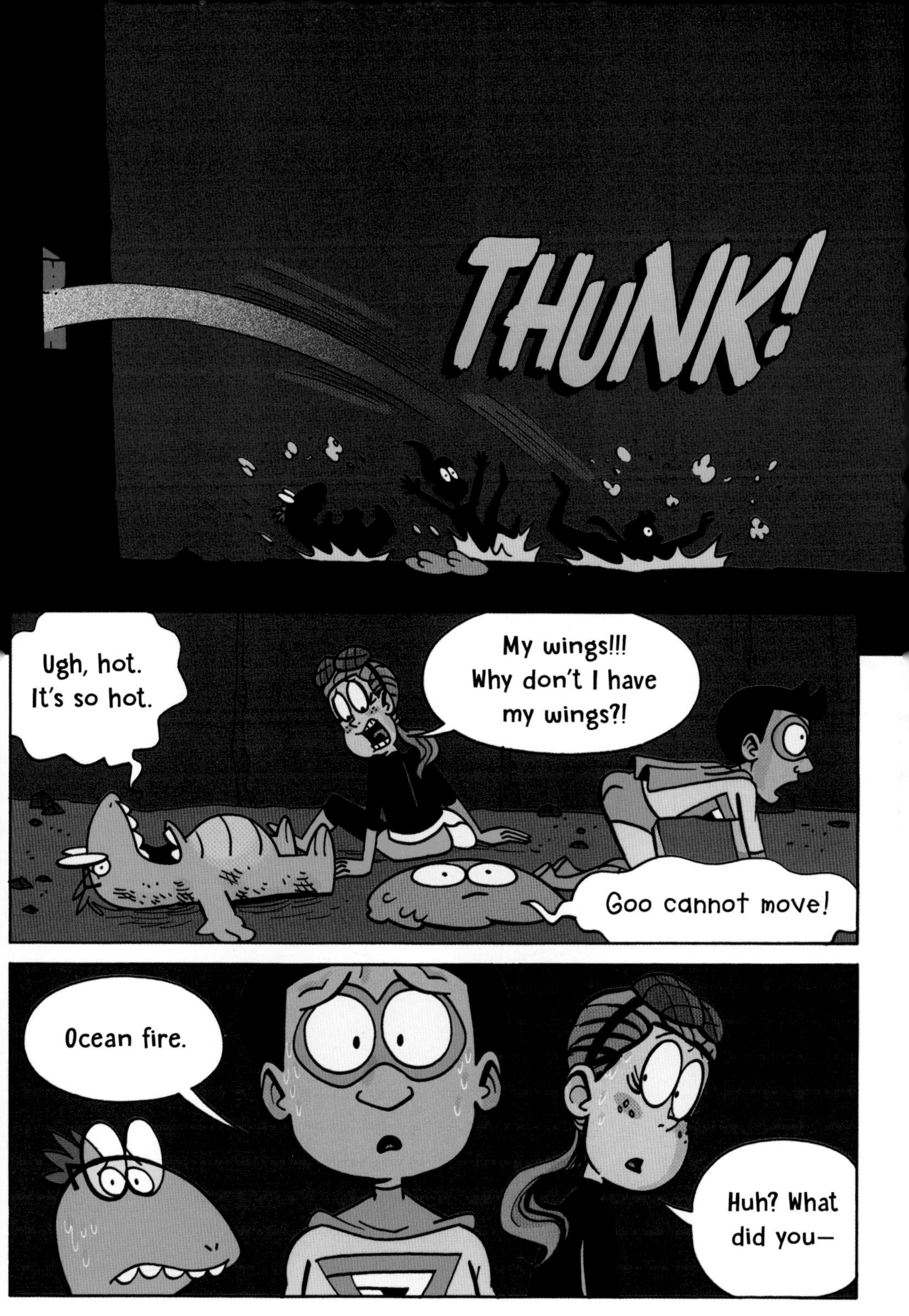
THUNK!
Ugh, hot. It's so hot.
My wings!!! Why don't I have my wings?!
Goo cannot move!
Ocean fire.
Huh? What did you—

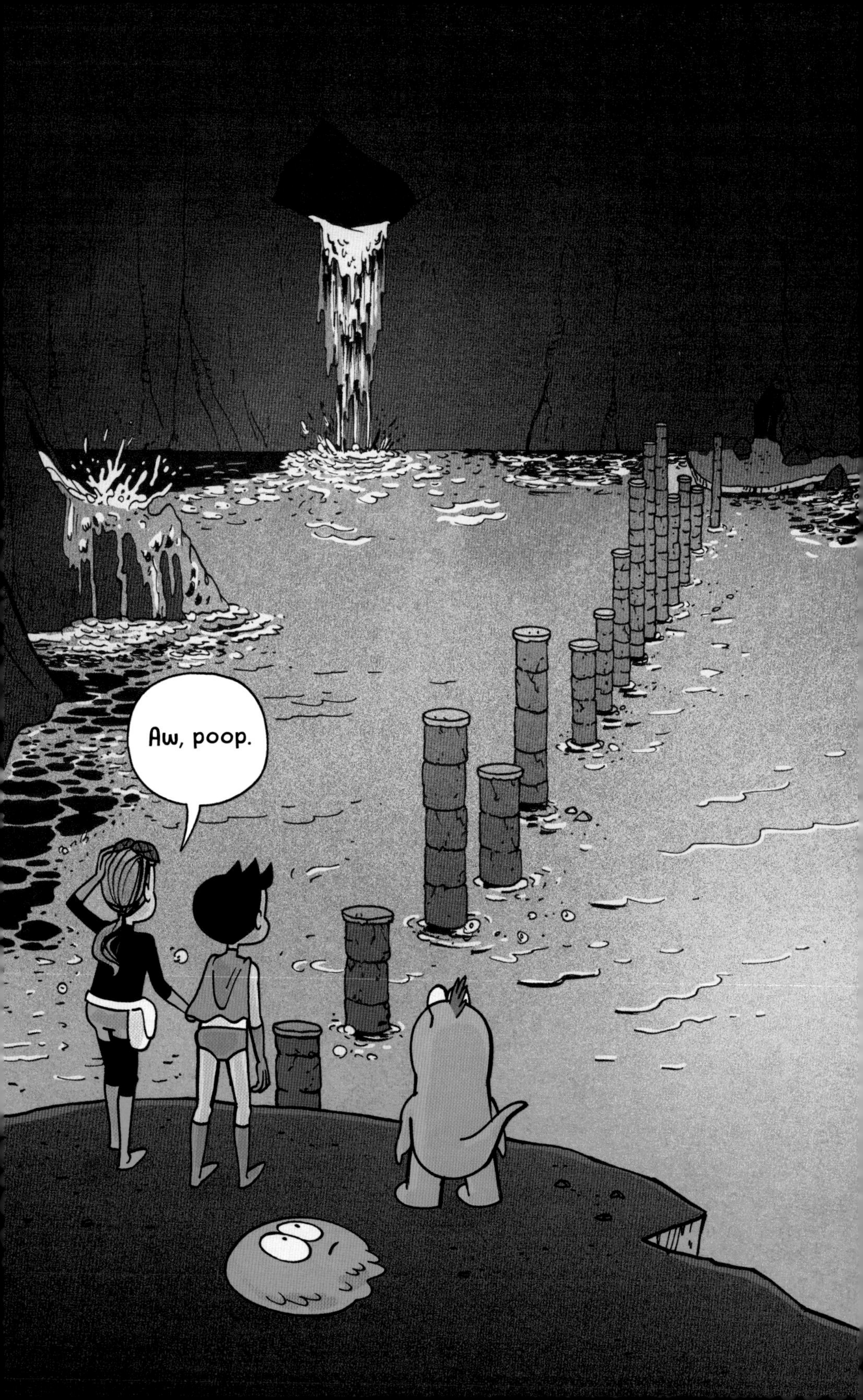
Aw, poop.

65

67

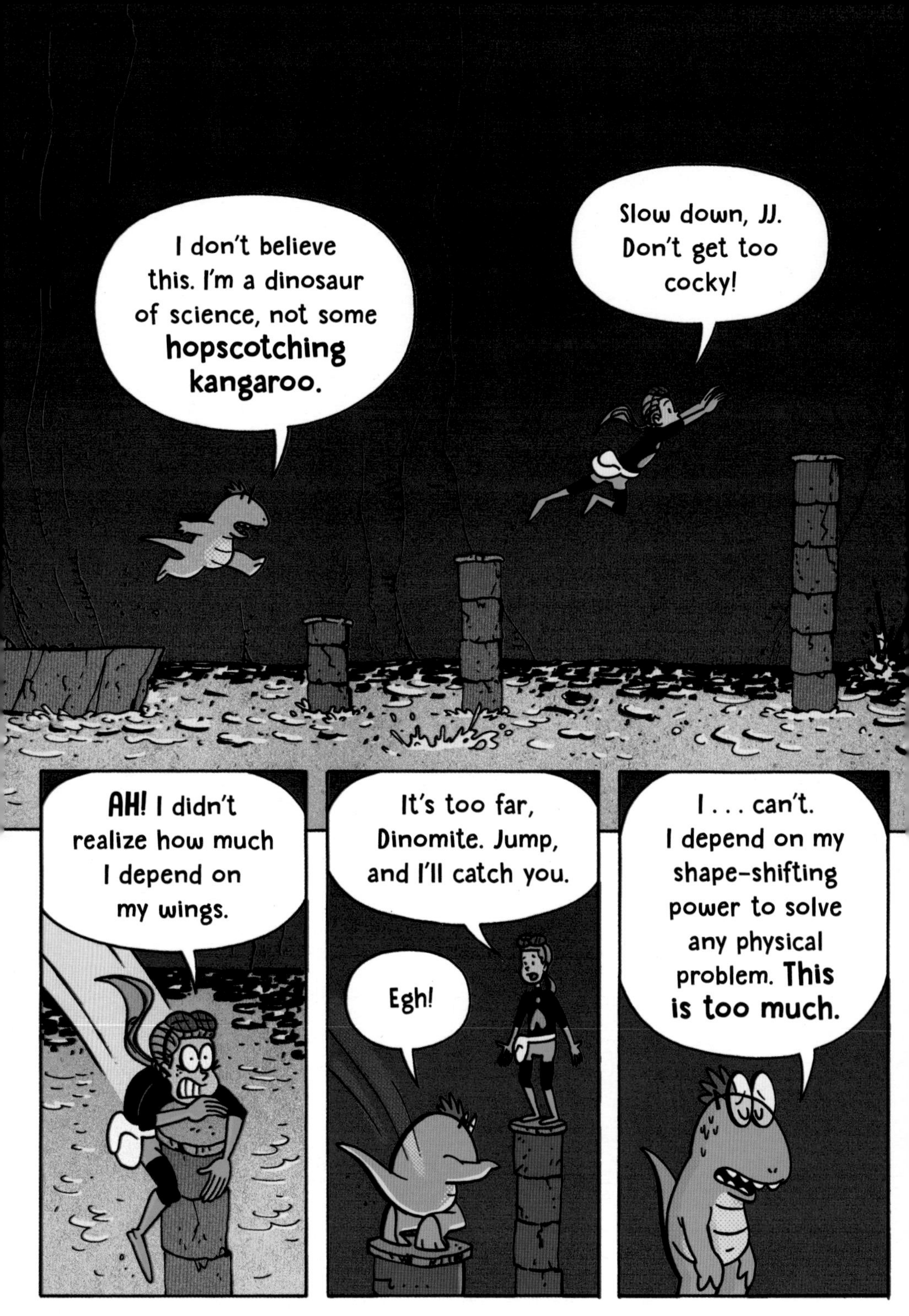
I don't believe this. I'm a dinosaur of science, not some **hopscotching kangaroo.**
Slow down, JJ. Don't get too cocky!
AH! I didn't realize how much I depend on my wings.
It's too far, Dinomite. Jump, and I'll catch you.
Egh!
I . . . can't. I depend on my shape-shifting power to solve any physical problem. **This is too much.**

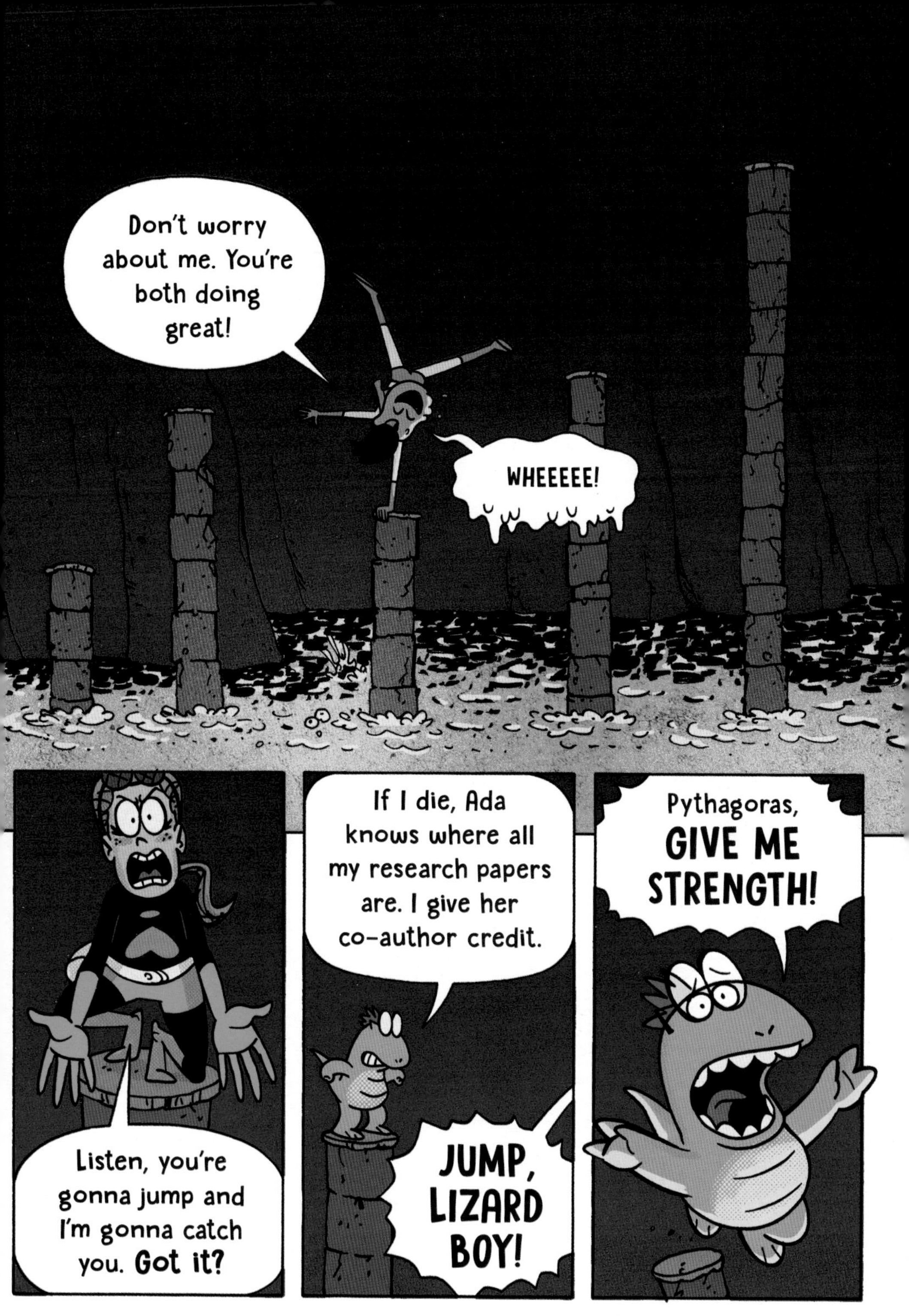
Don't worry about me. You're both doing great!
WHEEEEE!
Listen, you're gonna jump and I'm gonna catch you. Got it?
If I die, Ada knows where all my research papers are. I give her co-author credit.
JUMP, LIZARD BOY!
Pythagoras, GIVE ME STRENGTH!

GOTCHA!

AHHH!

SSSSSSSSSS

Forget about it. Just get up here!

I owe you my life, Flygirl.

We'll treat your wound once we're safe, Dinomite. Just move carefully . . .

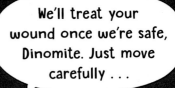

. . . I'm not sure how long these pillars are going to hold.

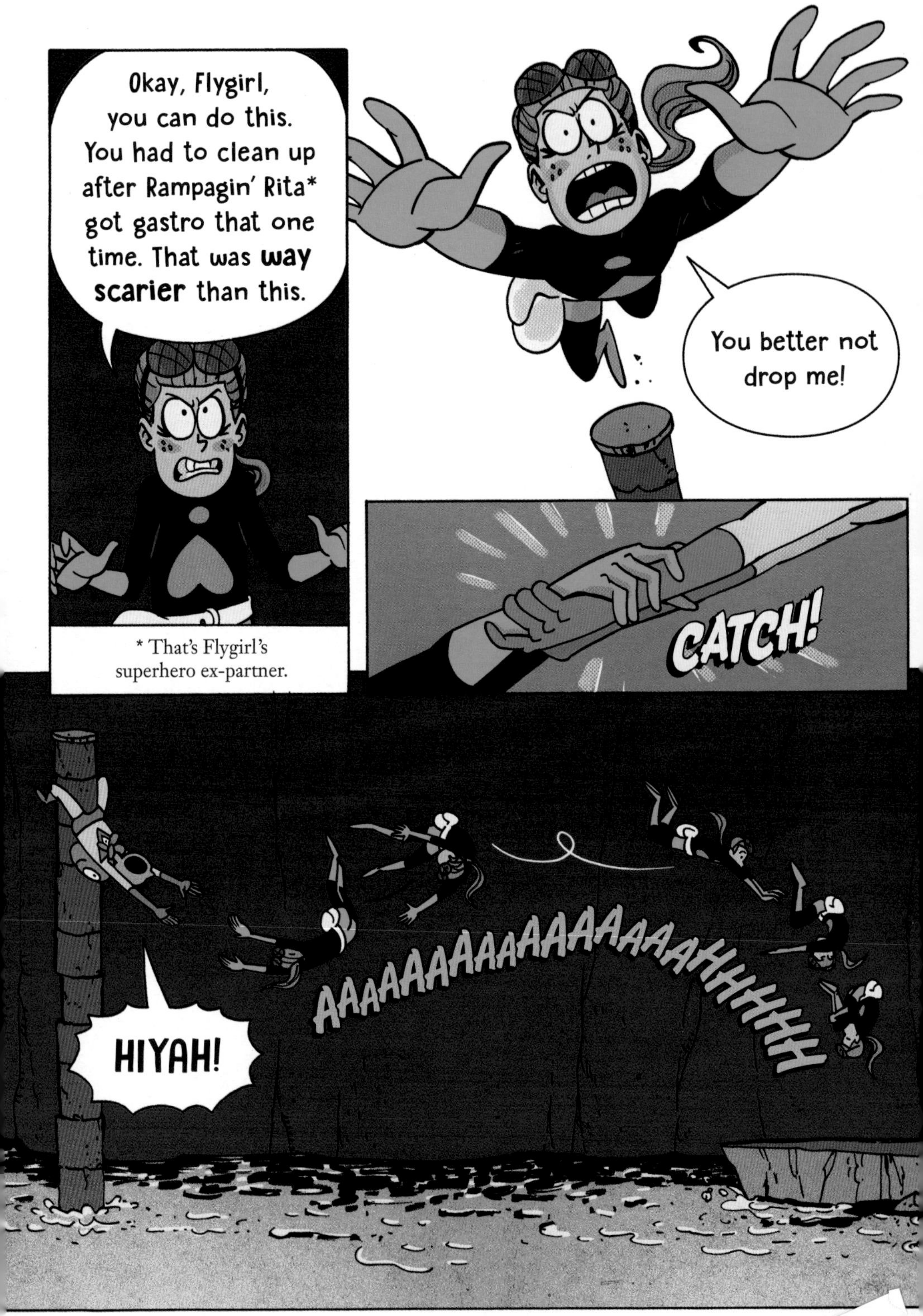

Okay, Flygirl, you can do this. You had to clean up after Rampagin' Rita* got gastro that one time. That was **way scarier** than this.
* That's Flygirl's superhero ex-partner.
You better not drop me!
CATCH!
HIYAH!
AAAAAAAAAAAAAAAAAHHHHHHH

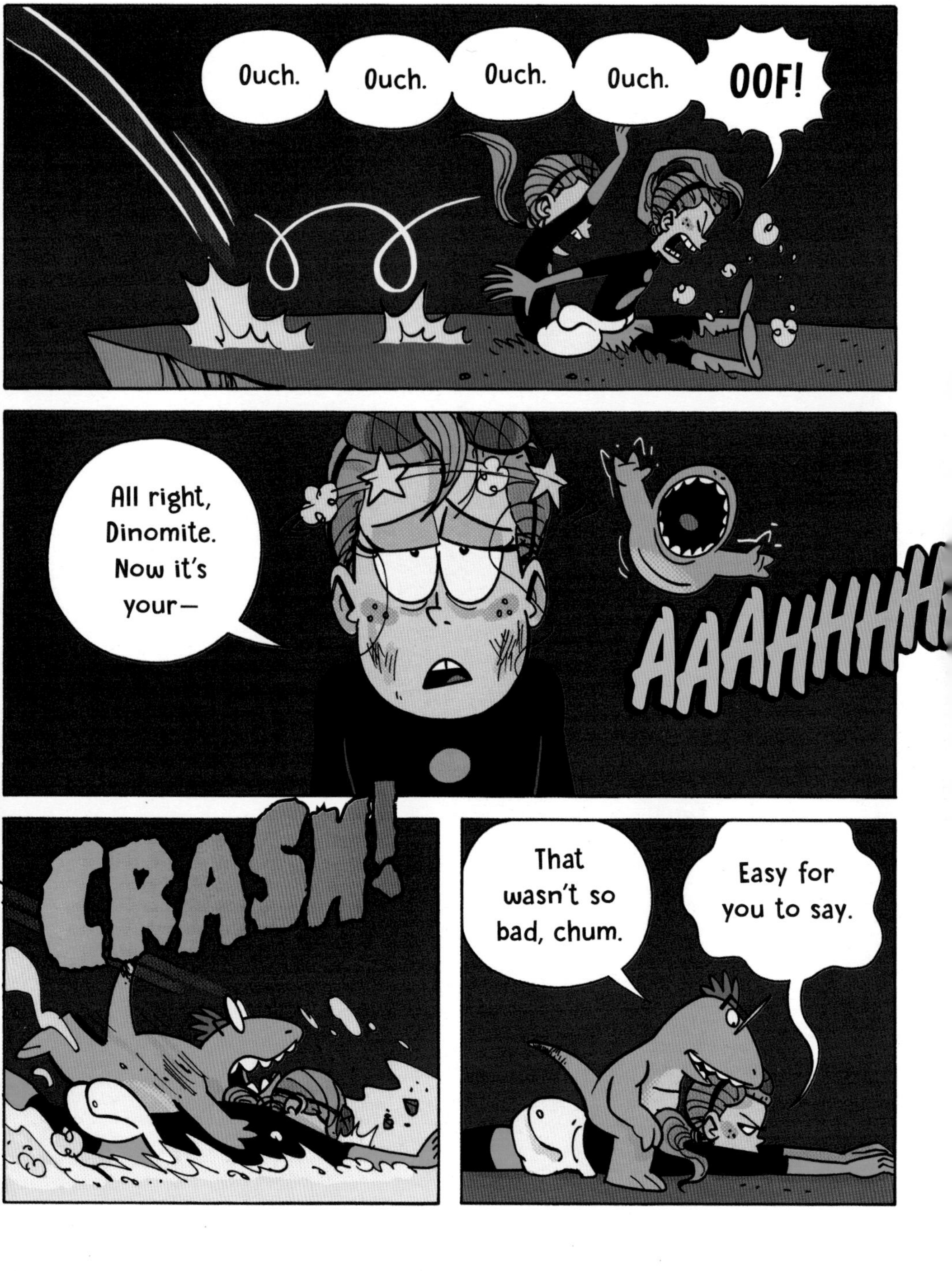
Ouch.
Ouch.
Ouch.
Ouch.
OOF!
All right, Dinomite. Now it's your—
AAAHHHH
CRASH!
That wasn't so bad, chum.
Easy for you to say.

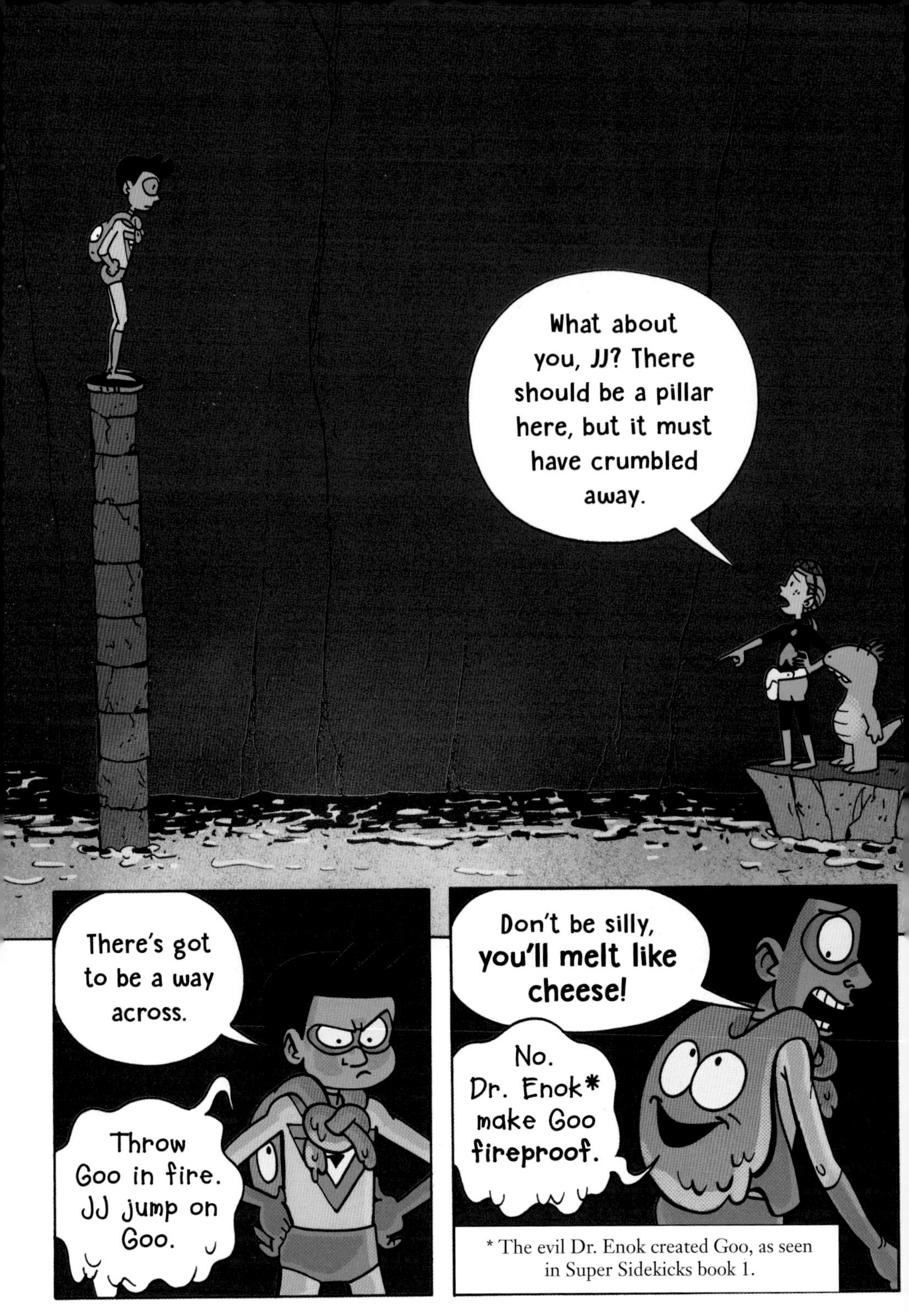
What about you, JJ? There should be a pillar here, but it must have crumbled away.
There's got to be a way across.
Throw Goo in fire. JJ jump on Goo.
Don't be silly, you'll melt like cheese!
No. Dr. Enok* make Goo fireproof.

* The evil Dr. Enok created Goo, as seen in Super Sidekicks book 1.

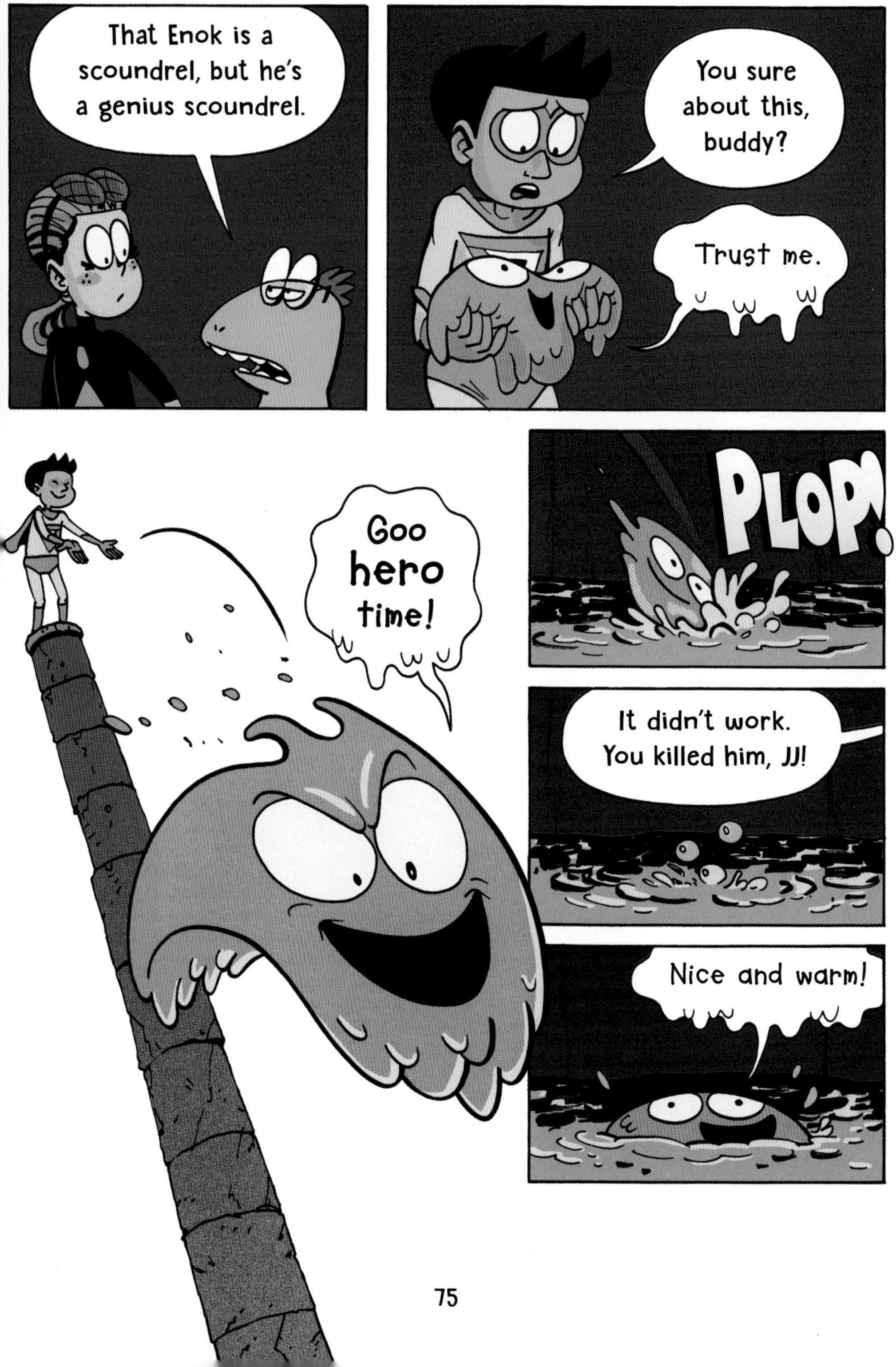
That Enok is a scoundrel, but he's a genius scoundrel.
You sure about this, buddy?
Trust me.
Goo hero time!
PLOP!
It didn't work. You killed him, JJ!
Nice and warm!

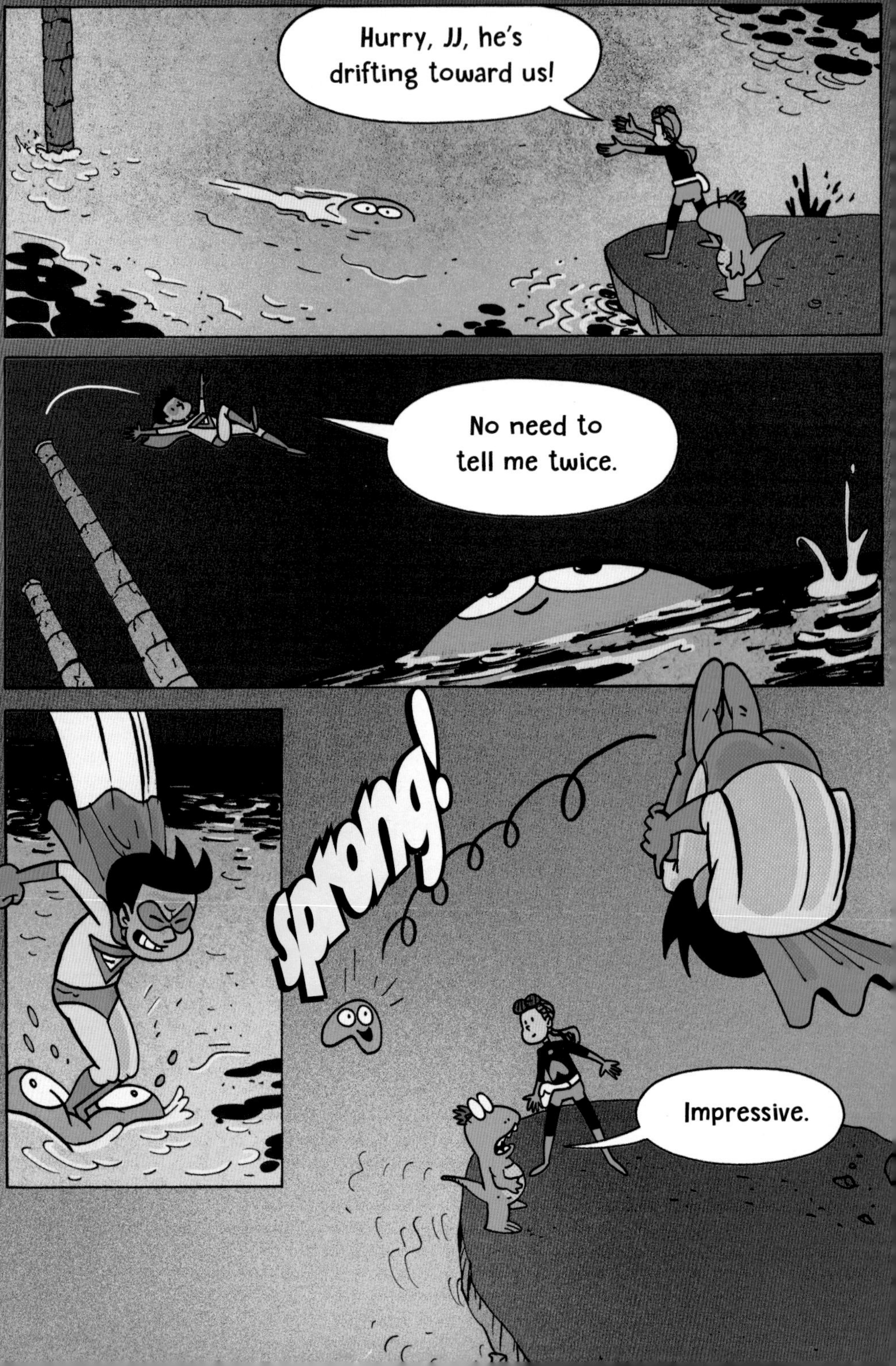
Hurry, JJ, he's drifting toward us!
No need to tell me twice.
sprong!
Impressive.

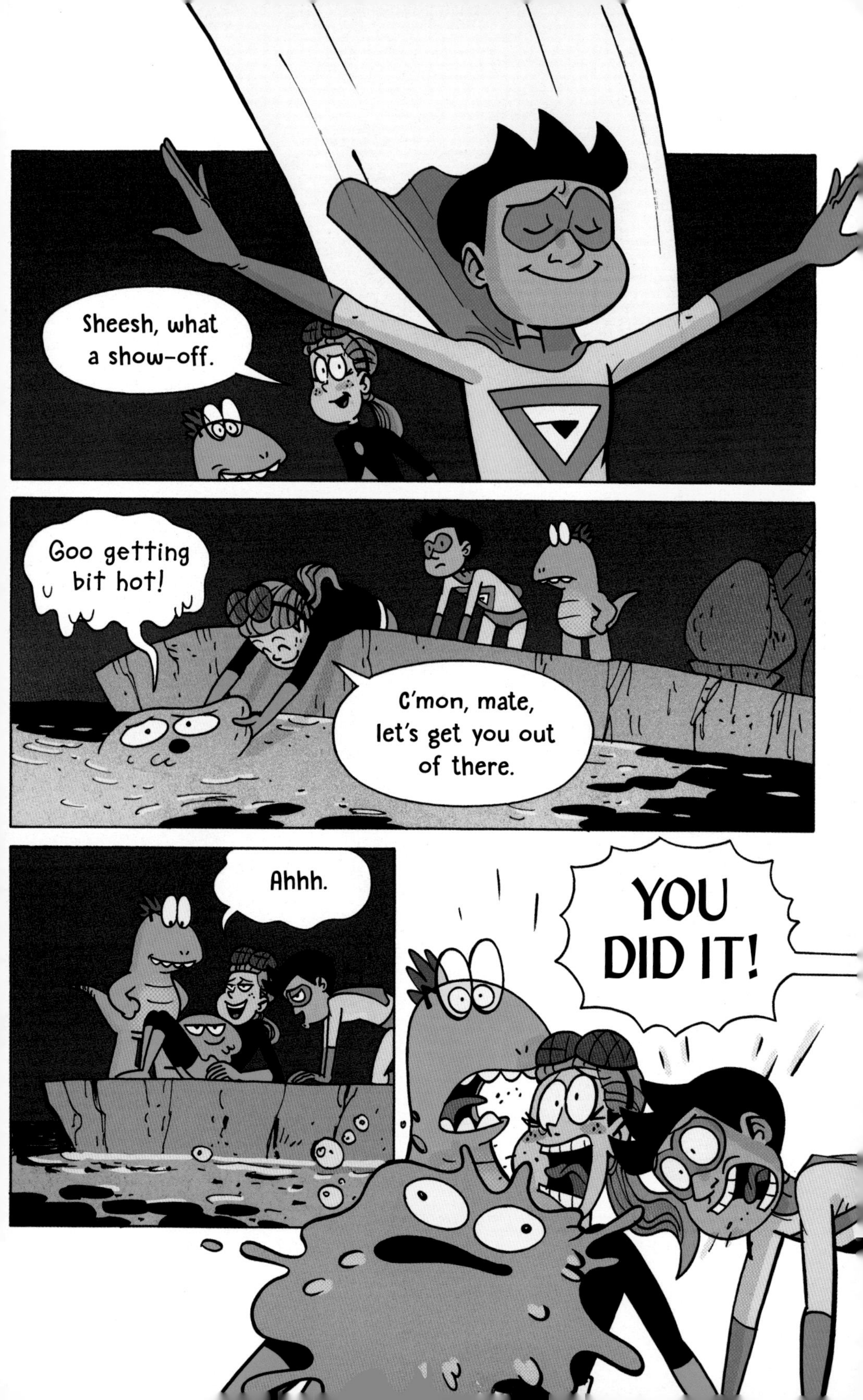

Sheesh, what a show-off.
Goo getting bit hot!
C'mon, mate, let's get you out of there.
Ahhh.
YOU DID IT!

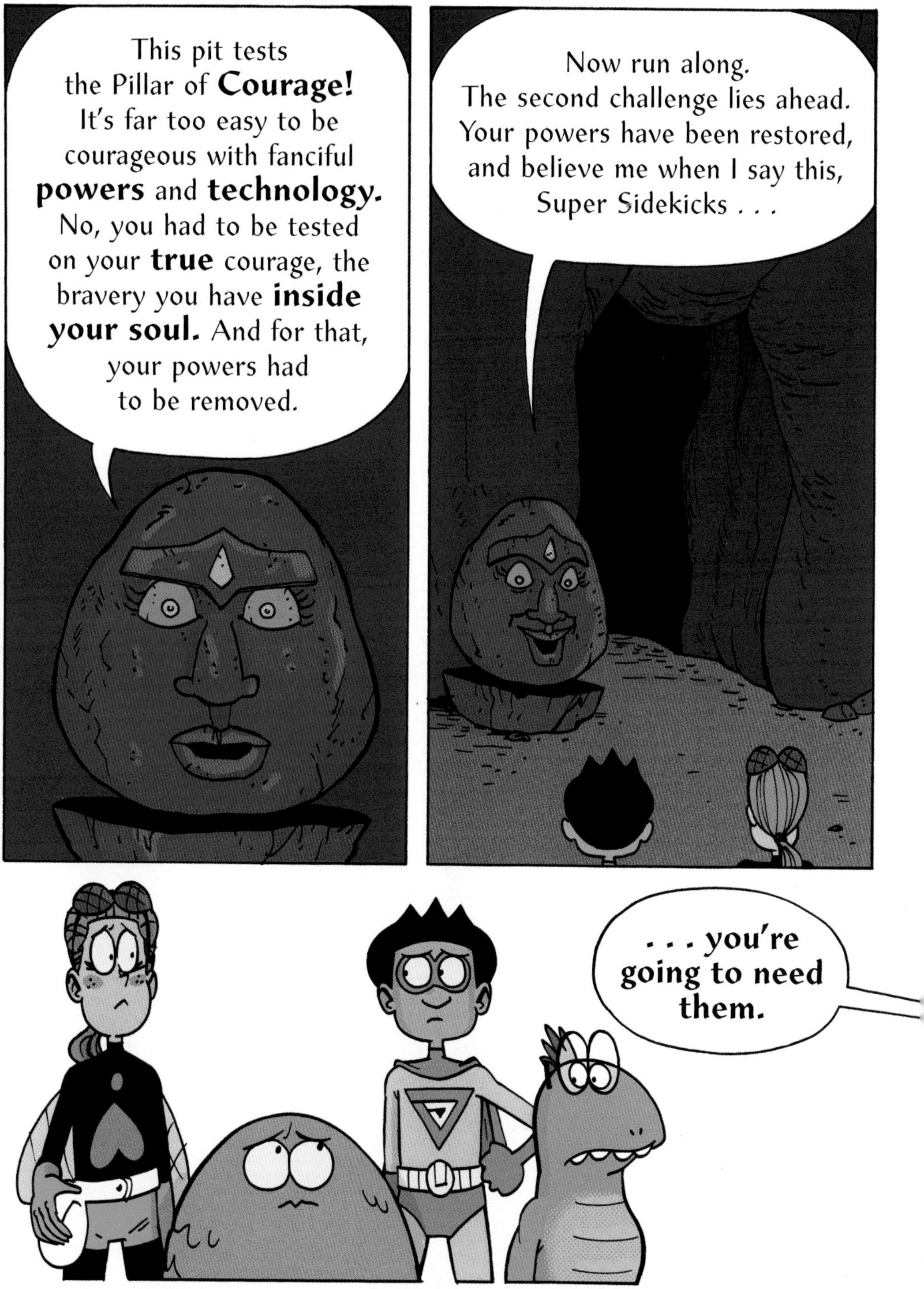
This pit tests the Pillar of **Courage!** It's far too easy to be courageous with fanciful **powers** and **technology.** No, you had to be tested on your **true** courage, the bravery you have **inside your soul.** And for that, your powers had to be removed.
Now run along. The second challenge lies ahead. Your powers have been restored, and believe me when I say this, Super Sidekicks . . .
. . . you're going to need them.

Chapter 4

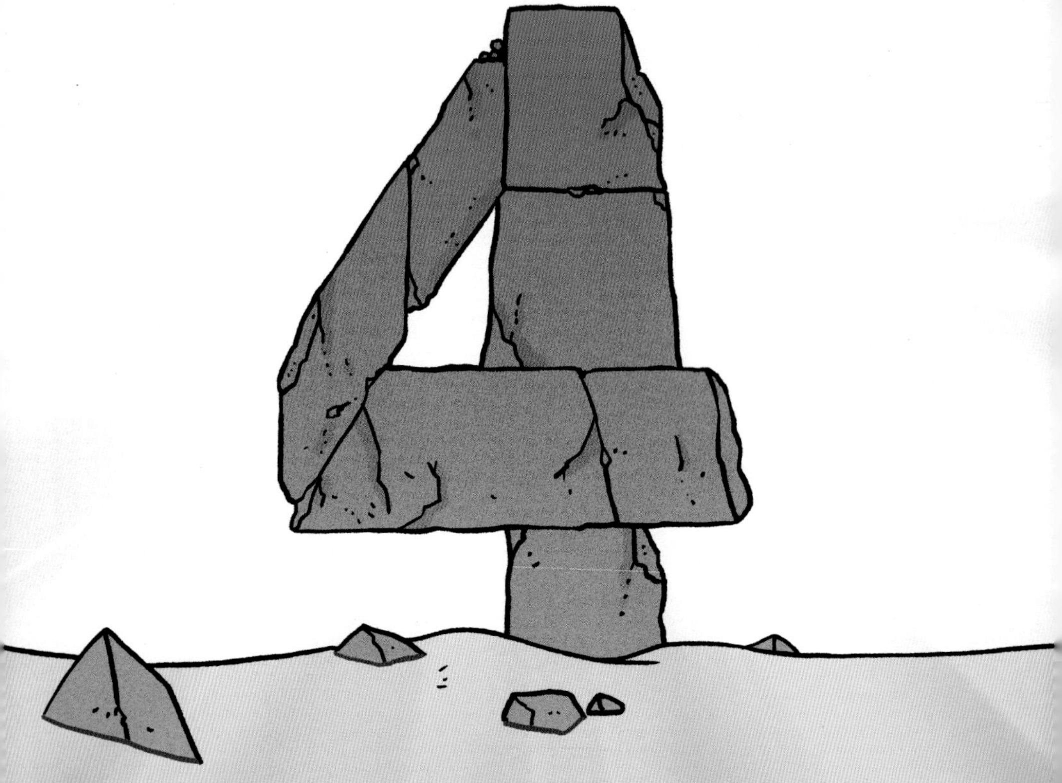

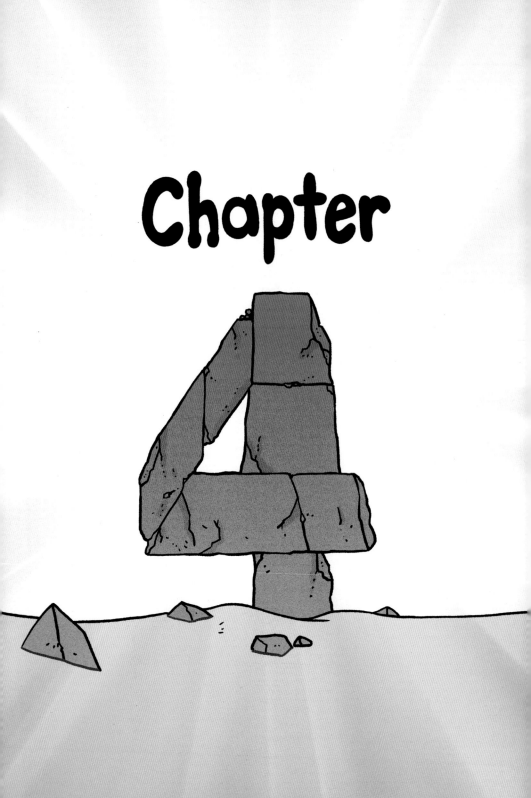

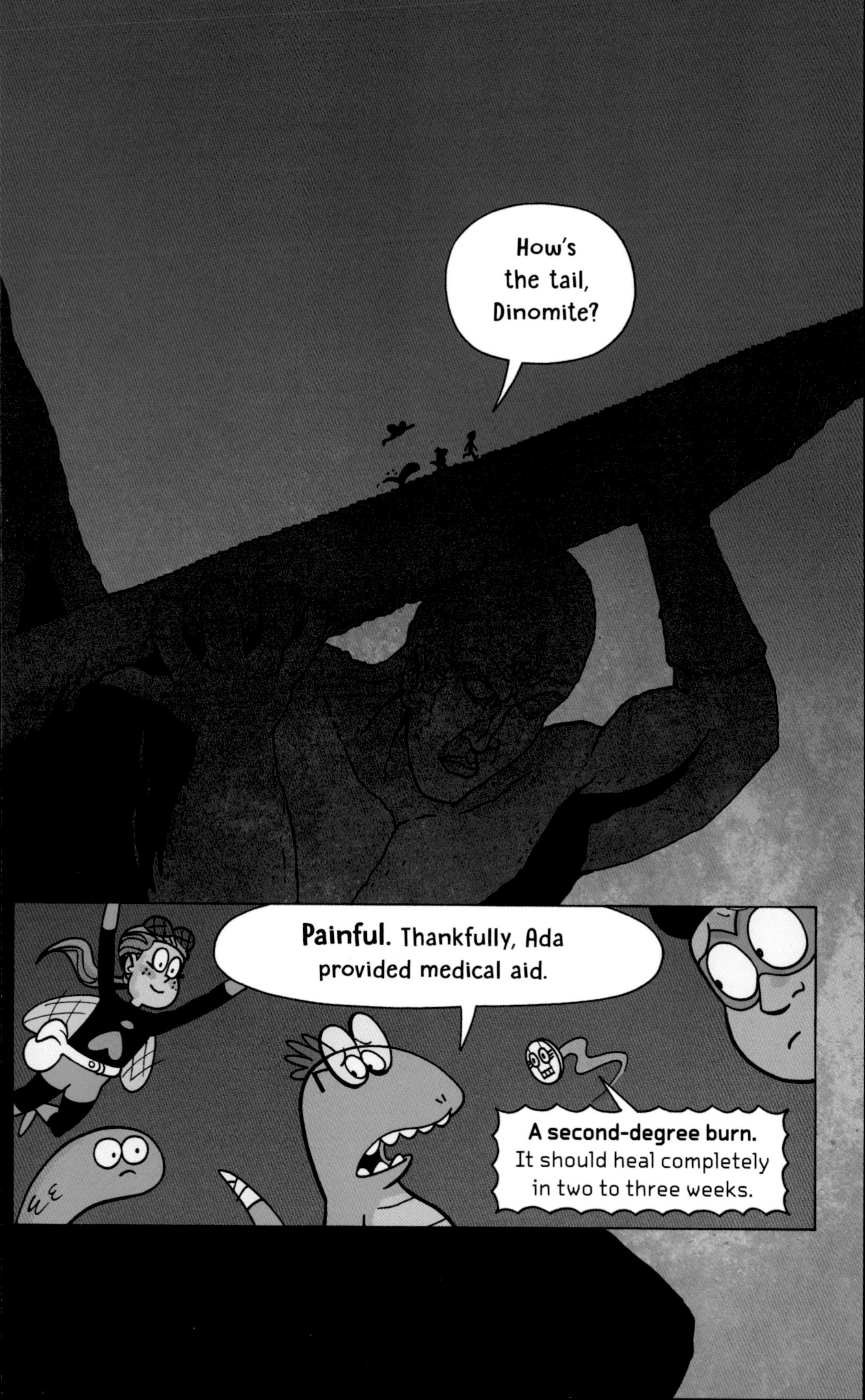
How's the tail, Dinomite?
Painful. Thankfully, Ada provided medical aid.
A second-degree burn. It should heal completely in two to three weeks.

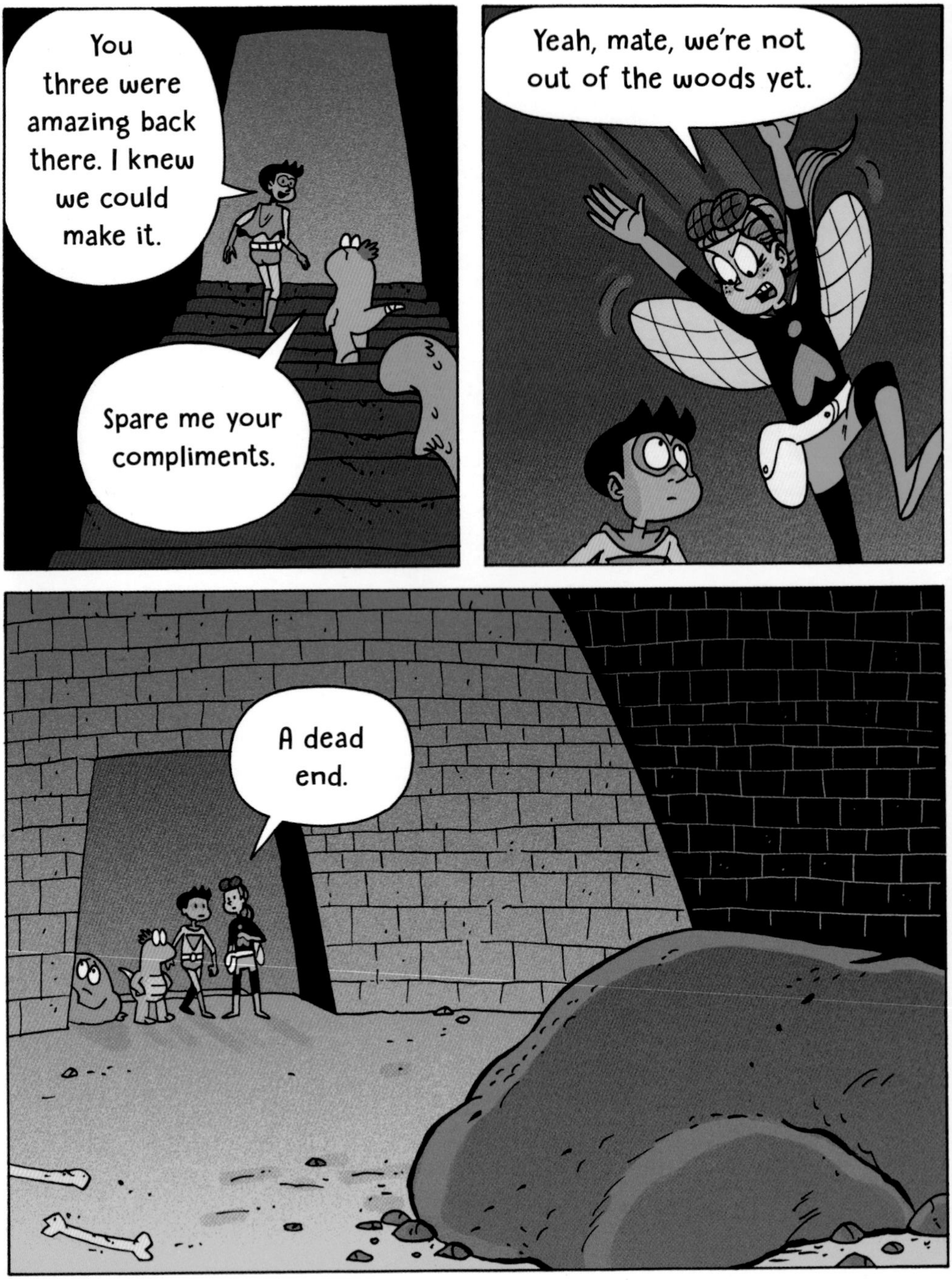
You three were amazing back there. I knew we could make it.
Spare me your compliments.
Yeah, mate, we're not out of the woods yet.
A dead end.

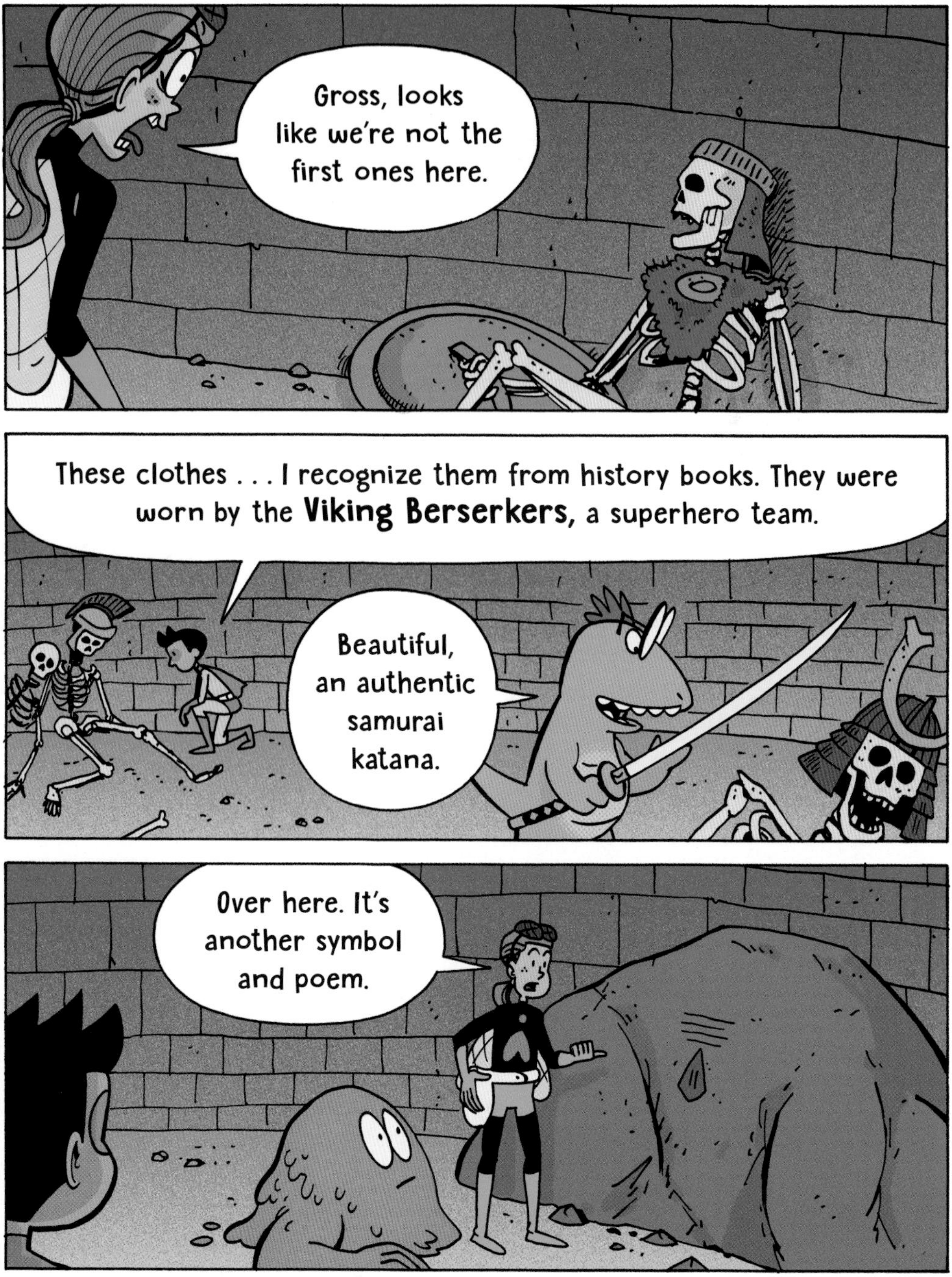
Gross, looks like we're not the first ones here.
These clothes . . . I recognize them from history books. They were worn by the **Viking Berserkers**, a superhero team.
Beautiful, an authentic samurai katana.
Over here. It's another symbol and poem.

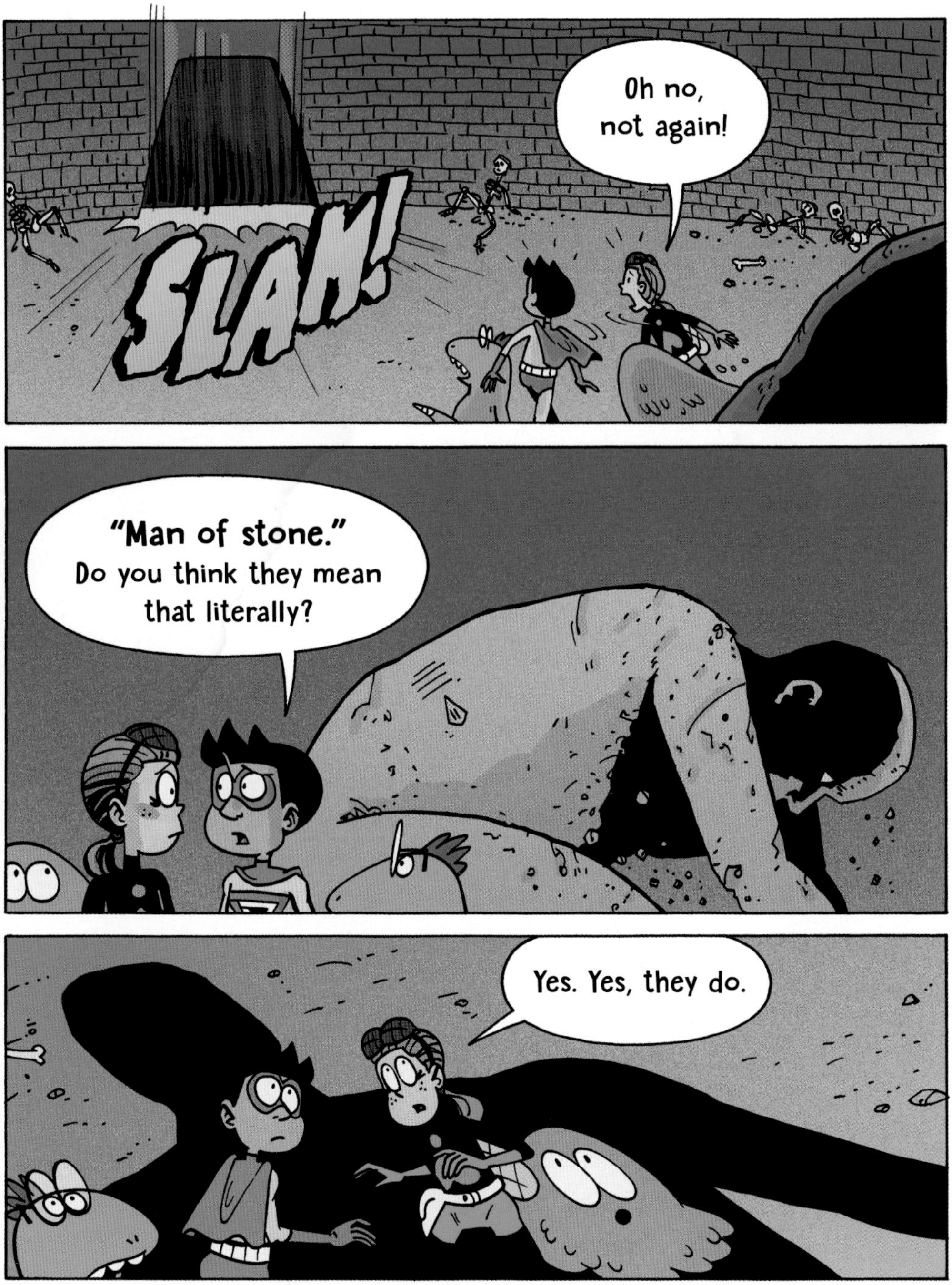
SLAM!
Oh no, not again!
"Man of stone." Do you think they mean that literally?
Yes. Yes, they do.

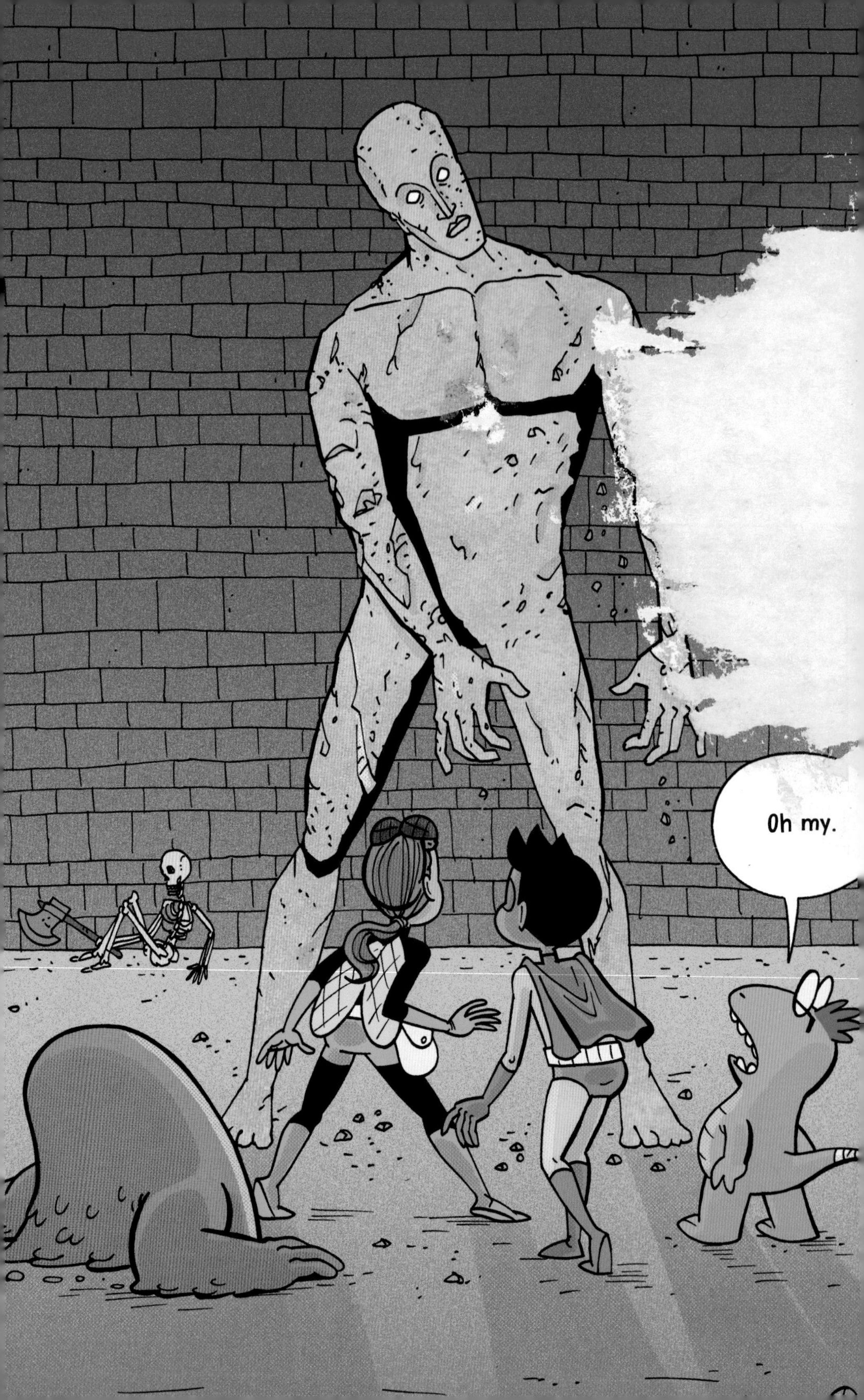
Oh my.

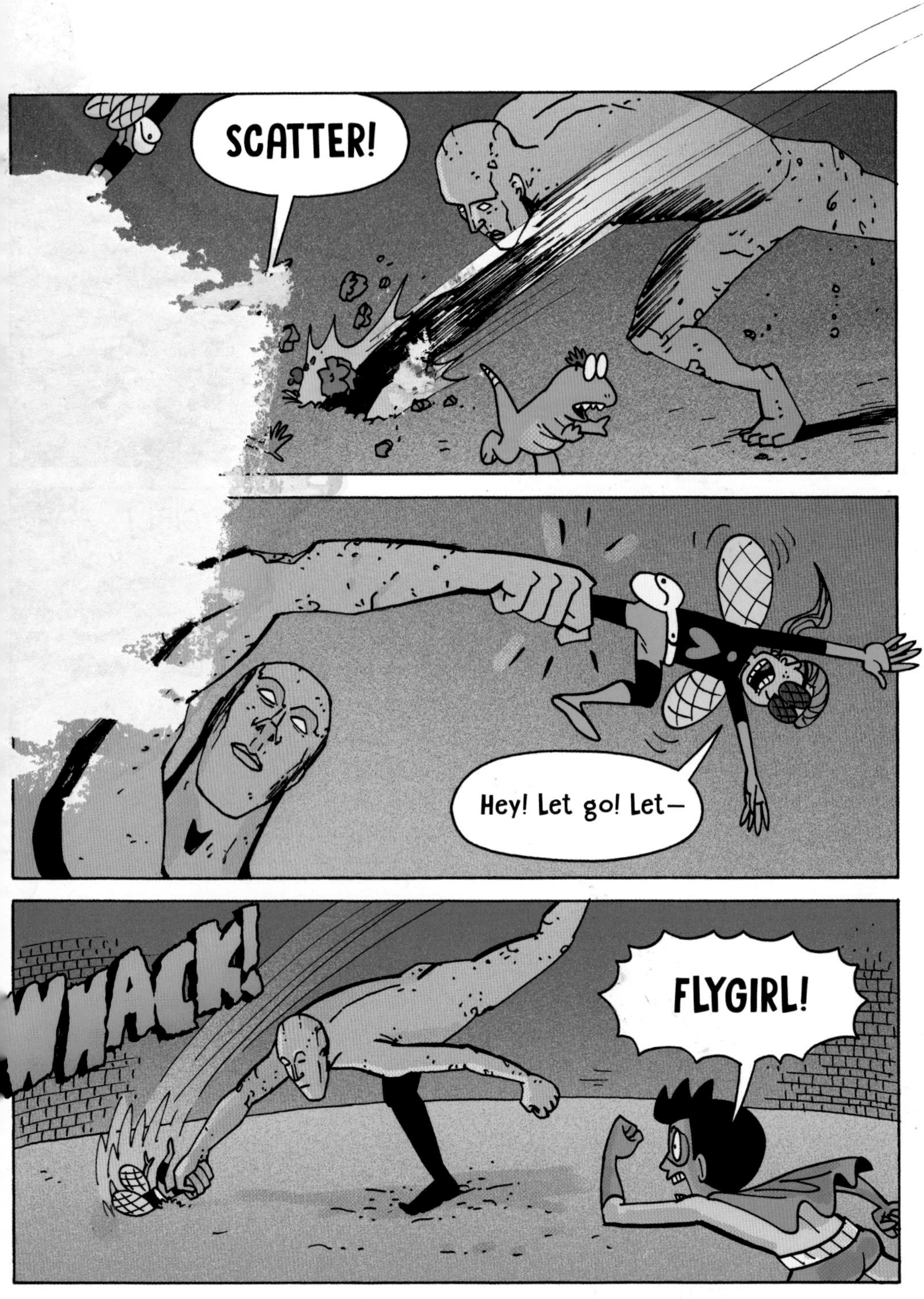
SCATTER!
Hey! Let go! Let–
WHACK!
FLYGIRL!

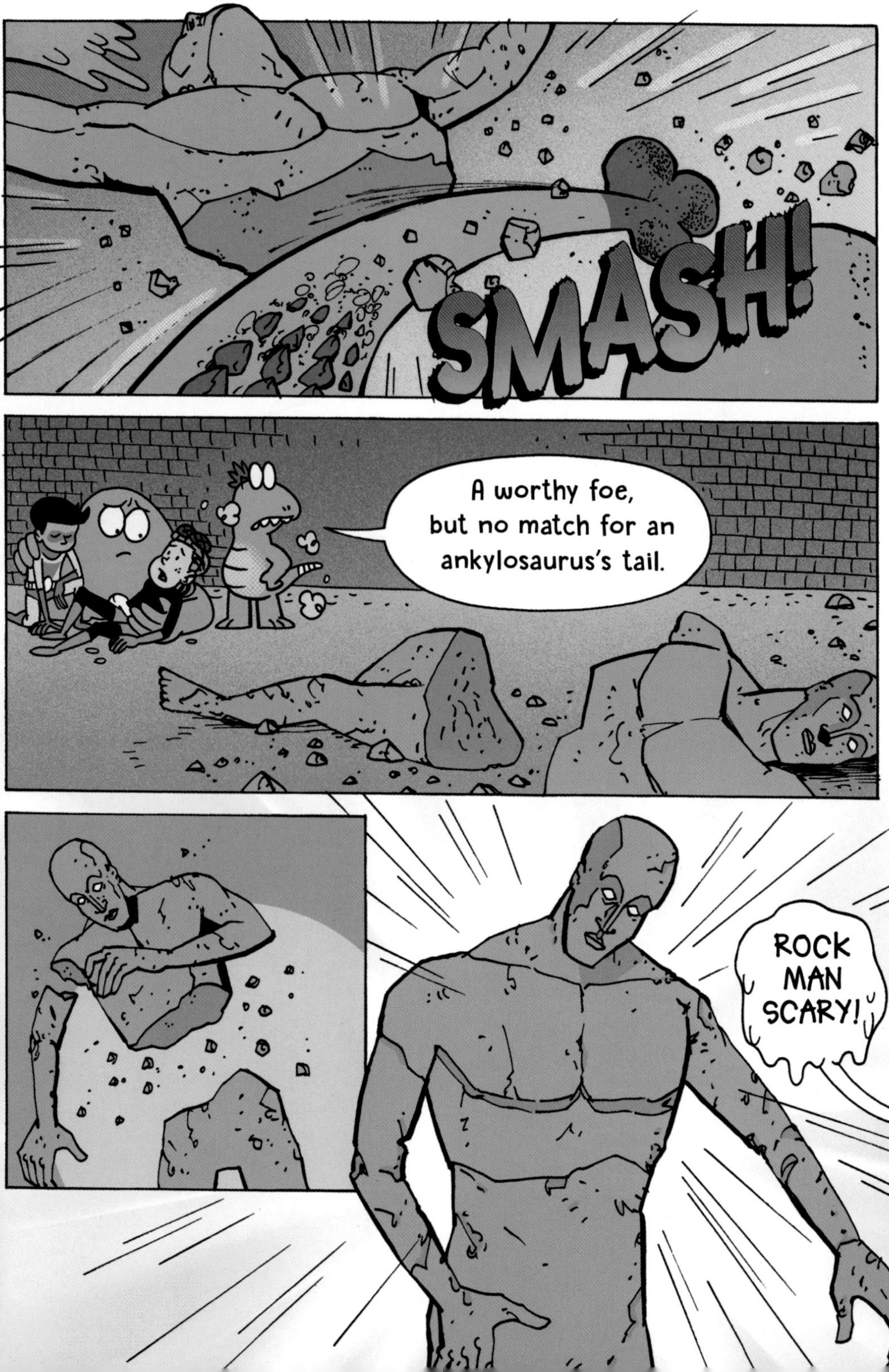
SMASH!
A worthy foe, but no match for an ankylosaurus's tail.
ROCK MAN SCARY!

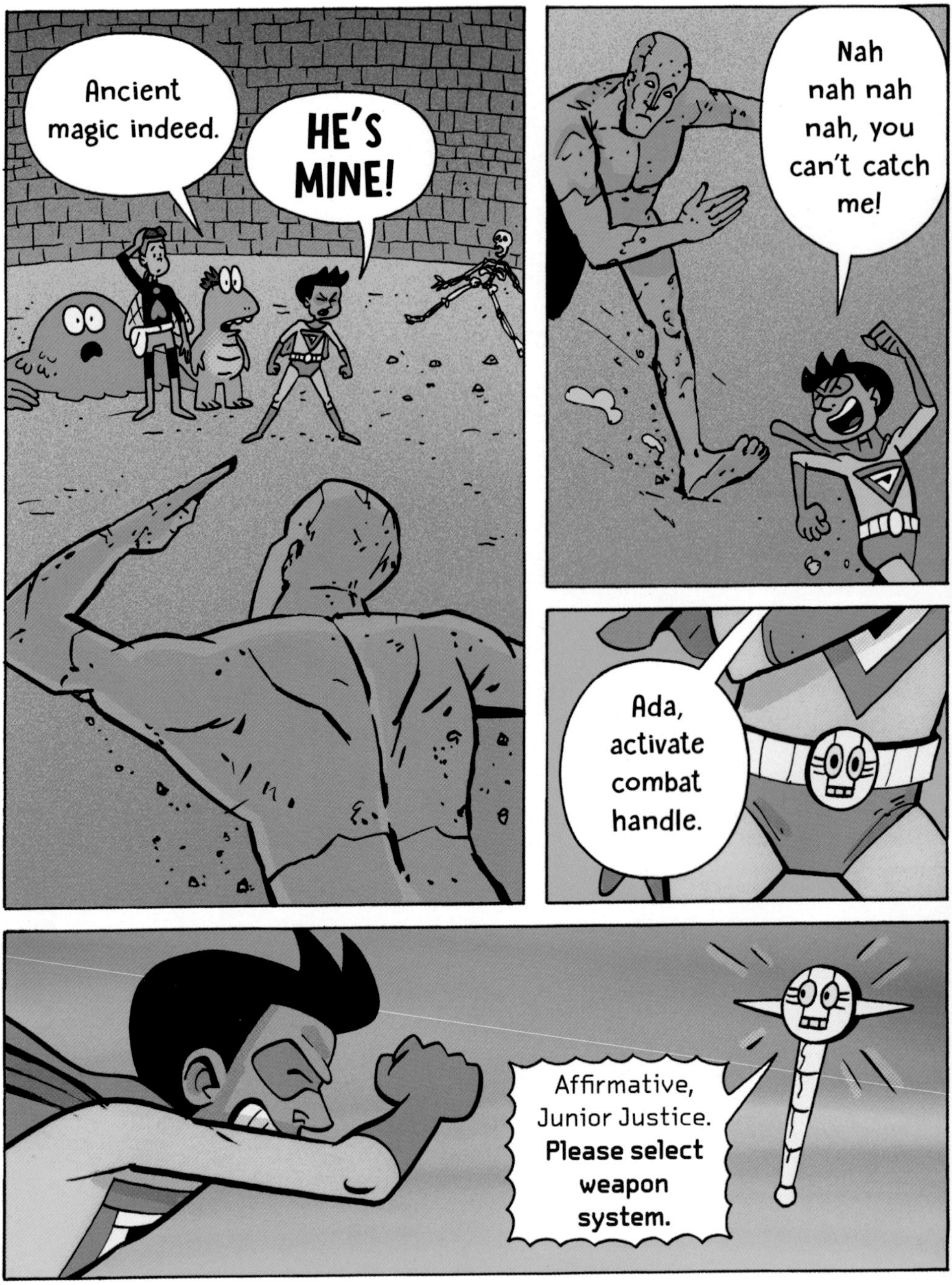
Ancient magic indeed.
HE'S MINE!
Nah nah nah nah, you can't catch me!
Ada, activate combat handle.
Affirmative, Junior Justice. **Please select weapon system.**

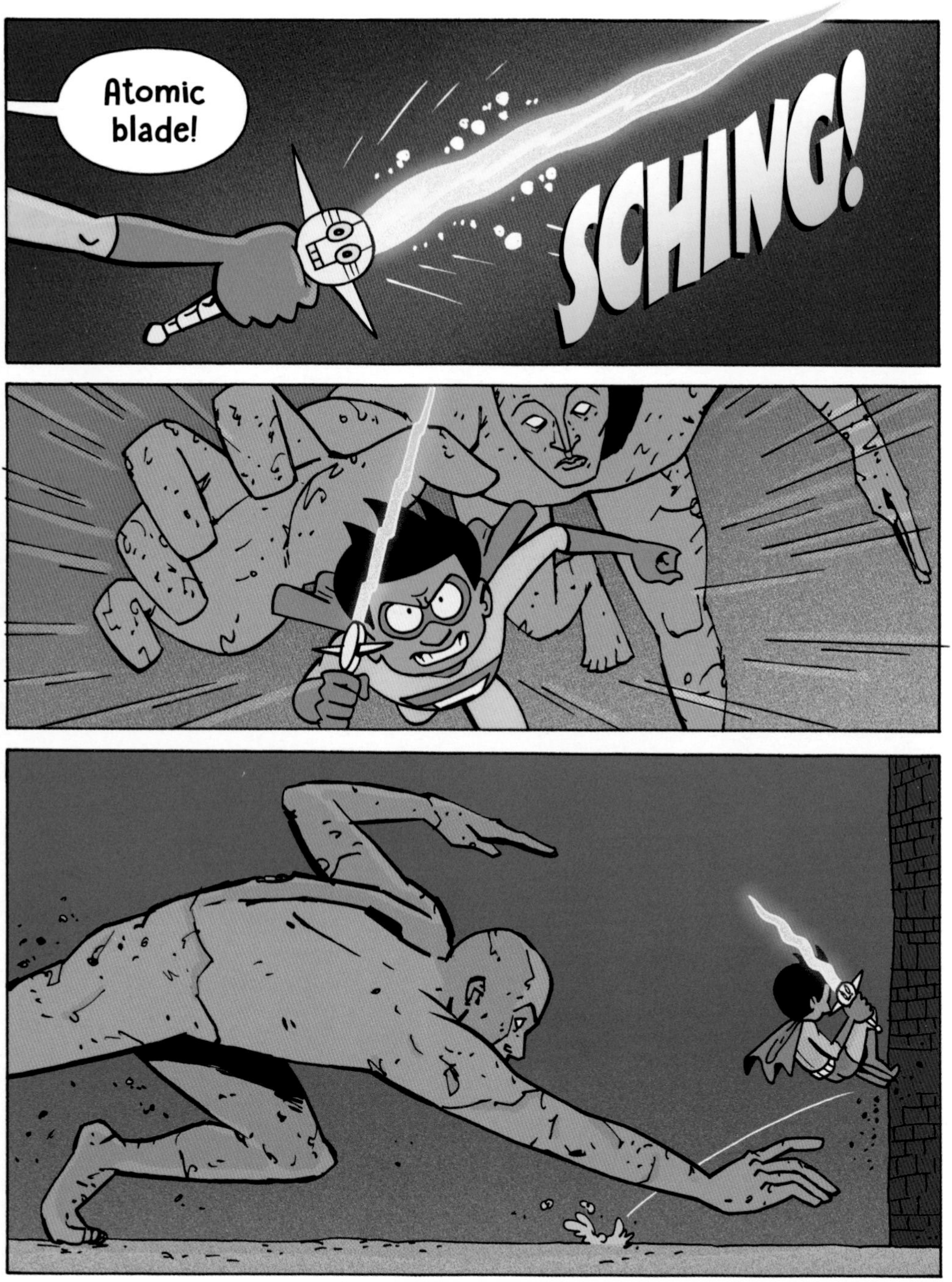
Atomic blade!
SCHING!

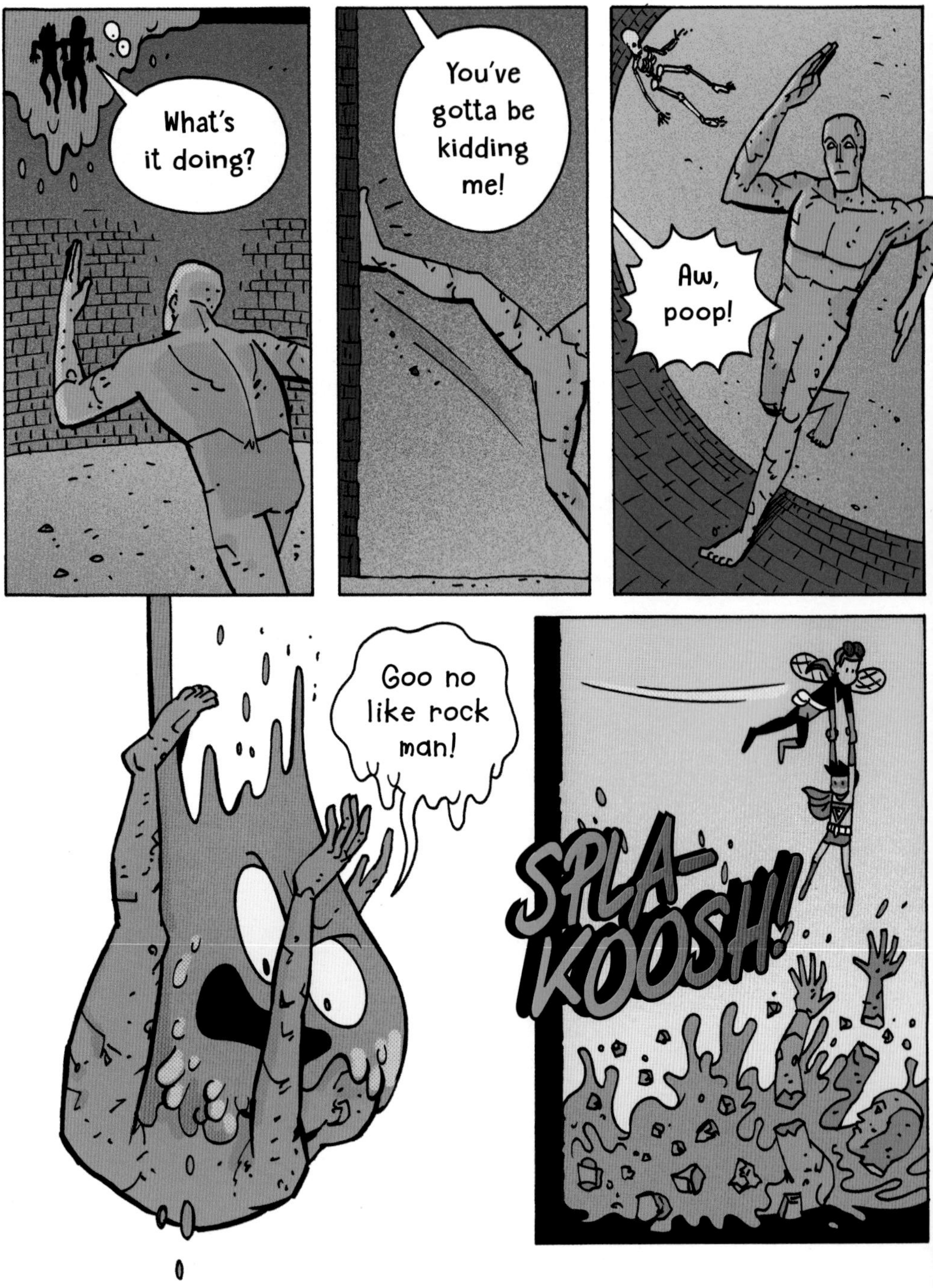
What's it doing?
You've gotta be kidding me!
Aw, poop!
Goo no like rock man!
SPLA-KOOSH!

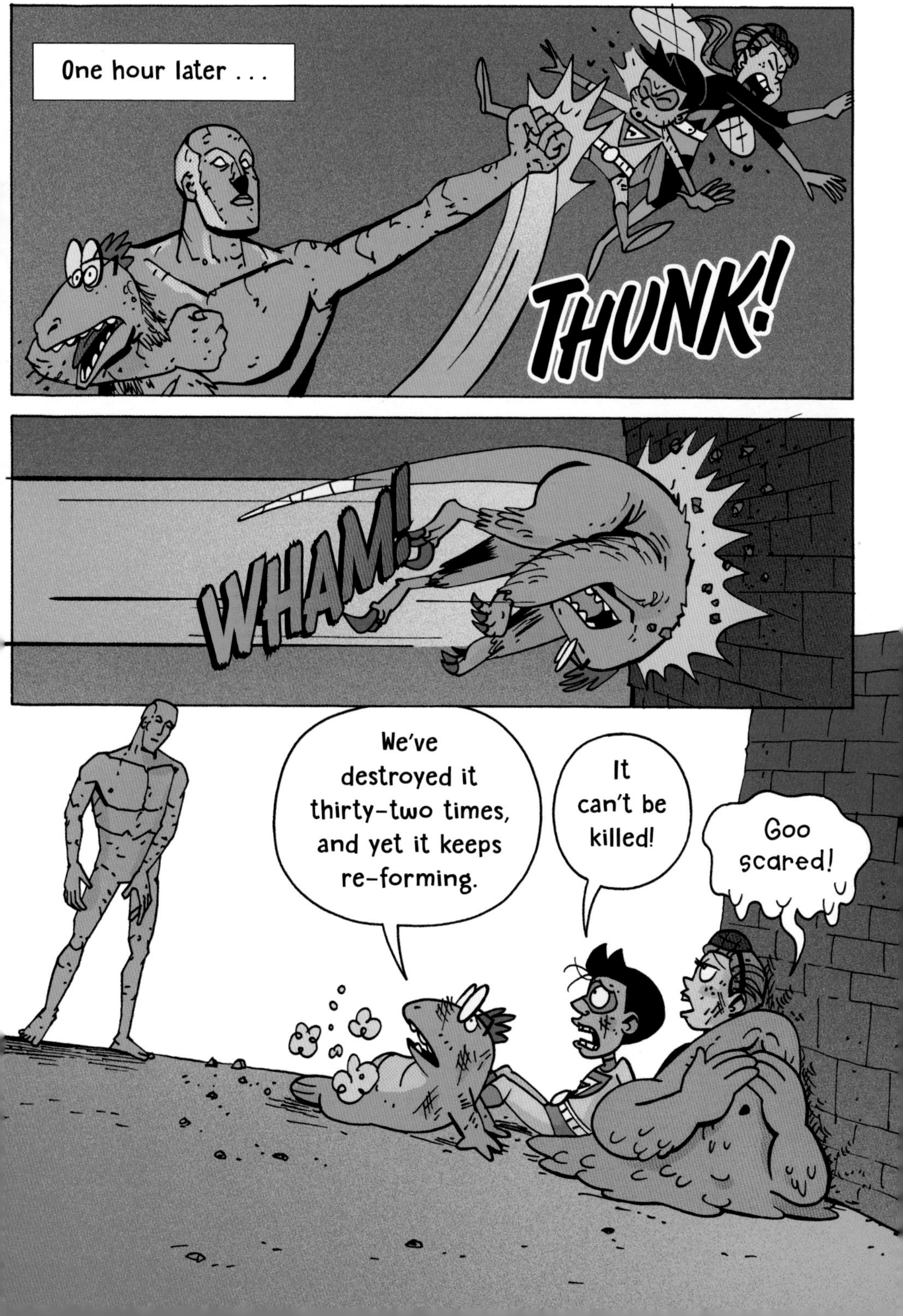
One hour later . . .
THUNK!
WHAM!
We've destroyed it thirty-two times, and yet it keeps re-forming.
It can't be killed!
Goo scared!

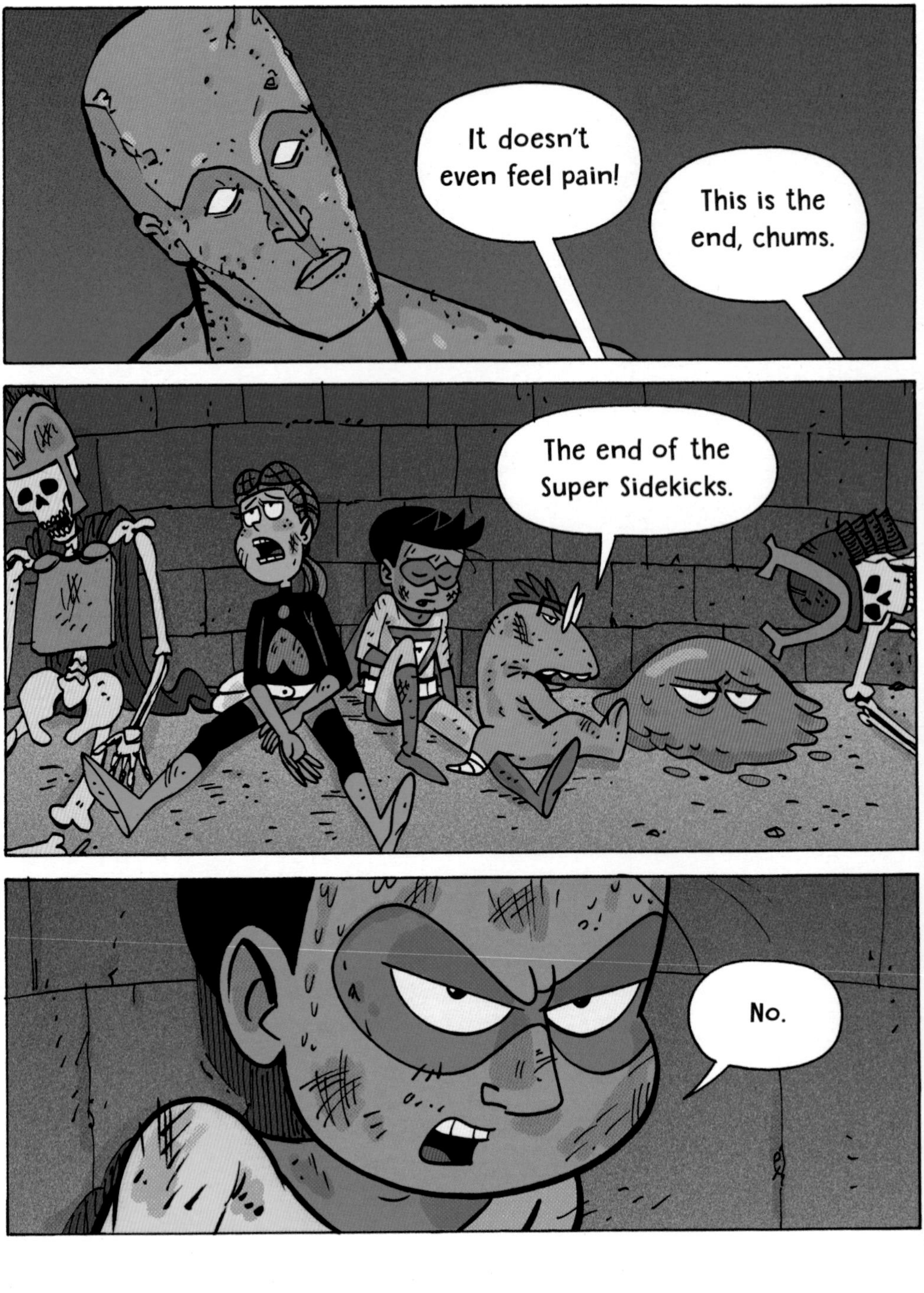
It doesn't even feel pain!
This is the end, chums.
The end of the Super Sidekicks.
No.

97

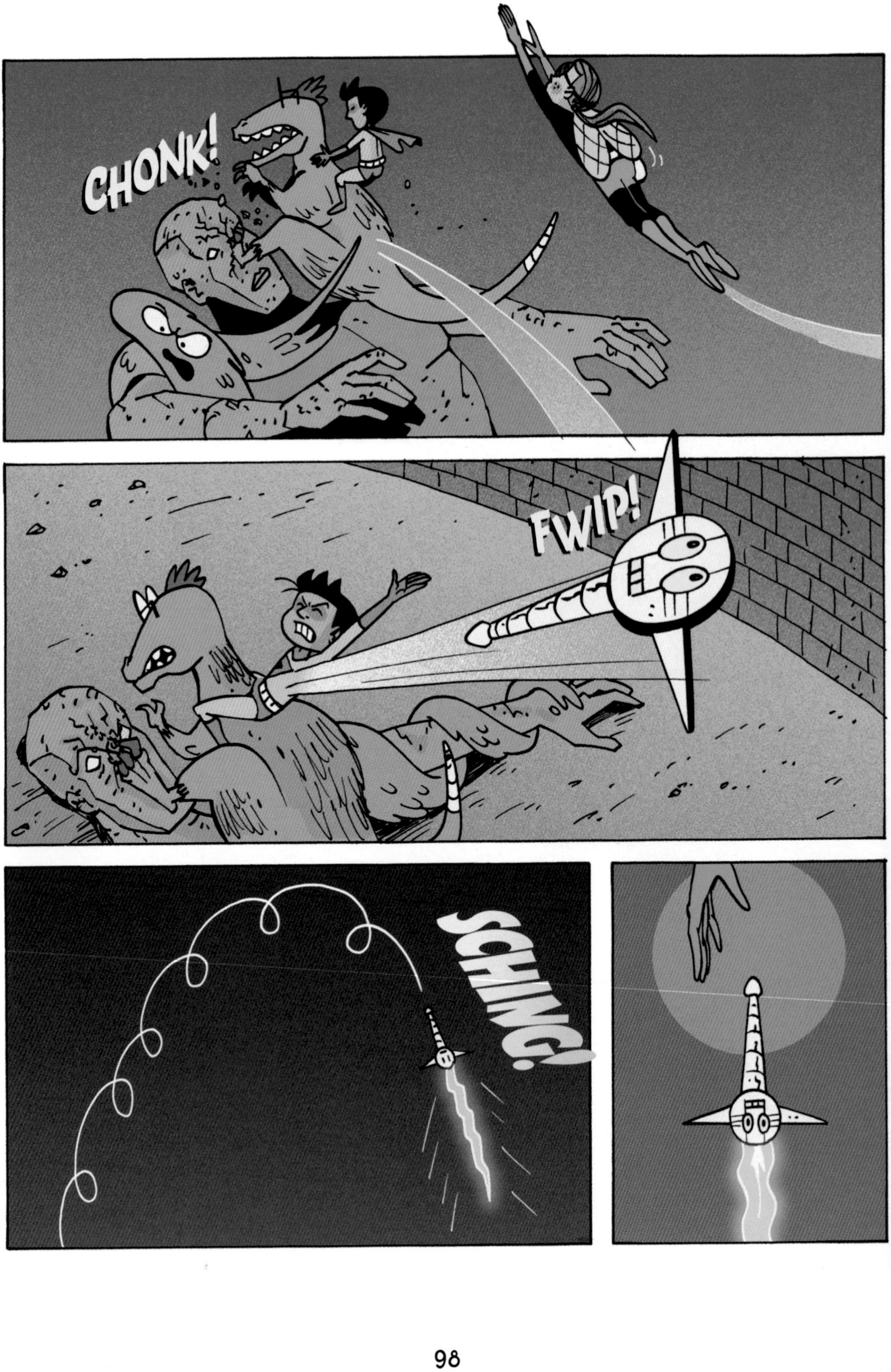
CHONK!
FWIP!
SCHING!

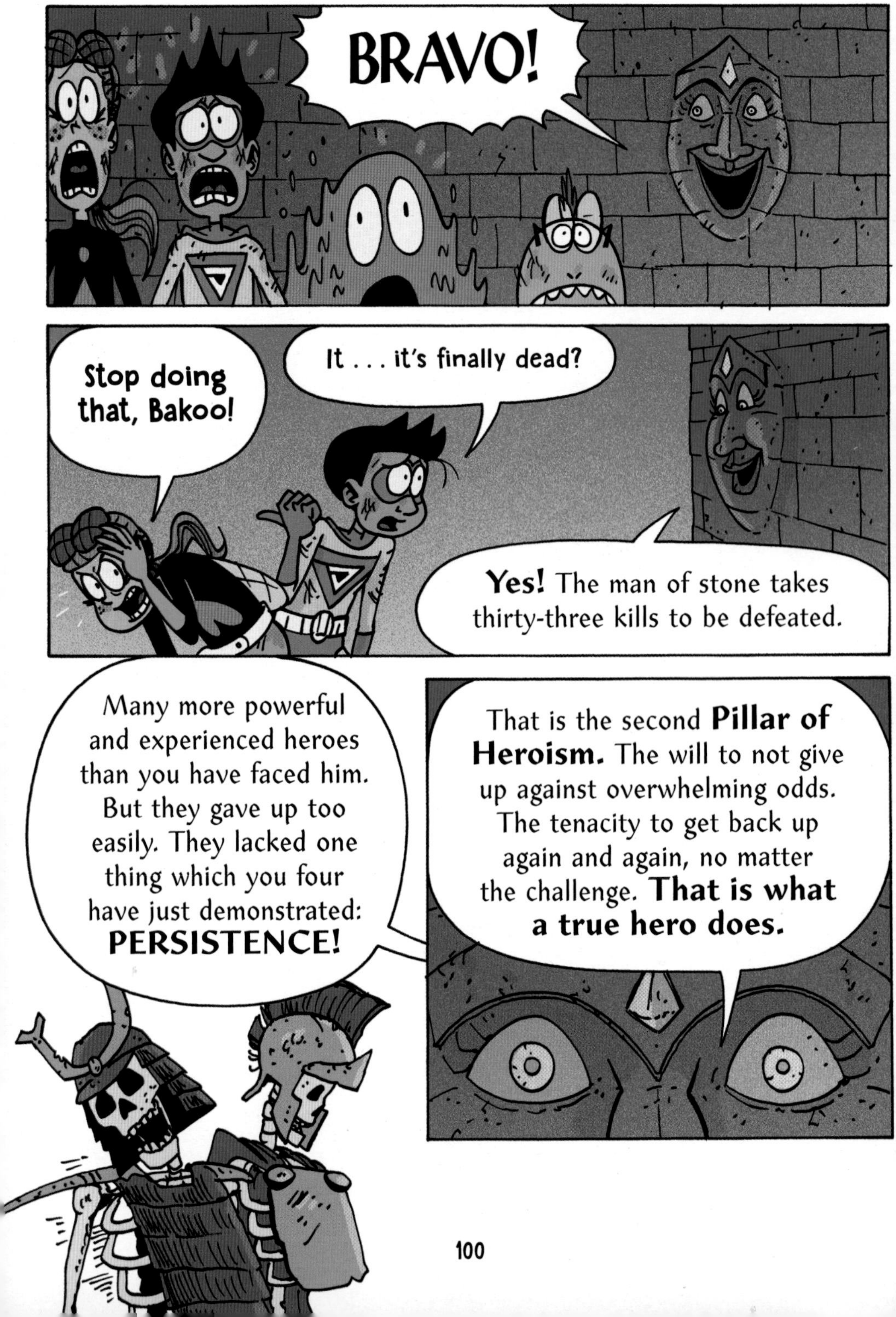
BRAVO!
Stop doing that, Bakoo!
It . . . it's finally dead?
Yes! The man of stone takes thirty-three kills to be defeated.
Many more powerful and experienced heroes than you have faced him. But they gave up too easily. They lacked one thing which you four have just demonstrated: **PERSISTENCE!**
That is the second **Pillar of Heroism.** The will to not give up against overwhelming odds. The tenacity to get back up again and again, no matter the challenge. **That is what a true hero does.**

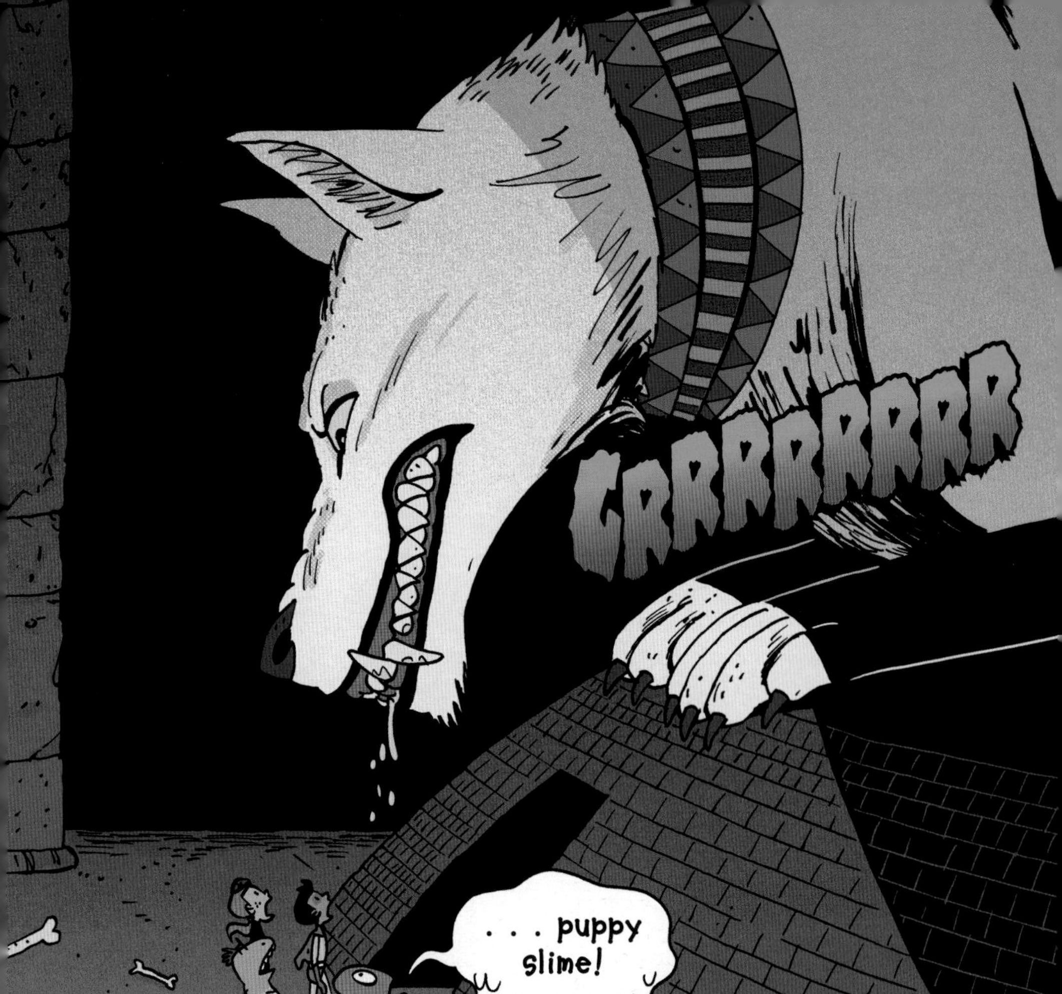
GRRRRRRRR
. . . puppy slime!

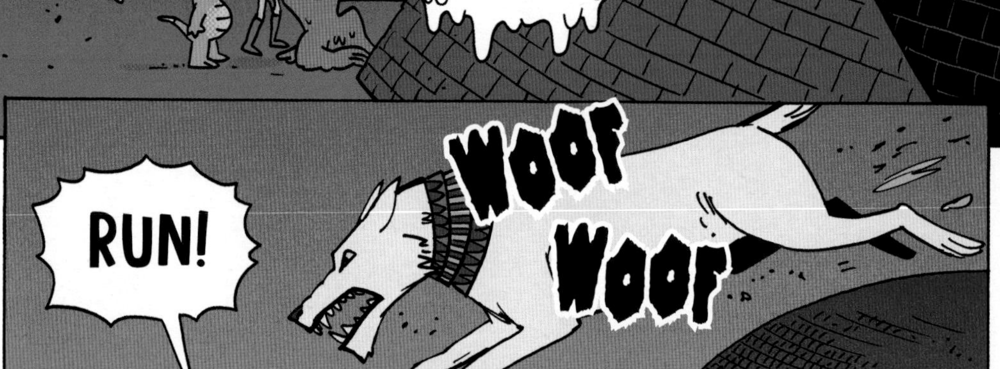
RUN!
WOOF
WOOF

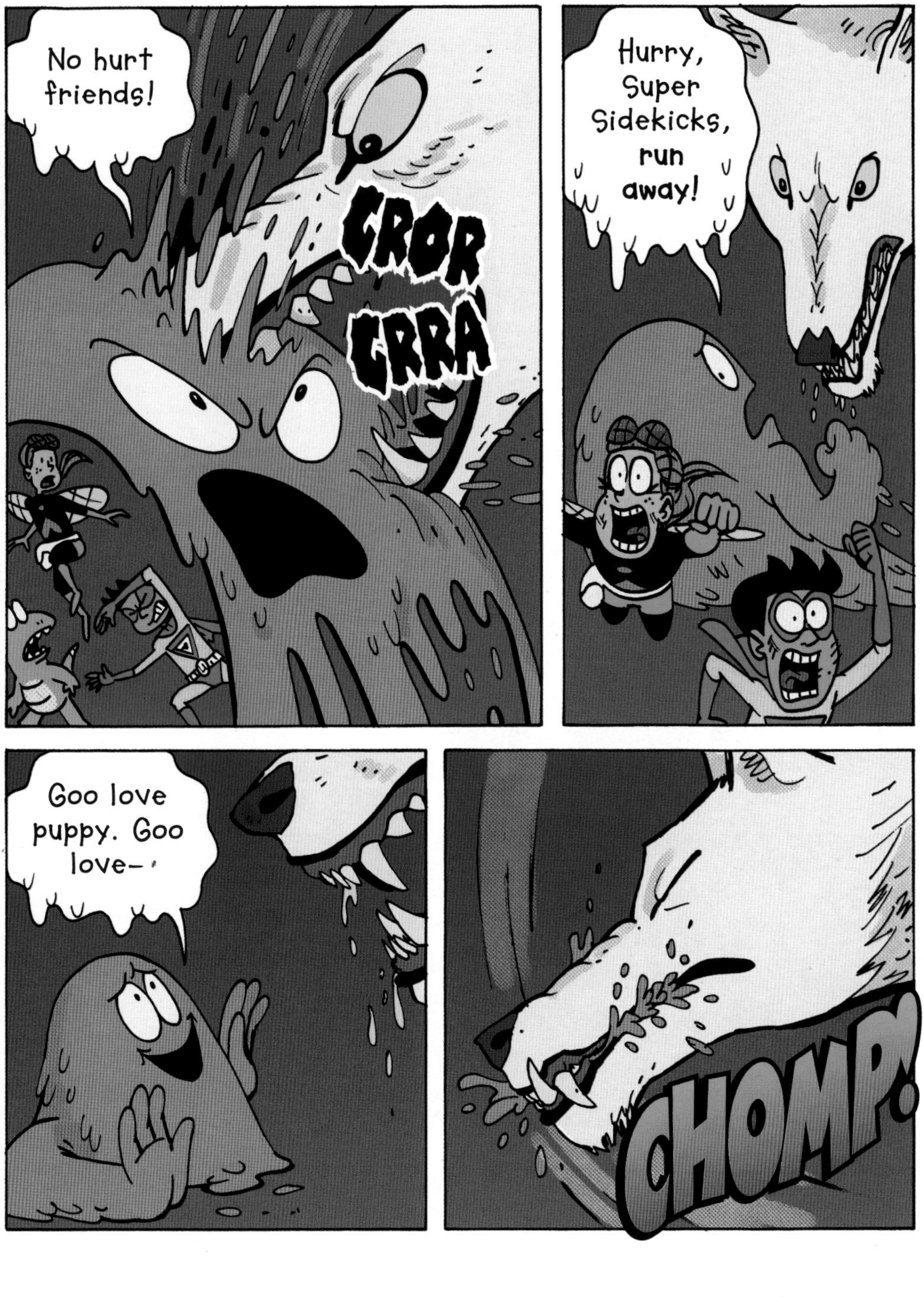
No hurt friends!
CROR GRRA
Hurry, Super Sidekicks, run away!
Goo love puppy. Goo love-
CHOMP!

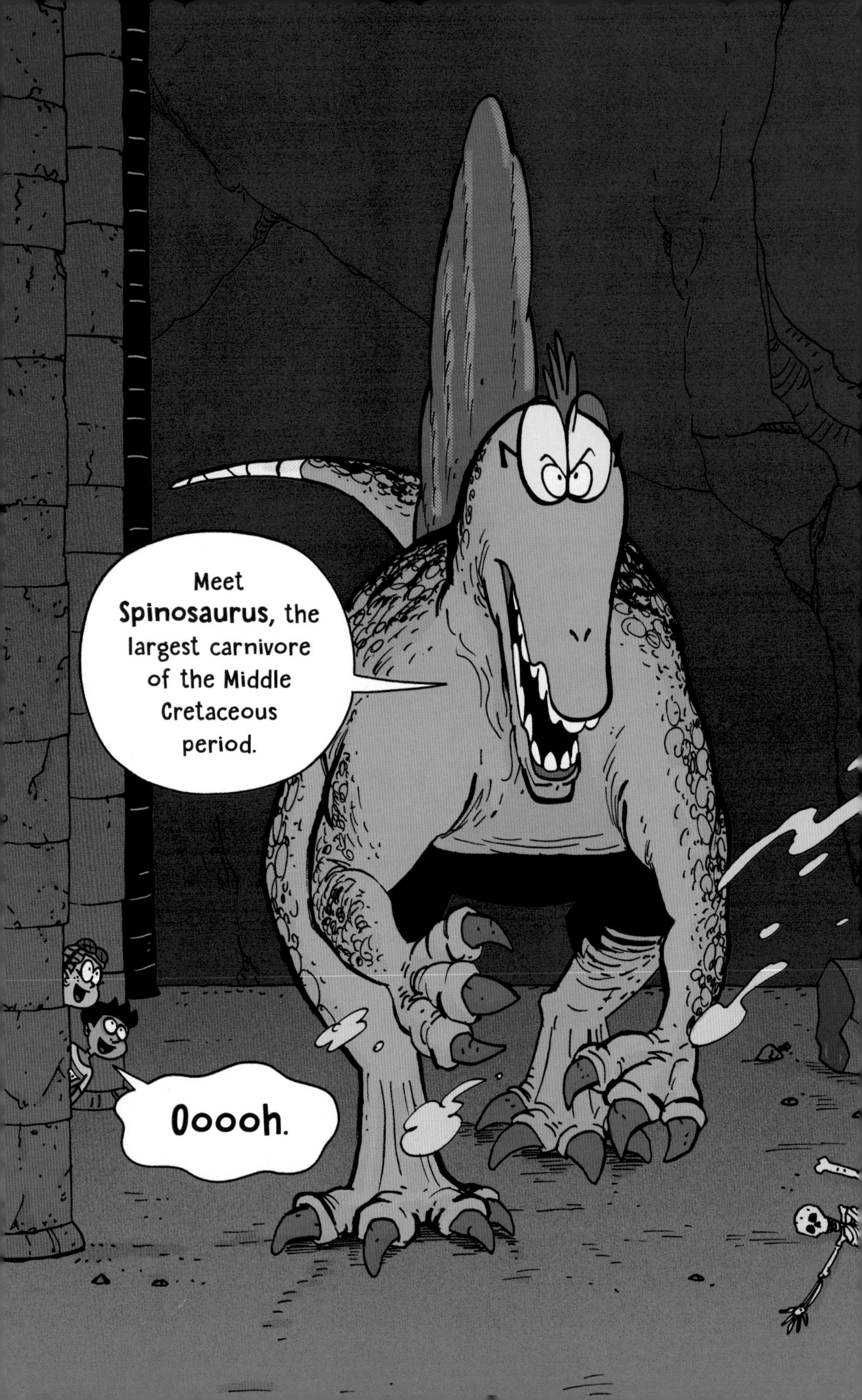
Meet **Spinosaurus**, the largest carnivore of the Middle Cretaceous period.
Ooooh.

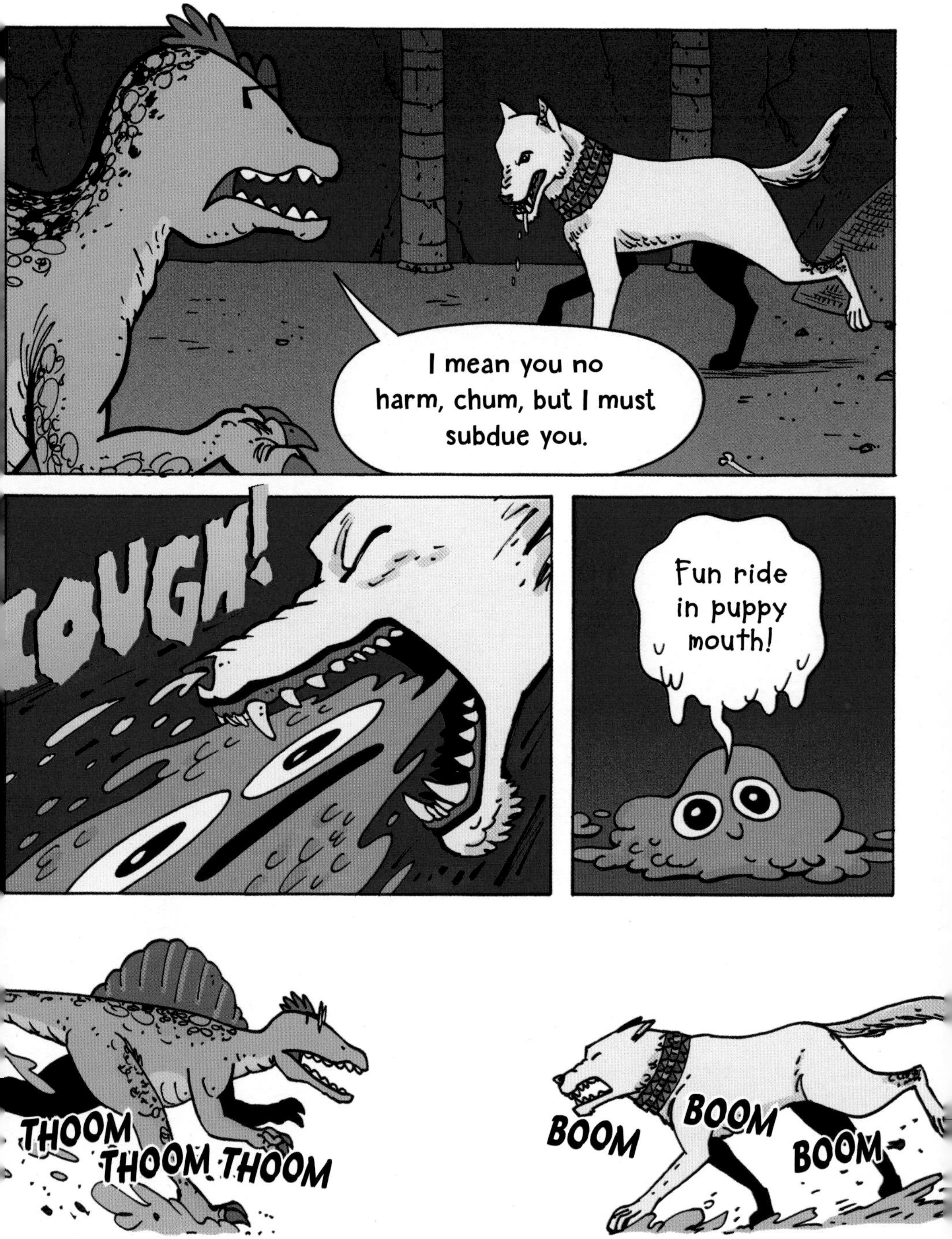
I mean you no harm, chum, but I must subdue you.
COUGH!
Fun ride in puppy mouth!
THOOM THOOM THOOM
BOOM BOOM BOOM

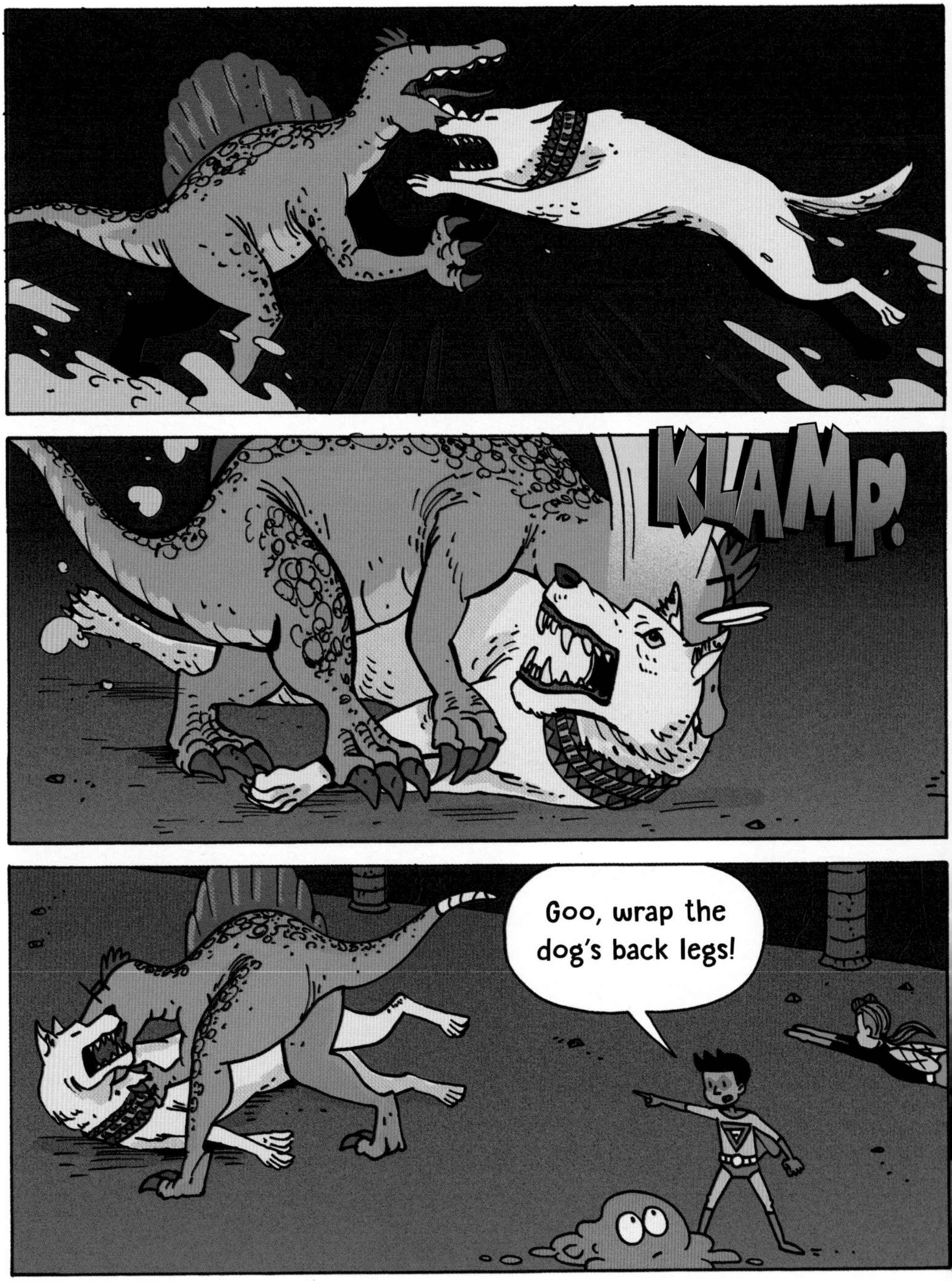
KLAMP!
Goo, wrap the dog's back legs!

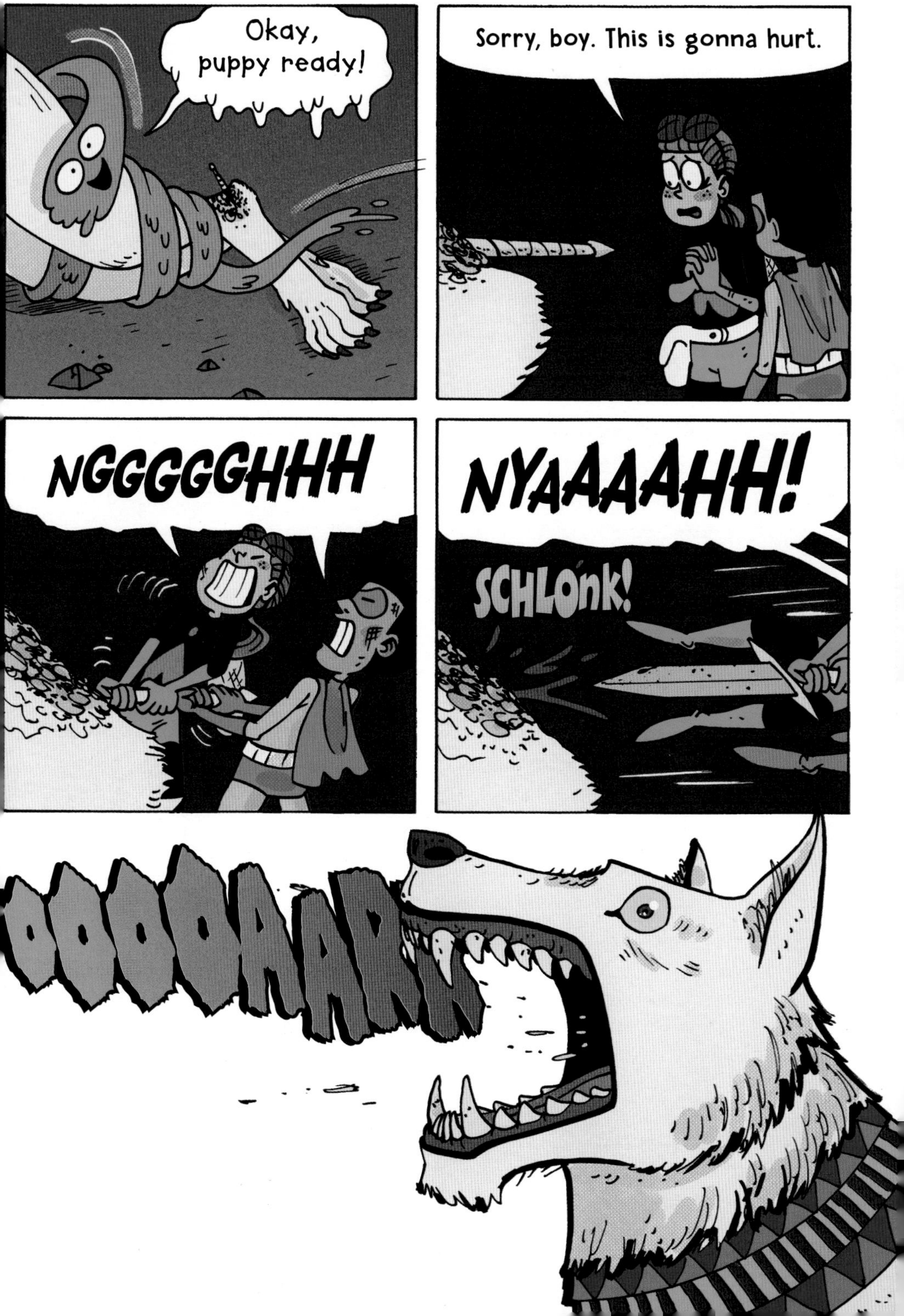
Okay, puppy ready!
Sorry, boy. This is gonna hurt.
NGGGGGHHH
NYAAAAHH!
SCHLONK!
OOOOOARR

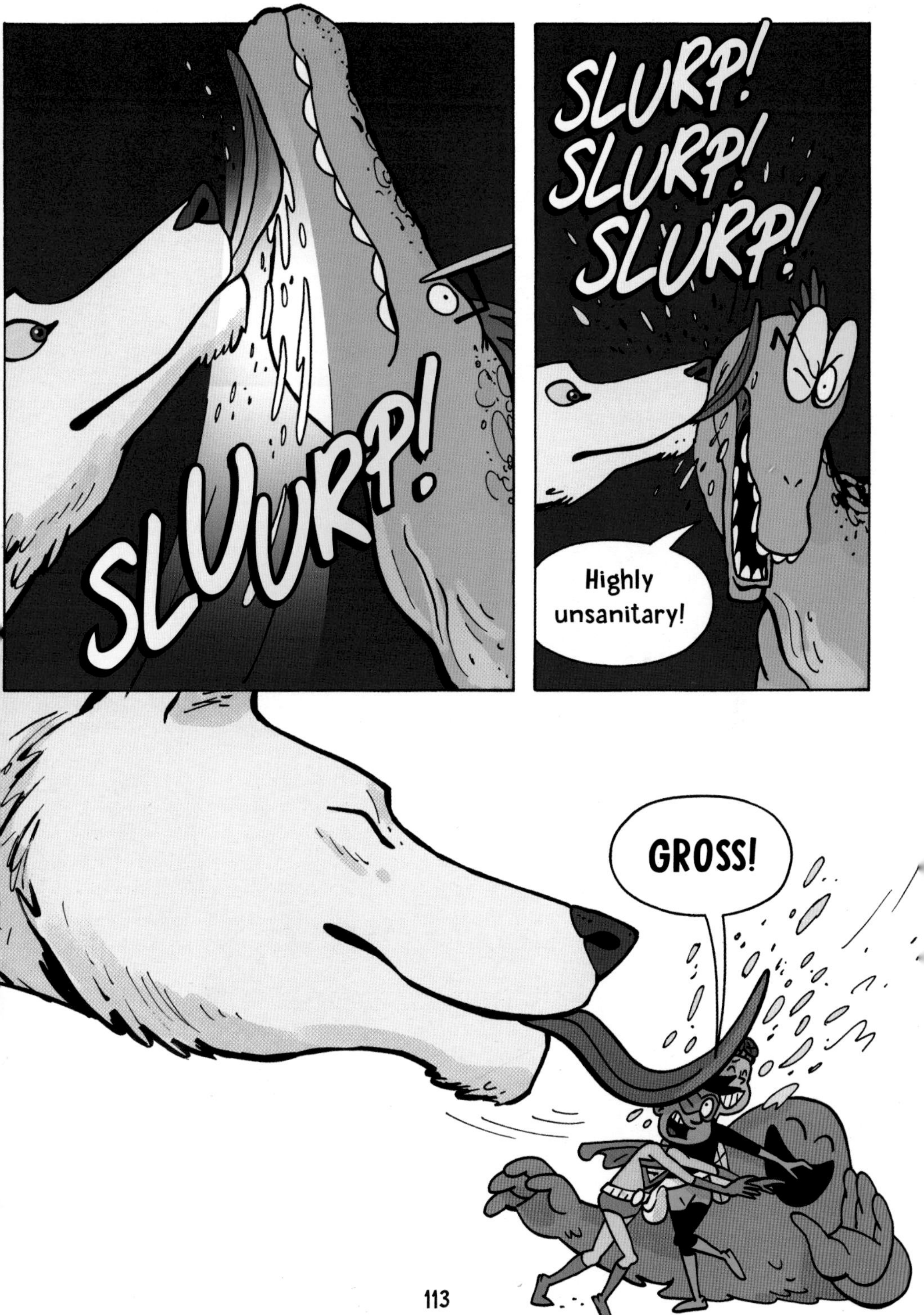
SLUUURP!
SLURP! SLURP! SLURP!
Highly unsanitary!
GROSS!

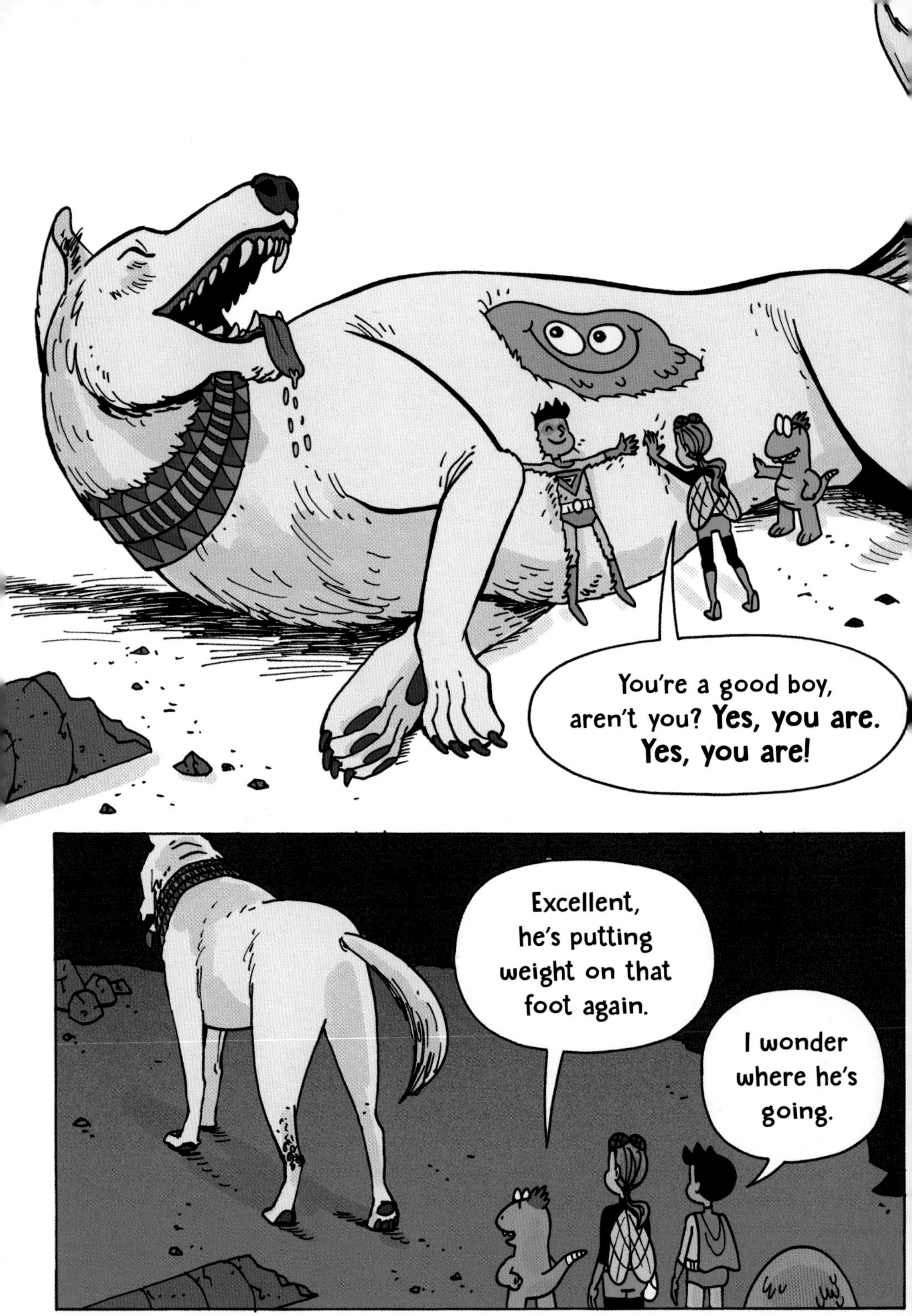
You're a good boy, aren't you? Yes, you are. Yes, you are!
Excellent, he's putting weight on that foot again.
I wonder where he's going.

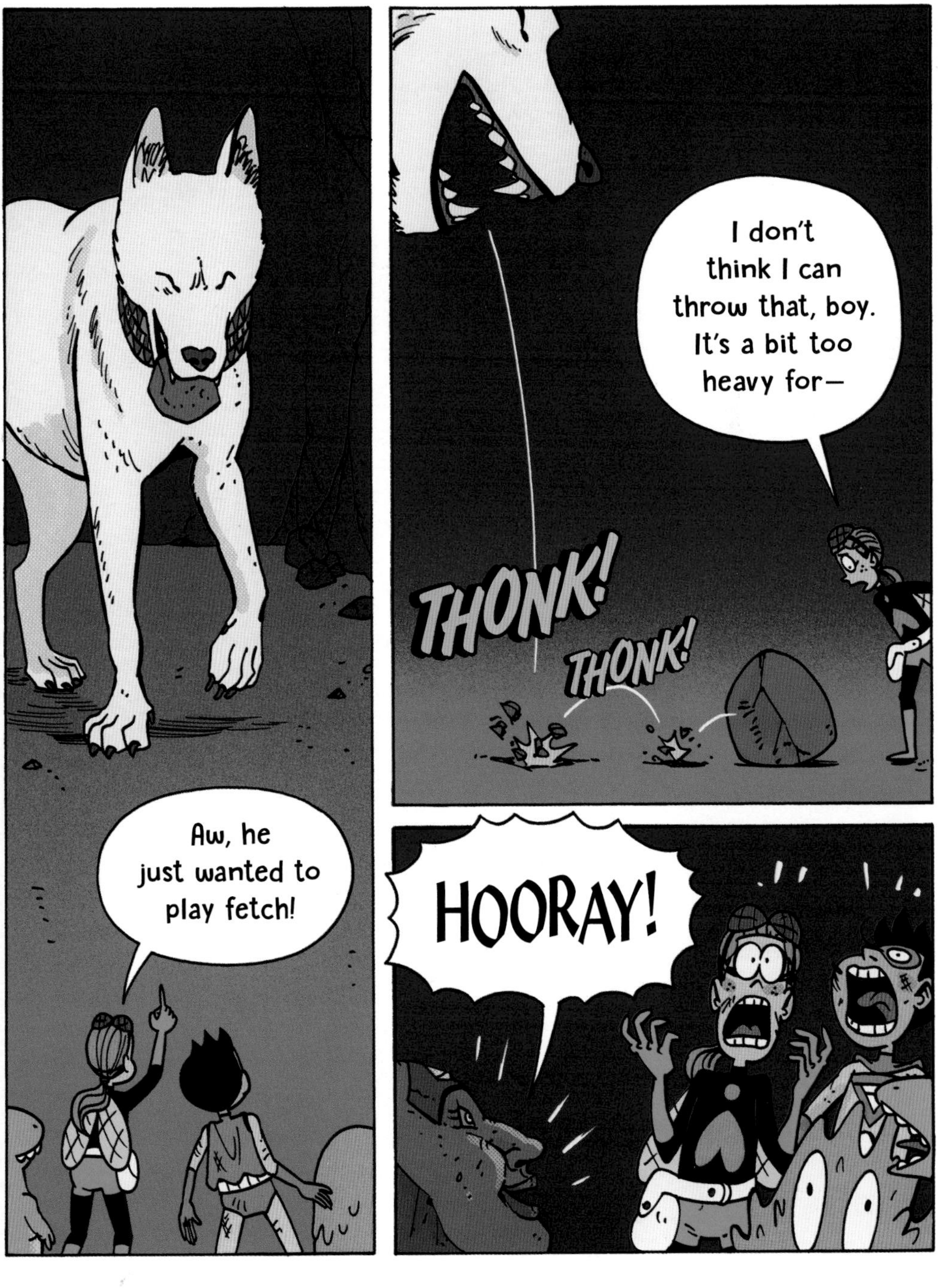
I don't think I can throw that, boy. It's a bit too heavy for—
THONK!
THONK!
Aw, he just wanted to play fetch!
HOORAY!

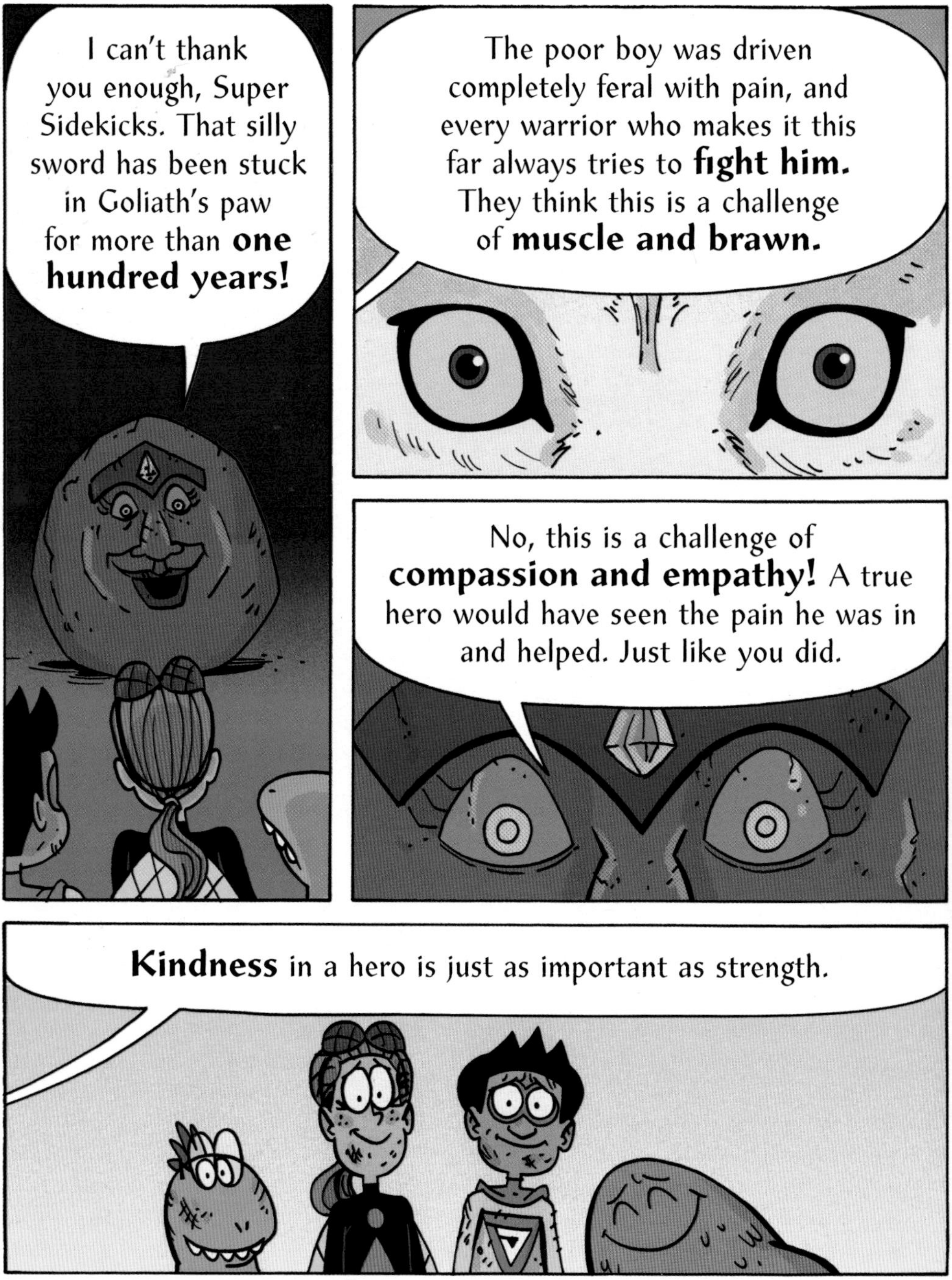
I can't thank you enough, Super Sidekicks. That silly sword has been stuck in Goliath's paw for more than **one hundred years!**
The poor boy was driven completely feral with pain, and every warrior who makes it this far always tries to **fight him.** They think this is a challenge of **muscle and brawn.**
No, this is a challenge of **compassion and empathy!** A true hero would have seen the pain he was in and helped. Just like you did.
Kindness in a hero is just as important as strength.

Chapter

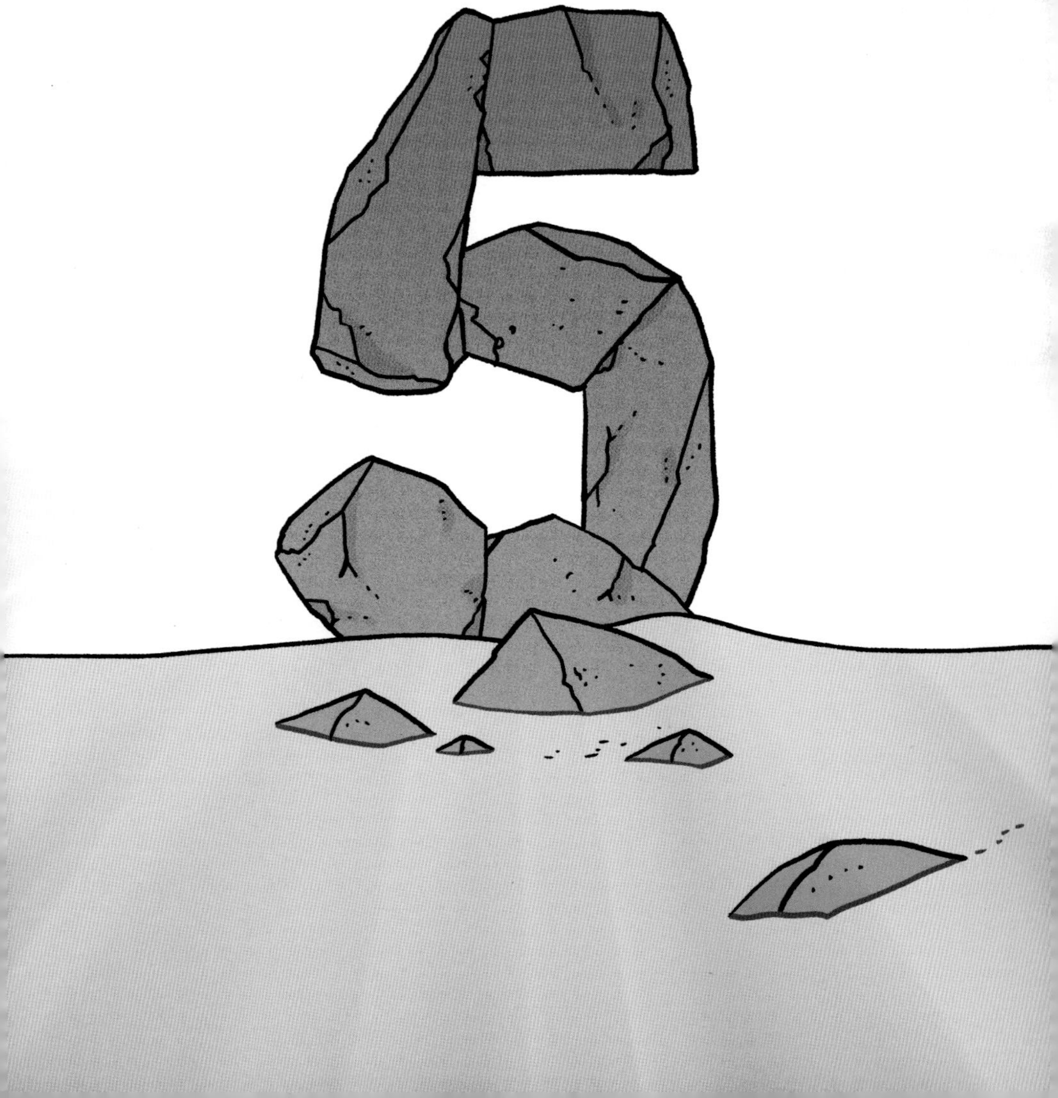
5

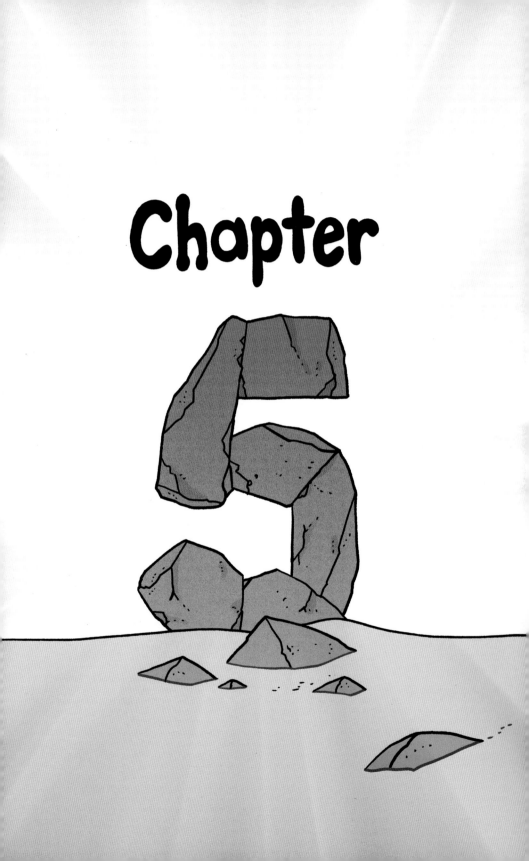

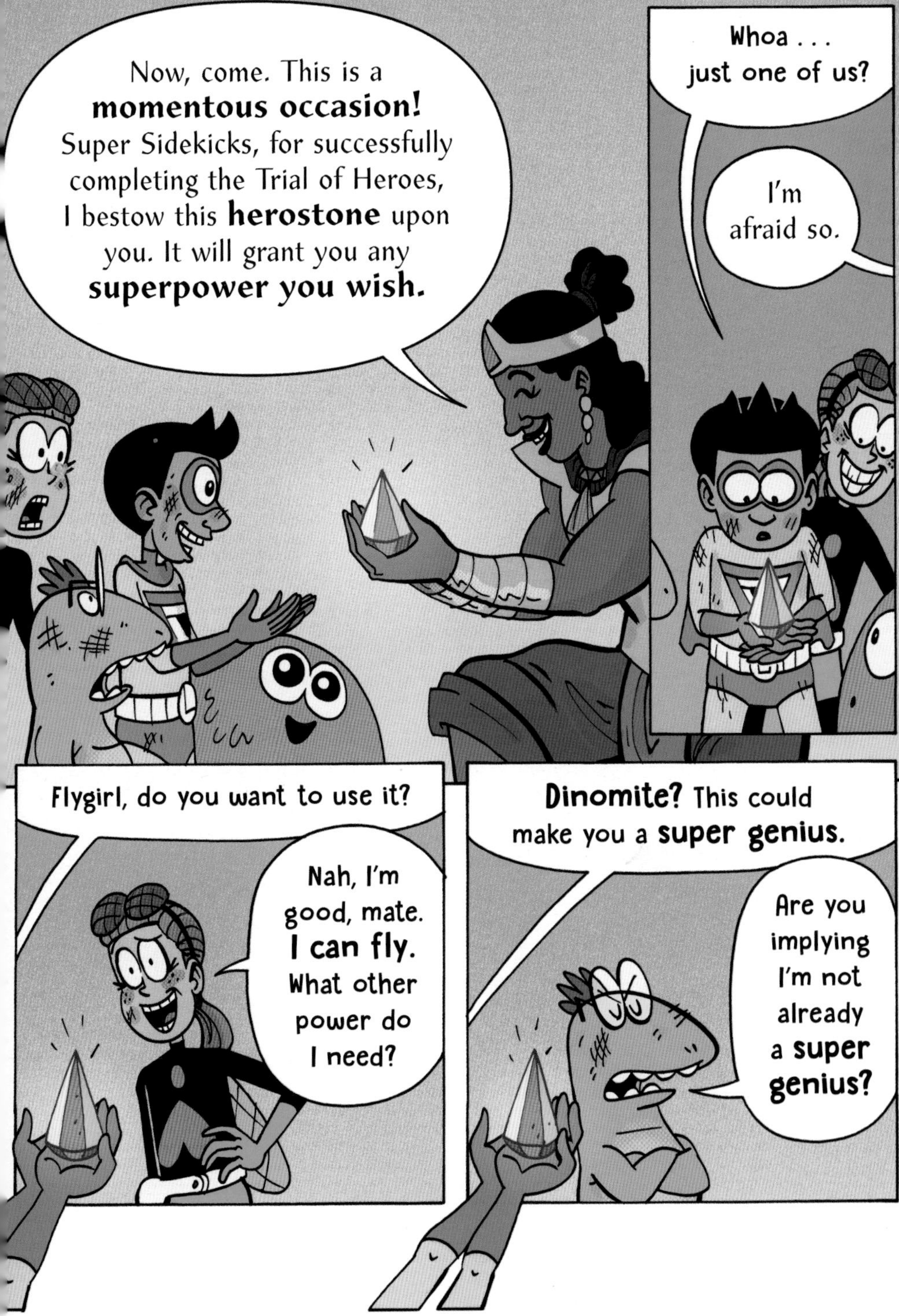
Now, come. This is a momentous occasion! Super Sidekicks, for successfully completing the Trial of Heroes, I bestow this herostone upon you. It will grant you any superpower you wish.
Whoa . . . just one of us?
I'm afraid so.
Flygirl, do you want to use it?
Nah, I'm good, mate. I can fly. What other power do I need?
Dinomite? This could make you a super genius.
Are you implying I'm not already a super genius?

127

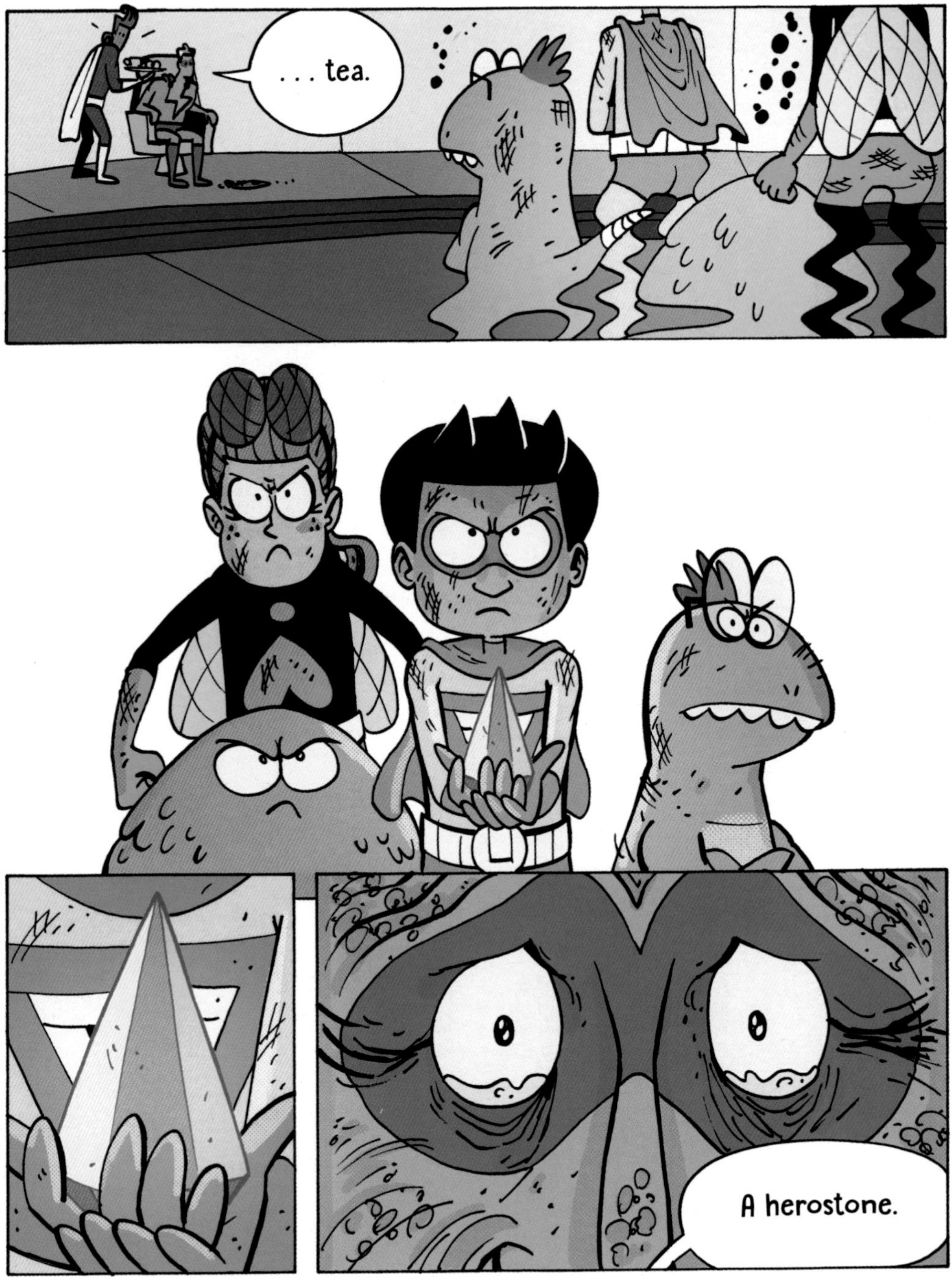
. . . tea.
A herostone.

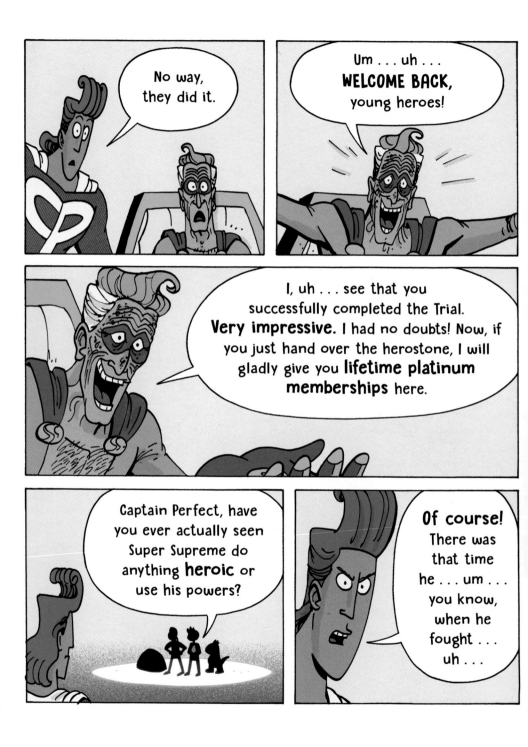

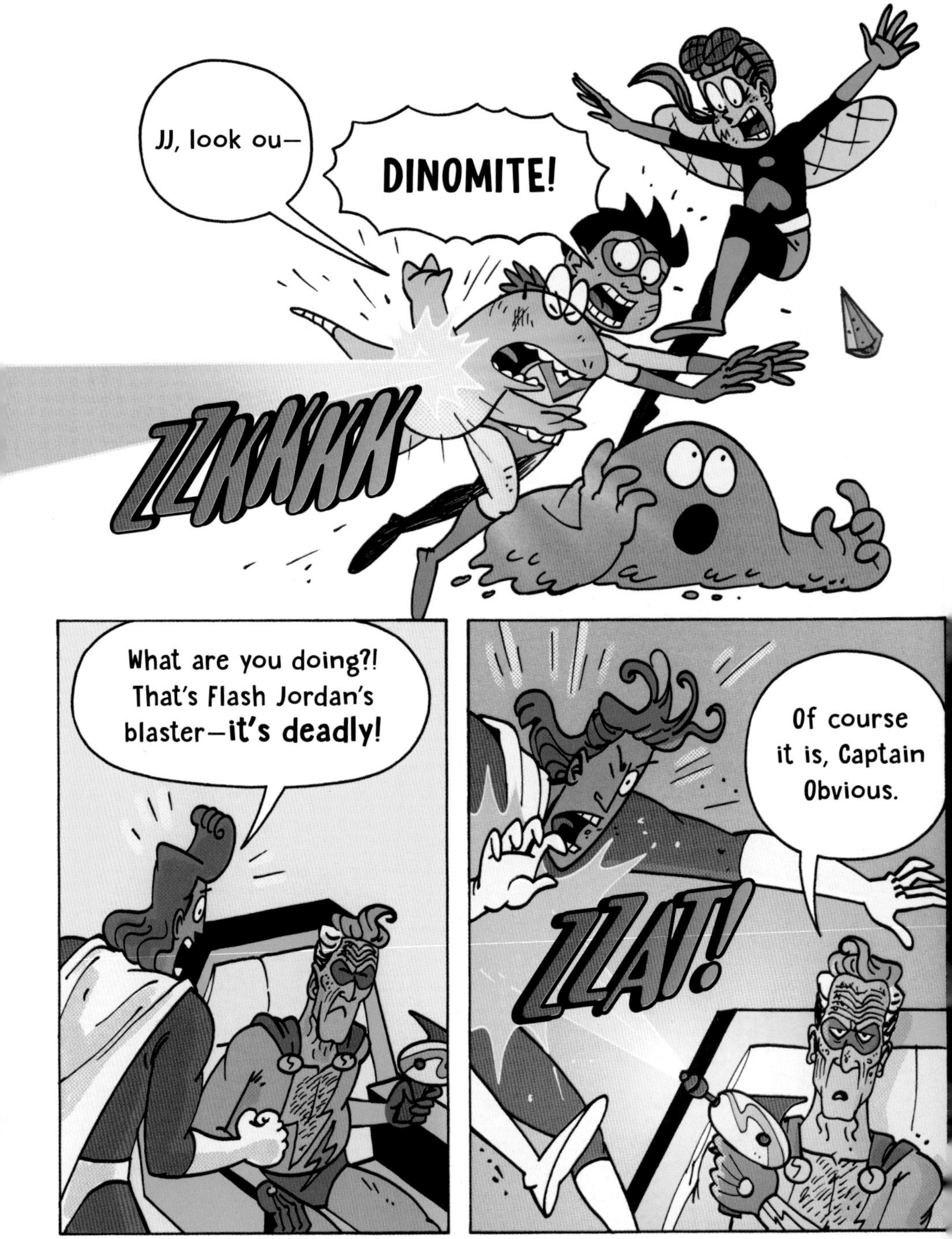
JJ, look ou—
DINOMITE!
What are you doing?! That's Flash Jordan's blaster—it's deadly!
Of course it is, Captain Obvious.
ZZAT!

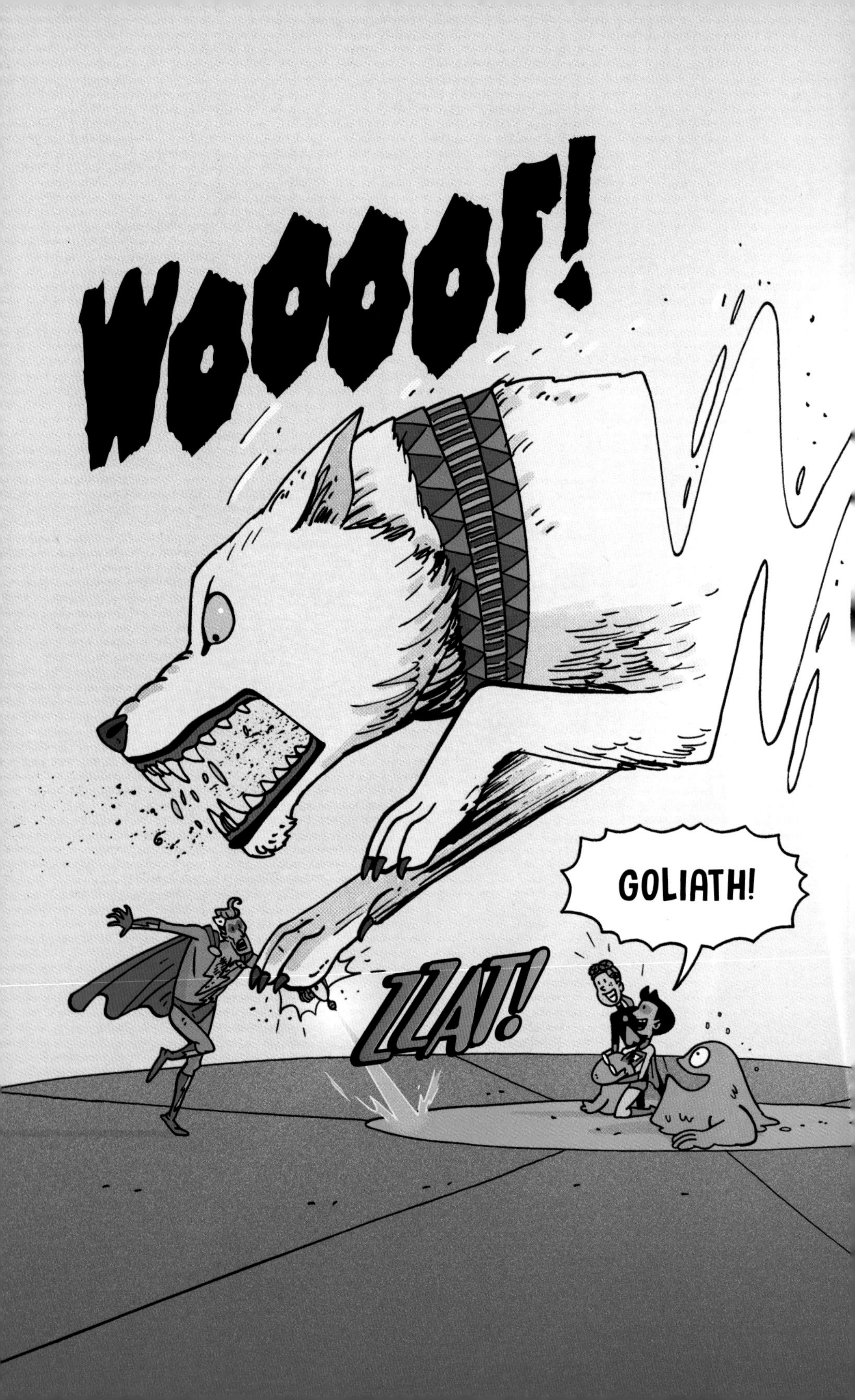
WOOOOF!
GOLIATH!
ZZAT!

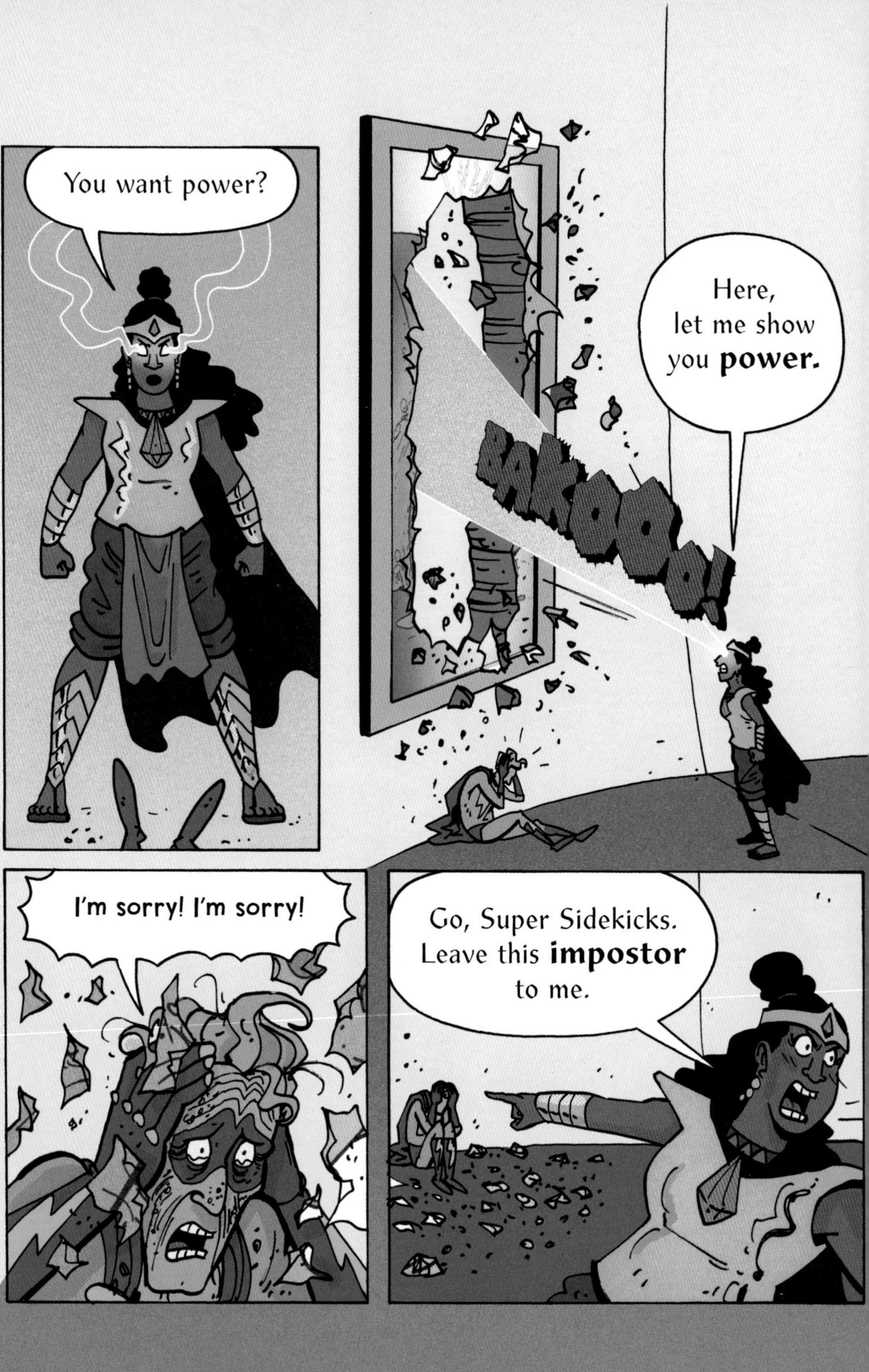
You want power?
Here, let me show you **power.**
BAKOOO!
I'm sorry! I'm sorry!
Go, Super Sidekicks. Leave this **impostor** to me.

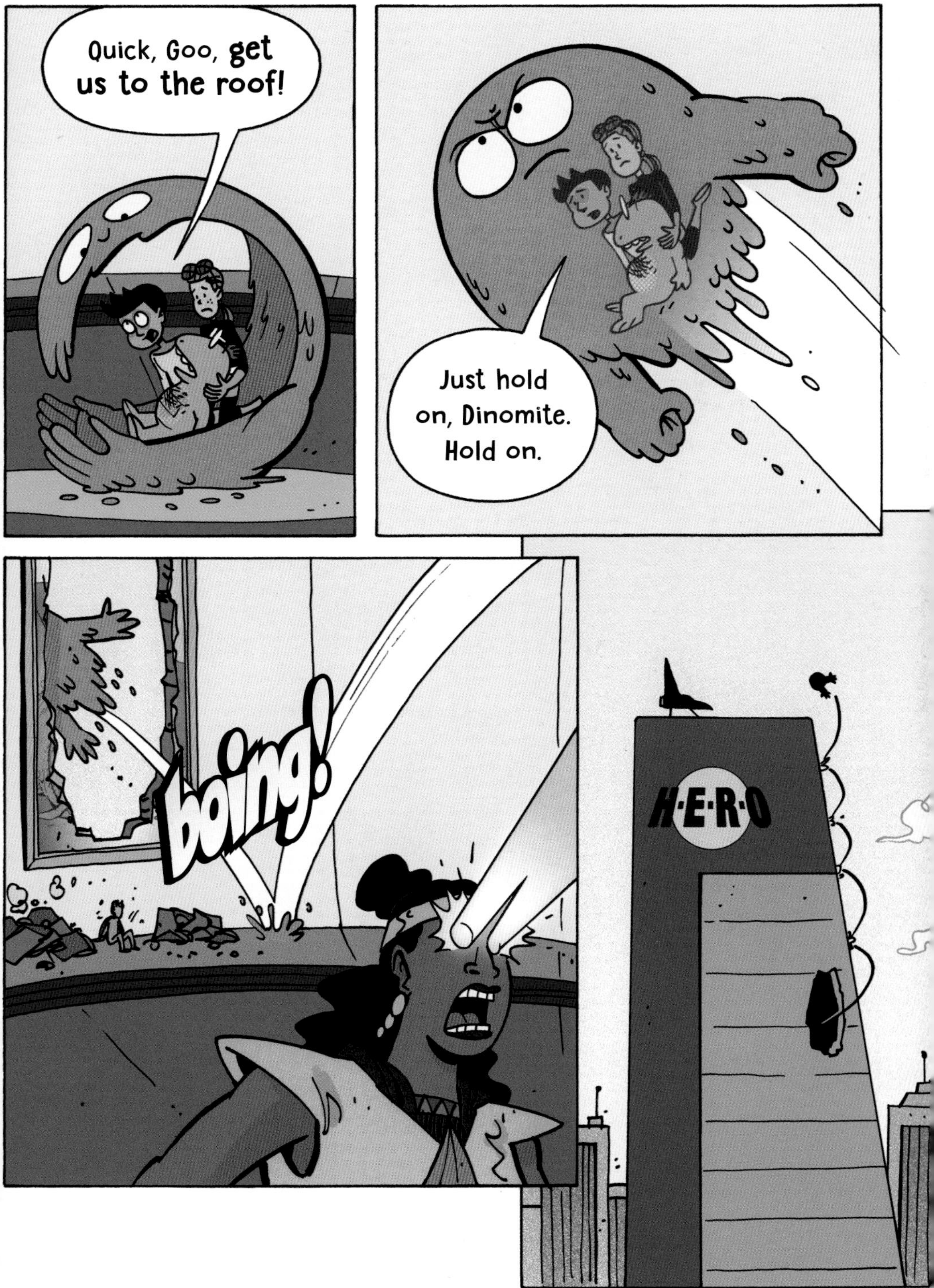
Quick, Goo, get us to the roof!
Just hold on, Dinomite. Hold on.
boing!
H·E·R·O

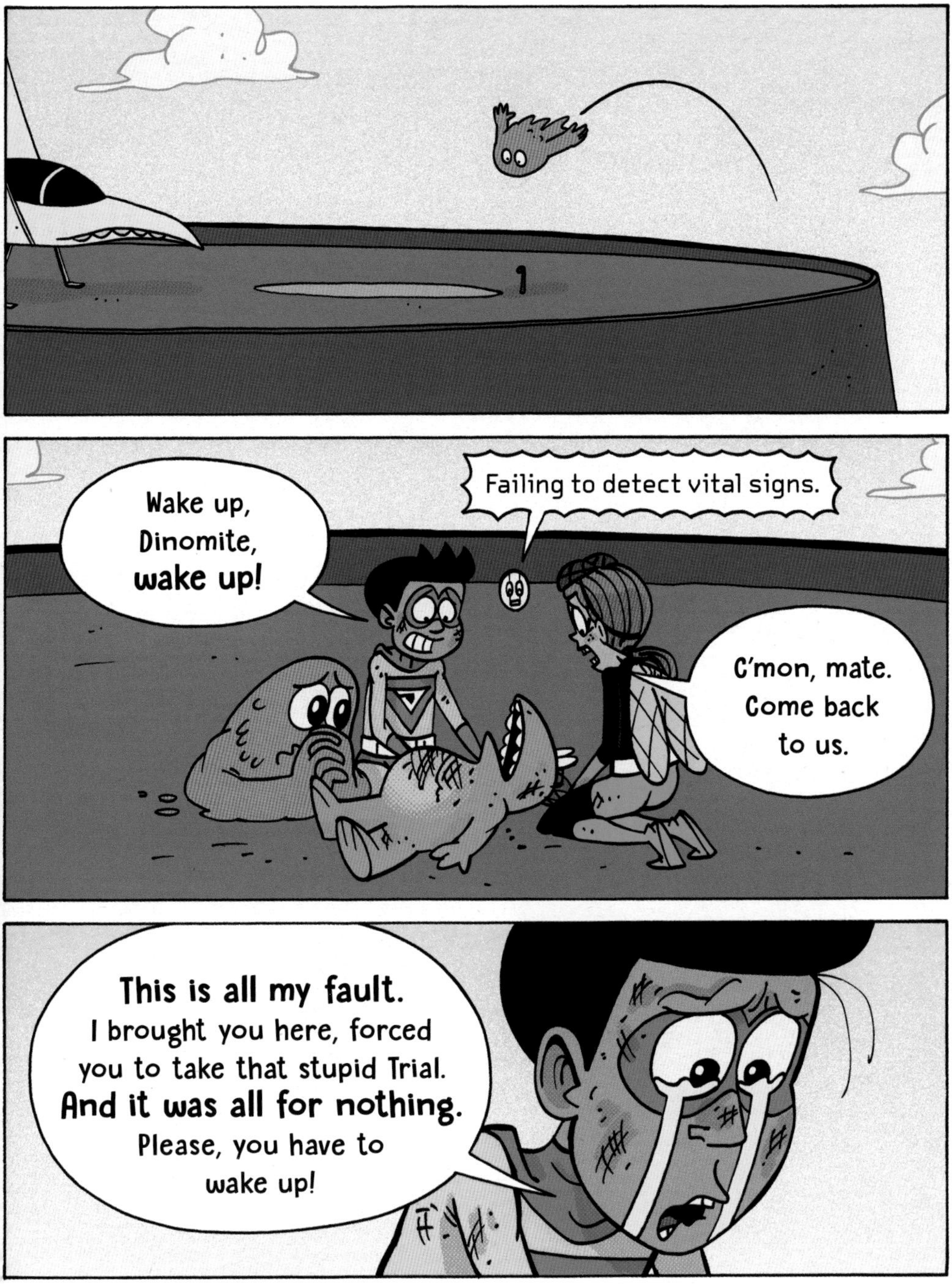

Wake up, Dinomite, wake up!
Failing to detect vital signs.
C'mon, mate. Come back to us.
This is all my fault. I brought you here, forced you to take that stupid Trial. And it was all for nothing. Please, you have to wake up!

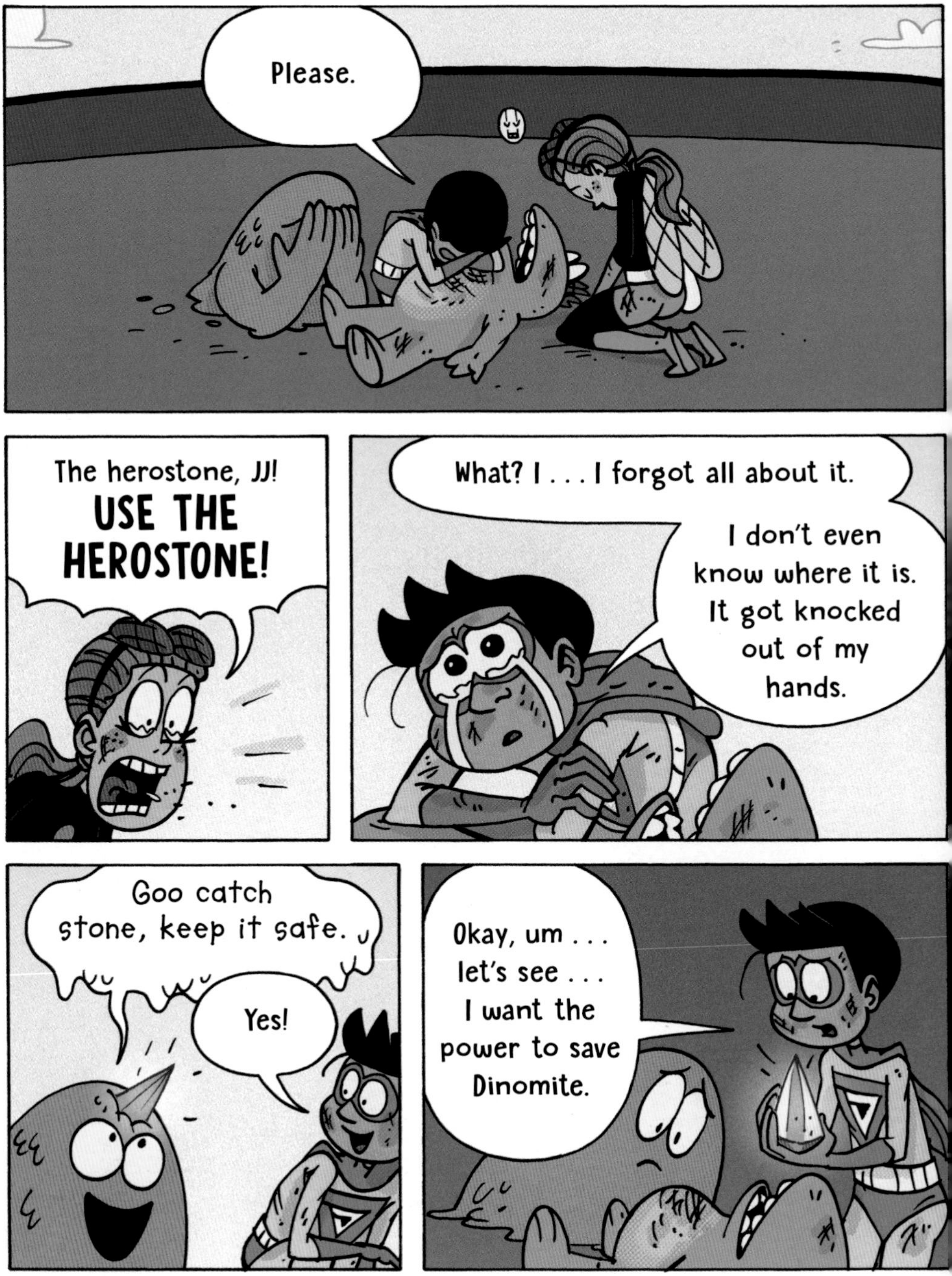
Please.
The herostone, JJ! USE THE HEROSTONE!
What? I . . . I forgot all about it.
I don't even know where it is. It got knocked out of my hands.
Goo catch stone, keep it safe.
Yes!
Okay, um . . . let's see . . . I want the power to save Dinomite.

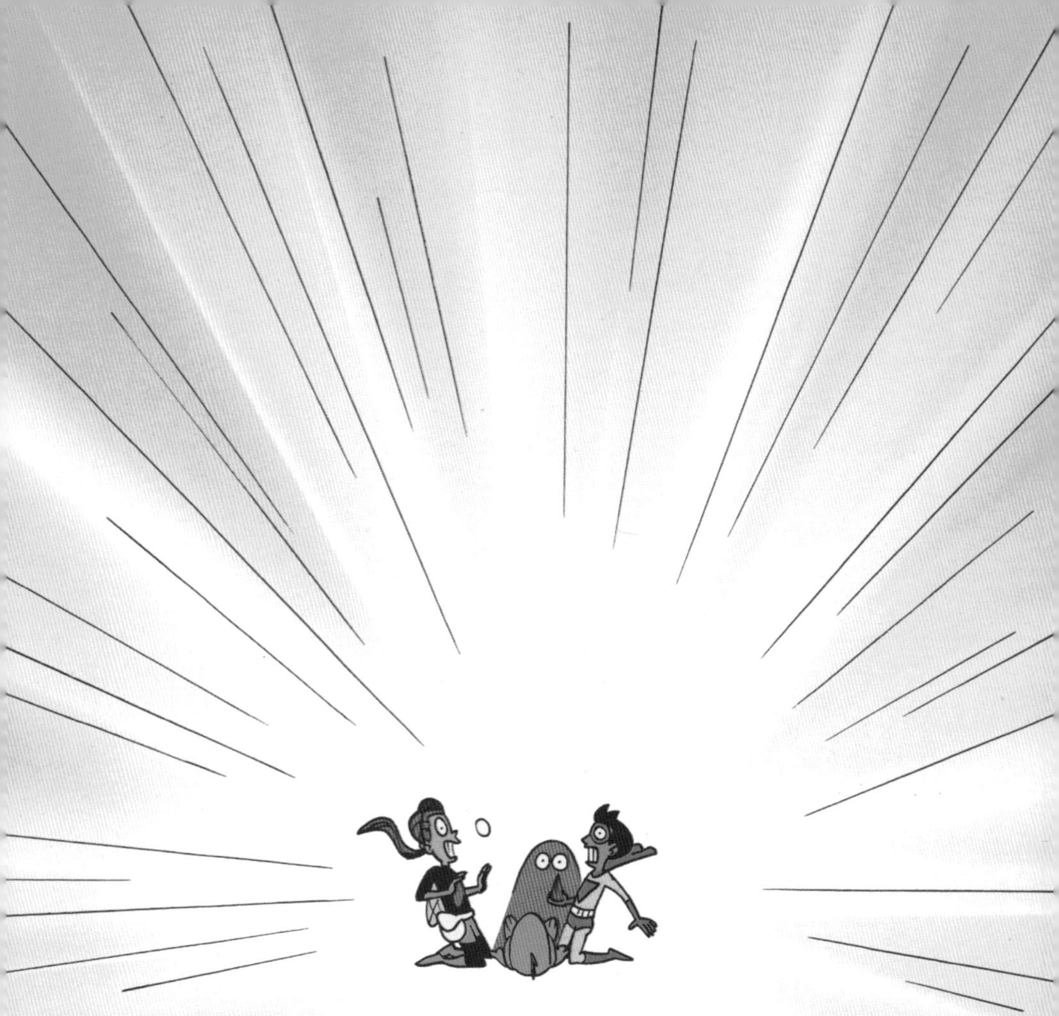

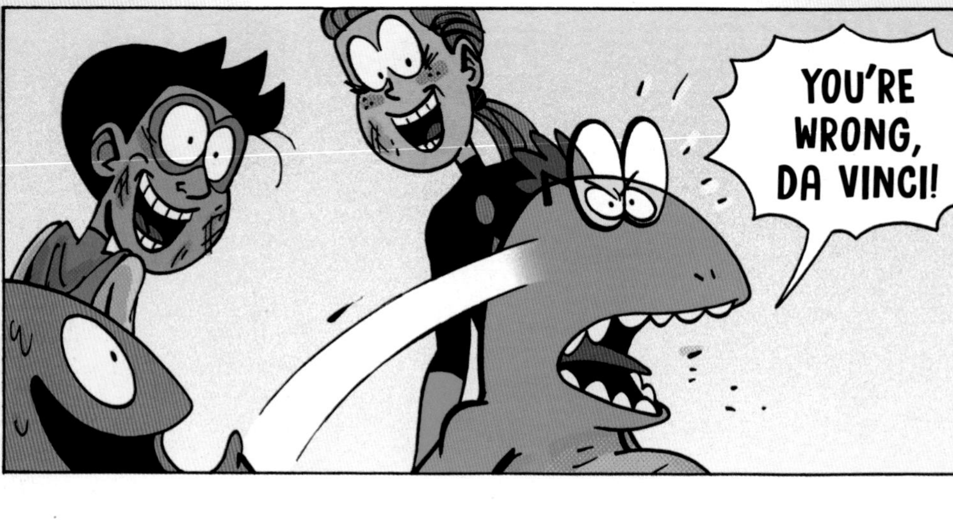
YOU'RE WRONG, DA VINCI!

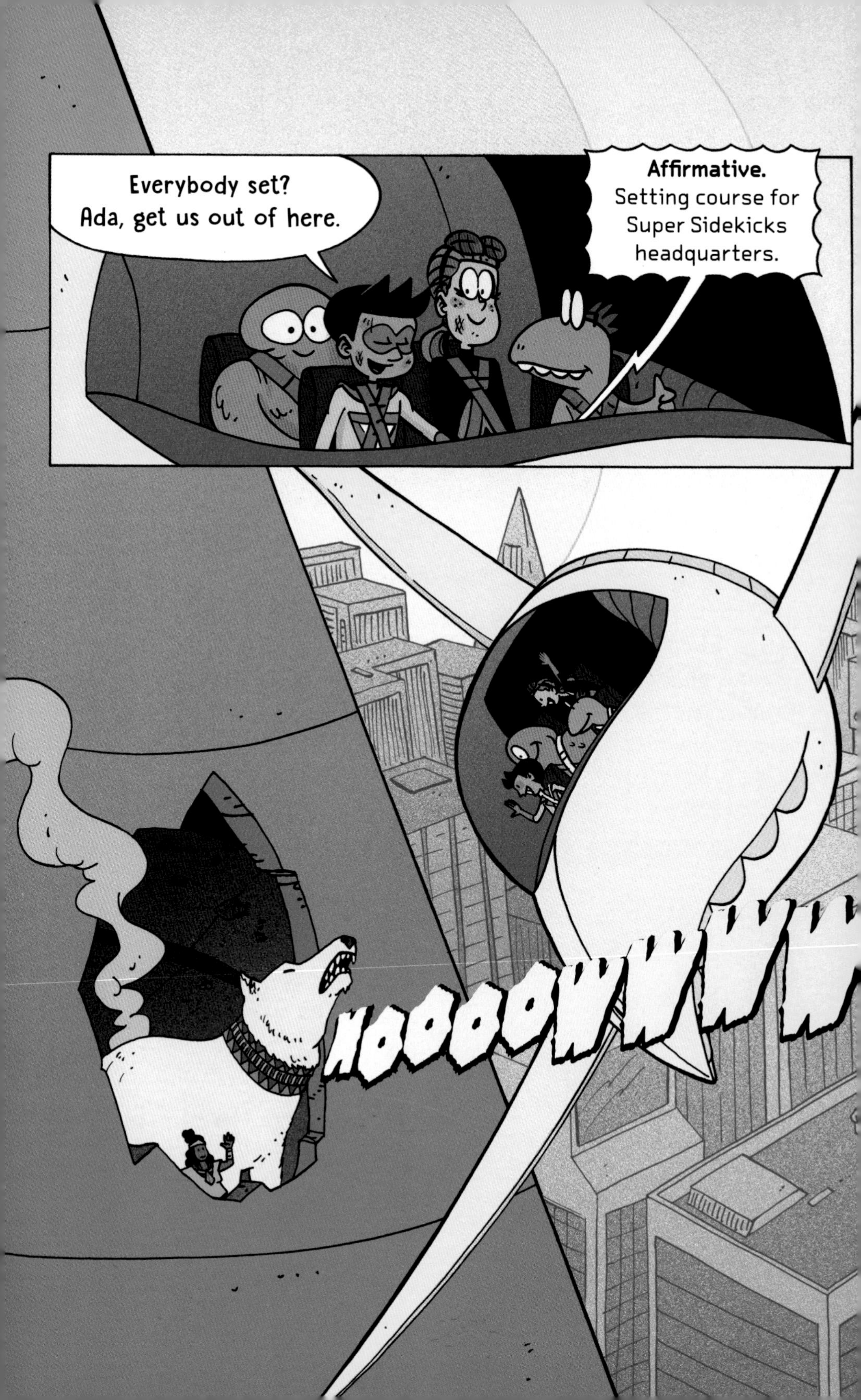
Everybody set?
Ada, get us out of here.
Affirmative.
Setting course for
Super Sidekicks
headquarters.
HOOOOOWWWWW

Chapter

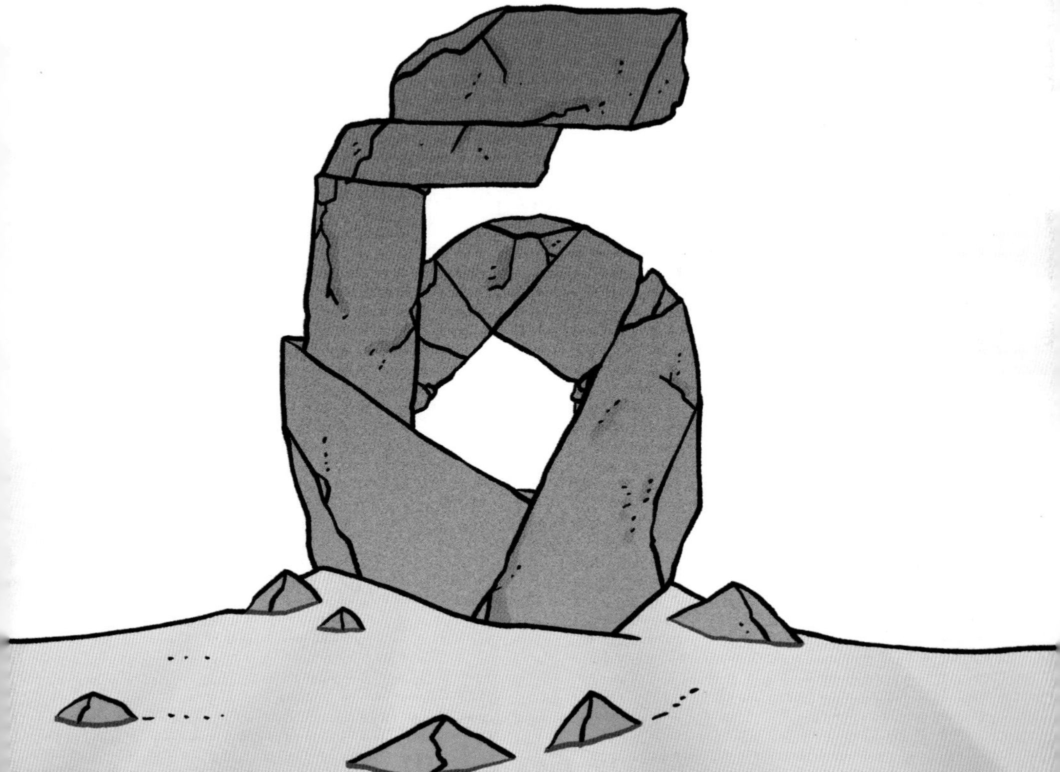
6

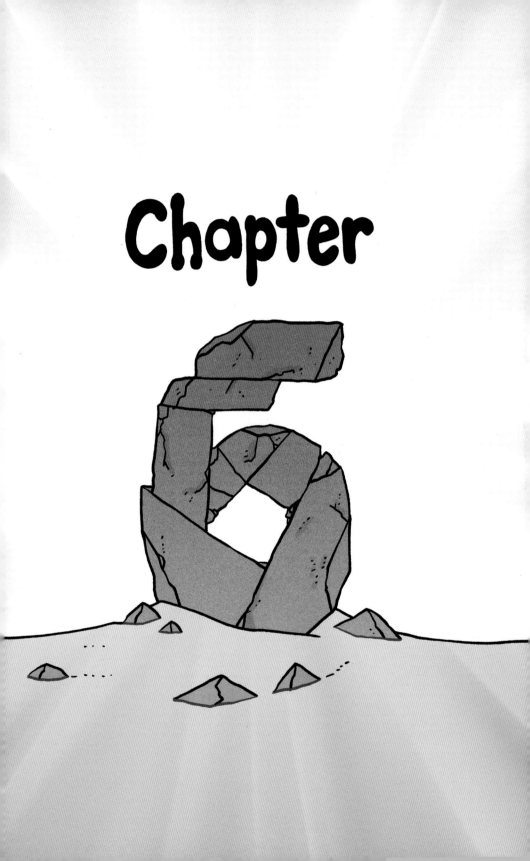

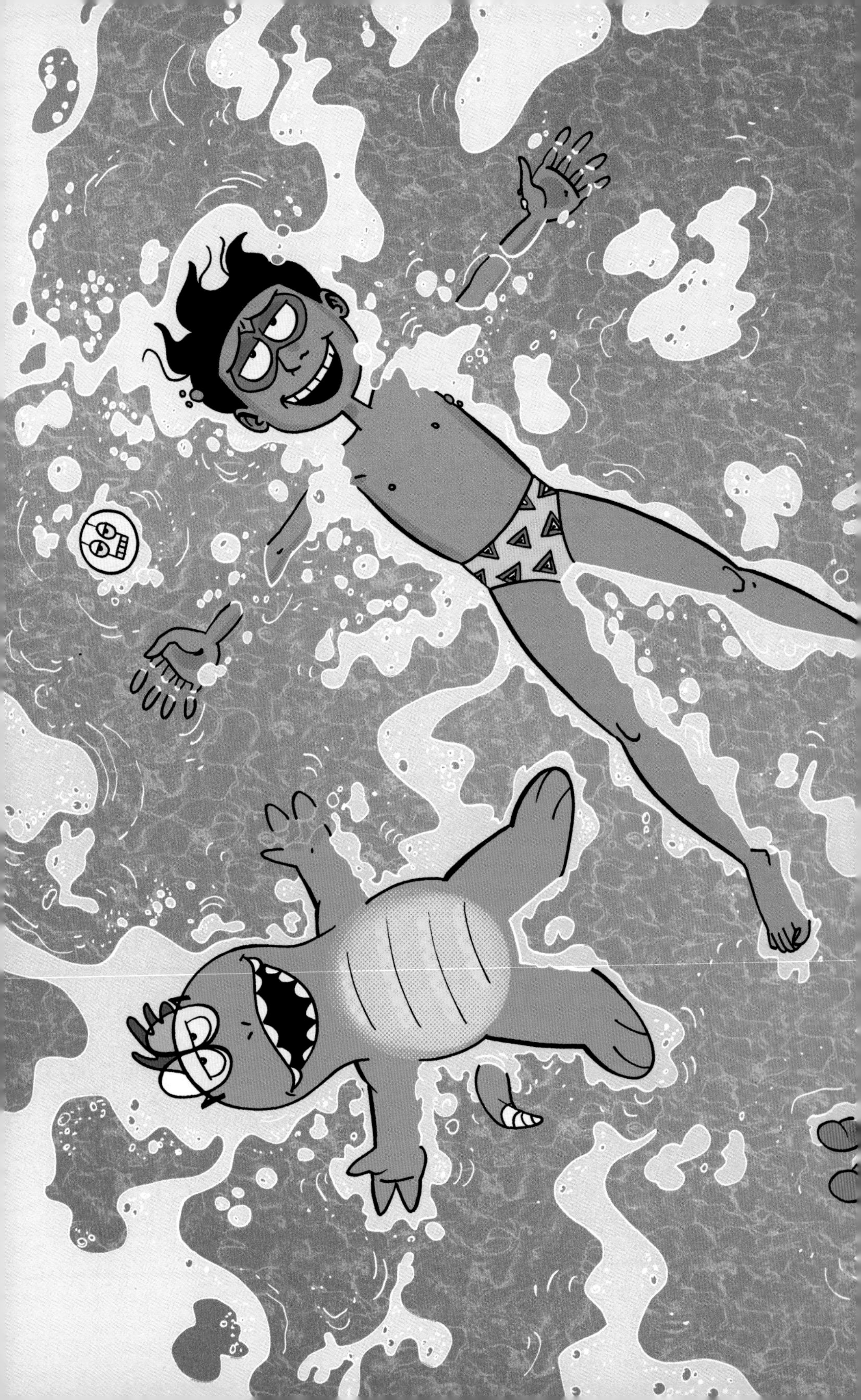

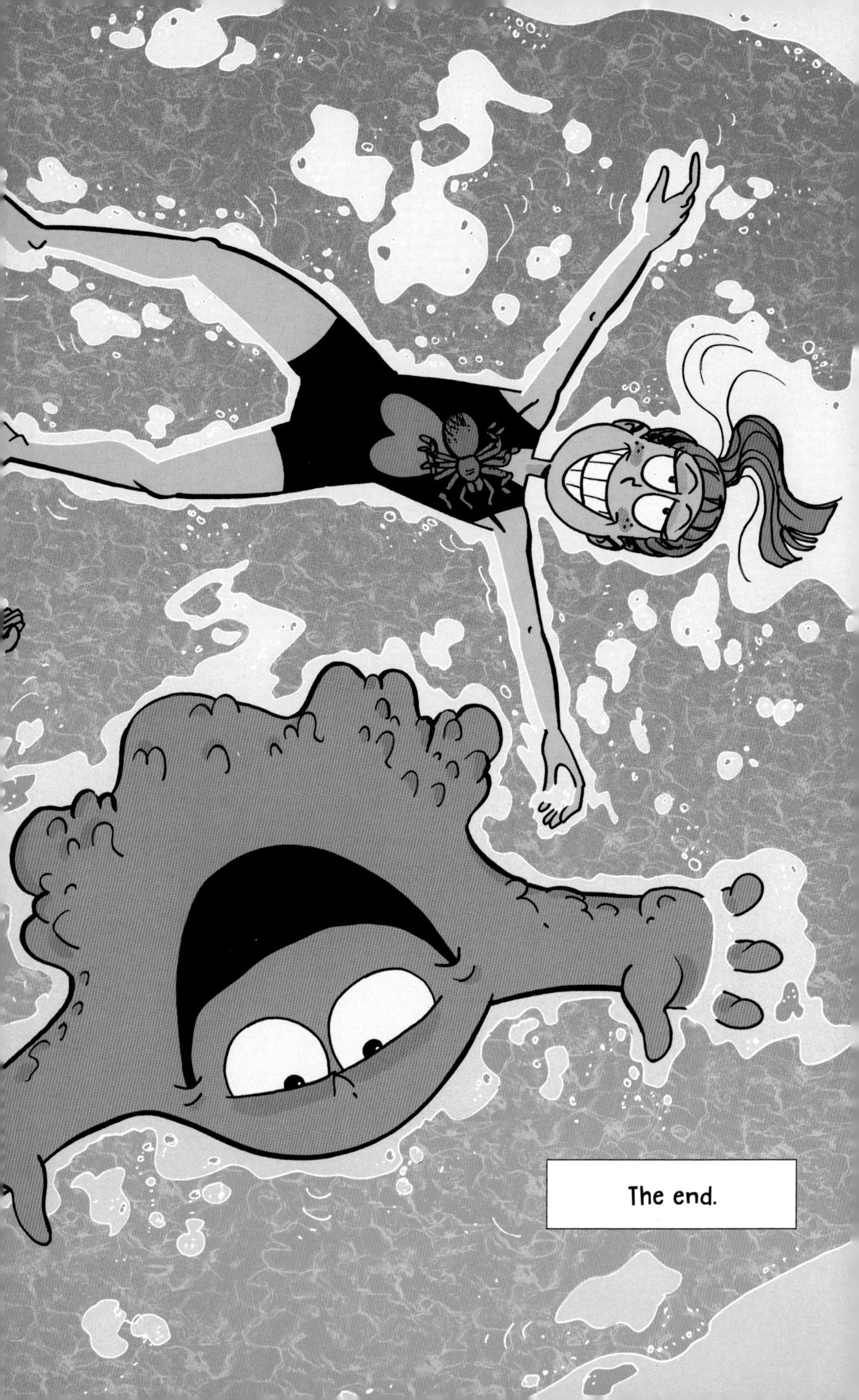
The end.

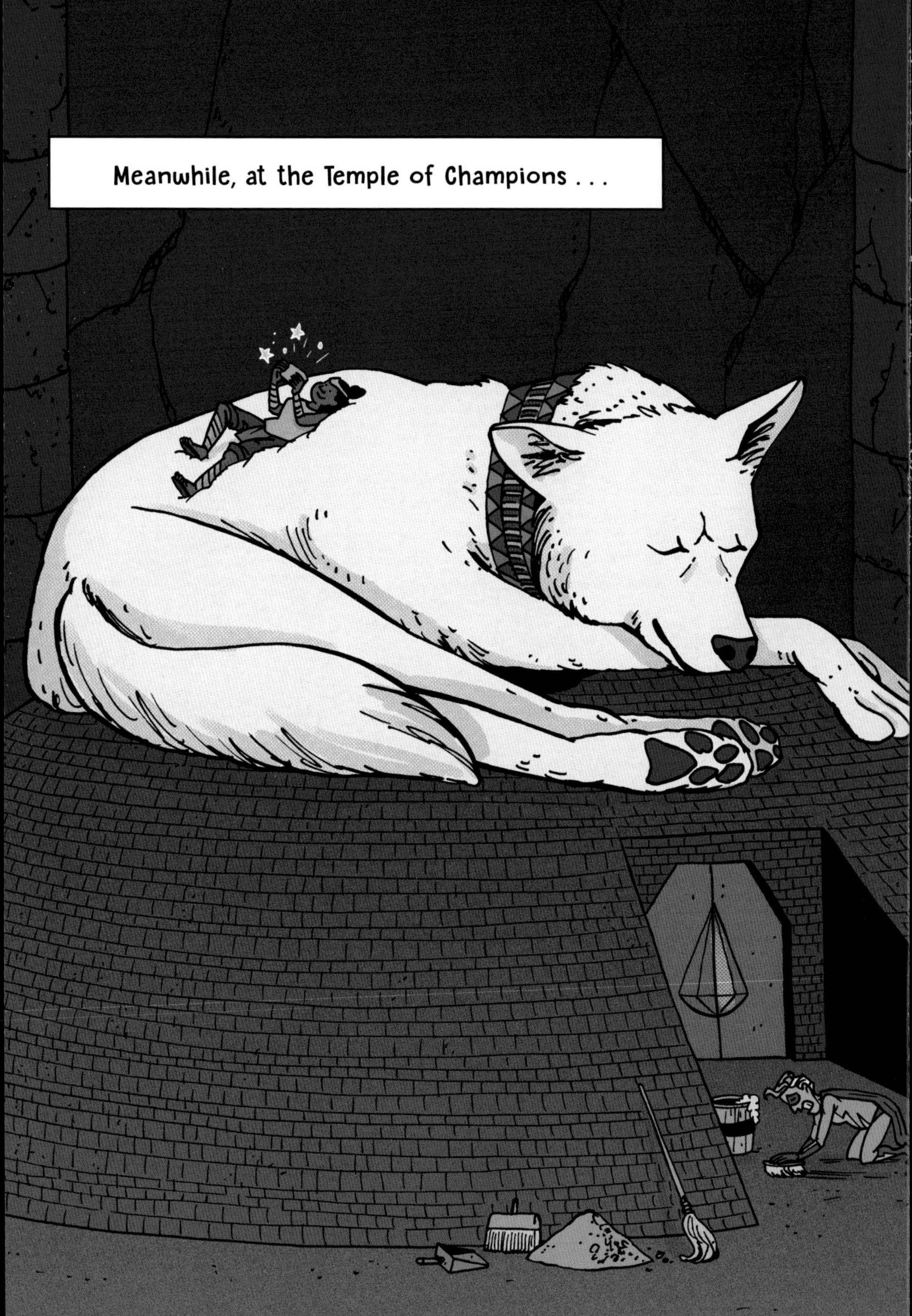
Meanwhile, at the Temple of Champions . . .

HOW HEROES ARE MADE

All heroes have origin stories. Check out how Gavin Aung Than takes the Super Sidekicks from early sketches to final art. It's super!

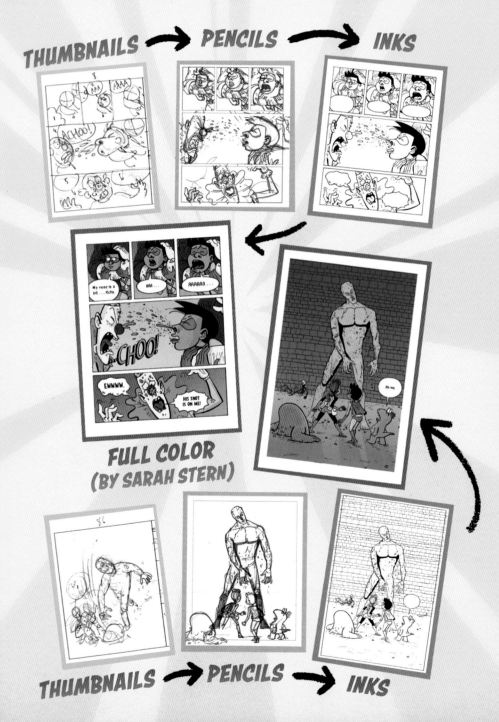

THUMBNAILS → PENCILS → INKS

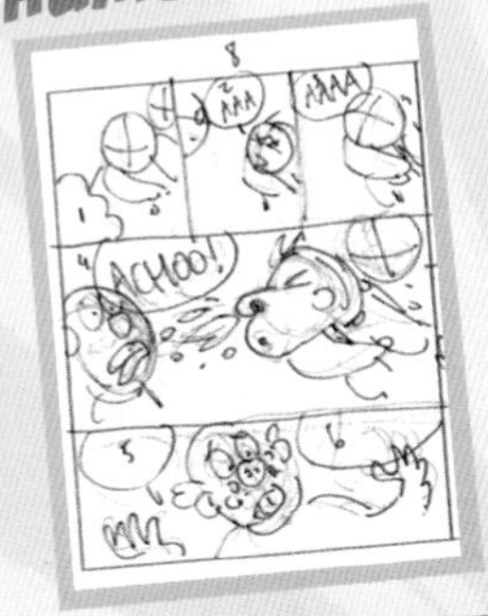

ACHOO!

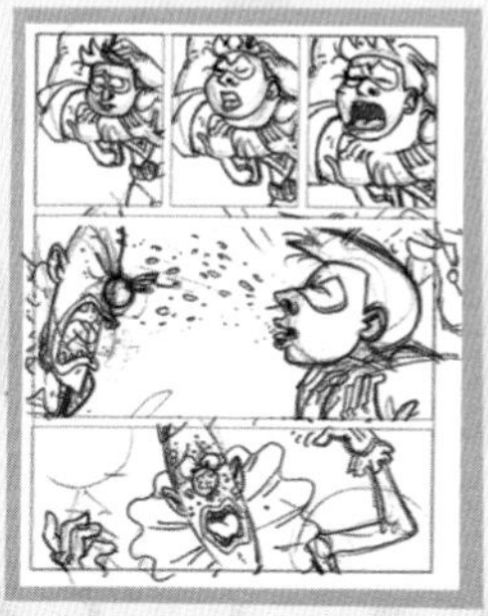

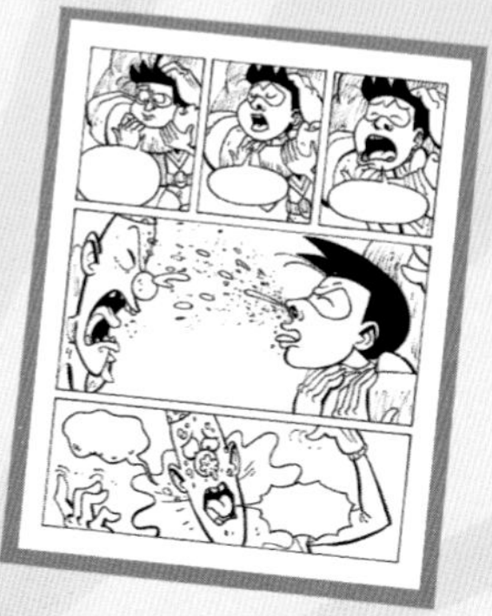

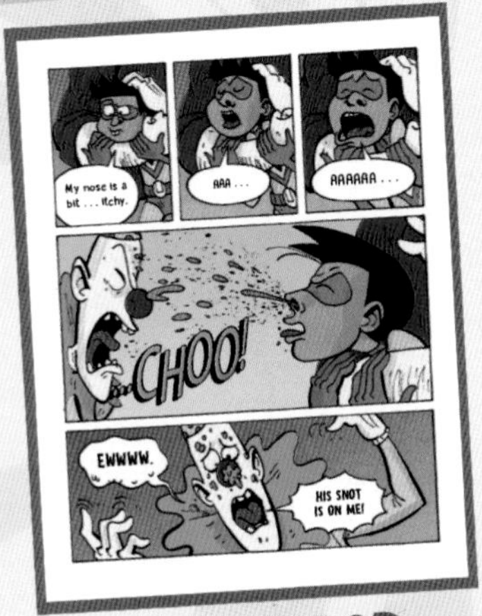

My nose is a bit . . . itchy.
AAA . . .
AAAAAA . . .
CHOO!
EWWWW.
HIS SNOT IS ON ME!

FULL COLOR (BY SARAH STERN)

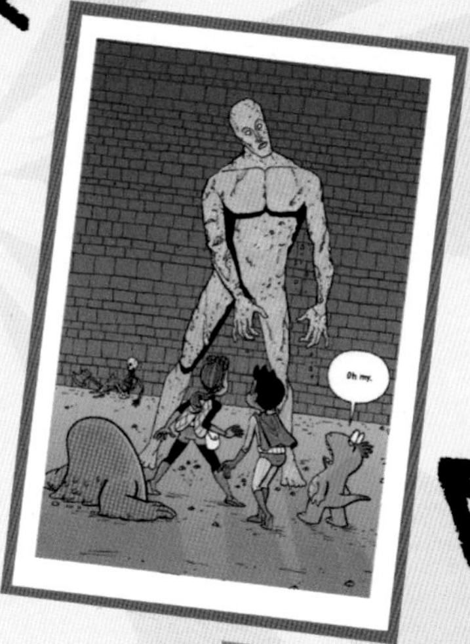

Oh my.

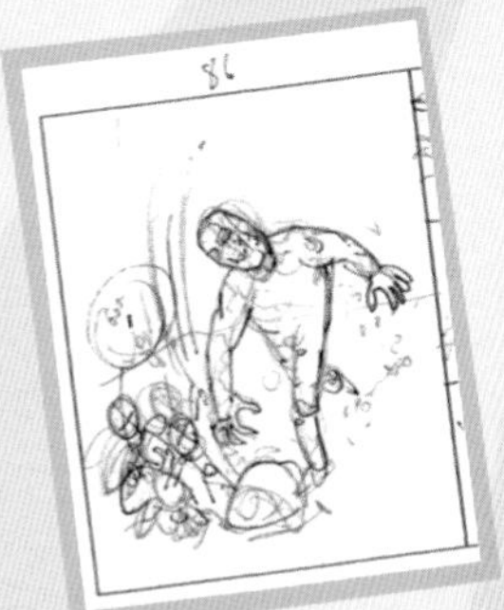

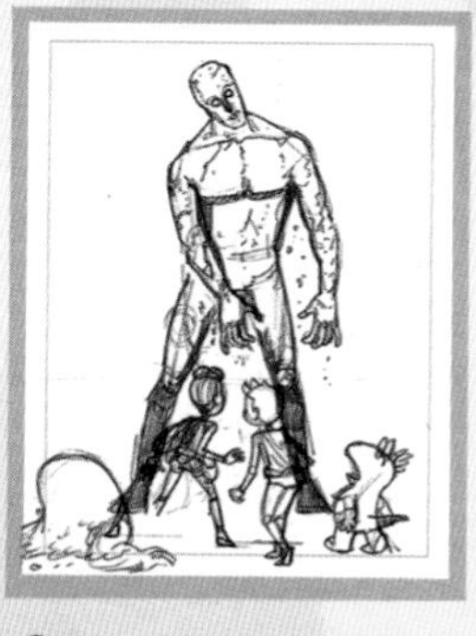

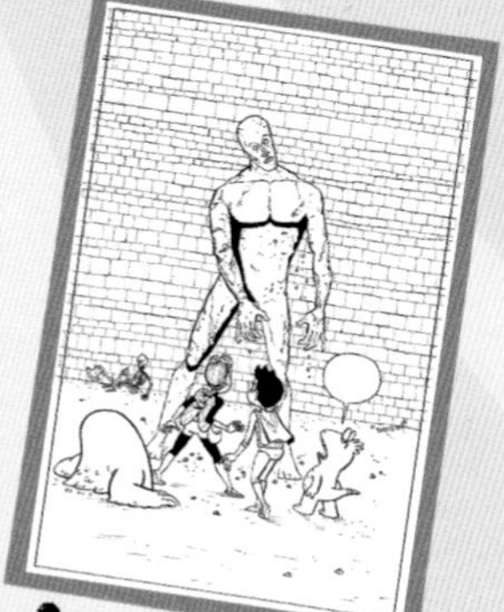

THUMBNAILS → PENCILS → INKS

Gavin Aung Than is a *New York Times* bestselling cartoonist and the creator of the Super Sidekicks series. He once attempted the Trial of Heroes but got a heat rash in the desert and had to turn back before making it to the Temple of Champions.

Visit Gav's website at aungthan.com and follow him on social media!

@ZenPencils

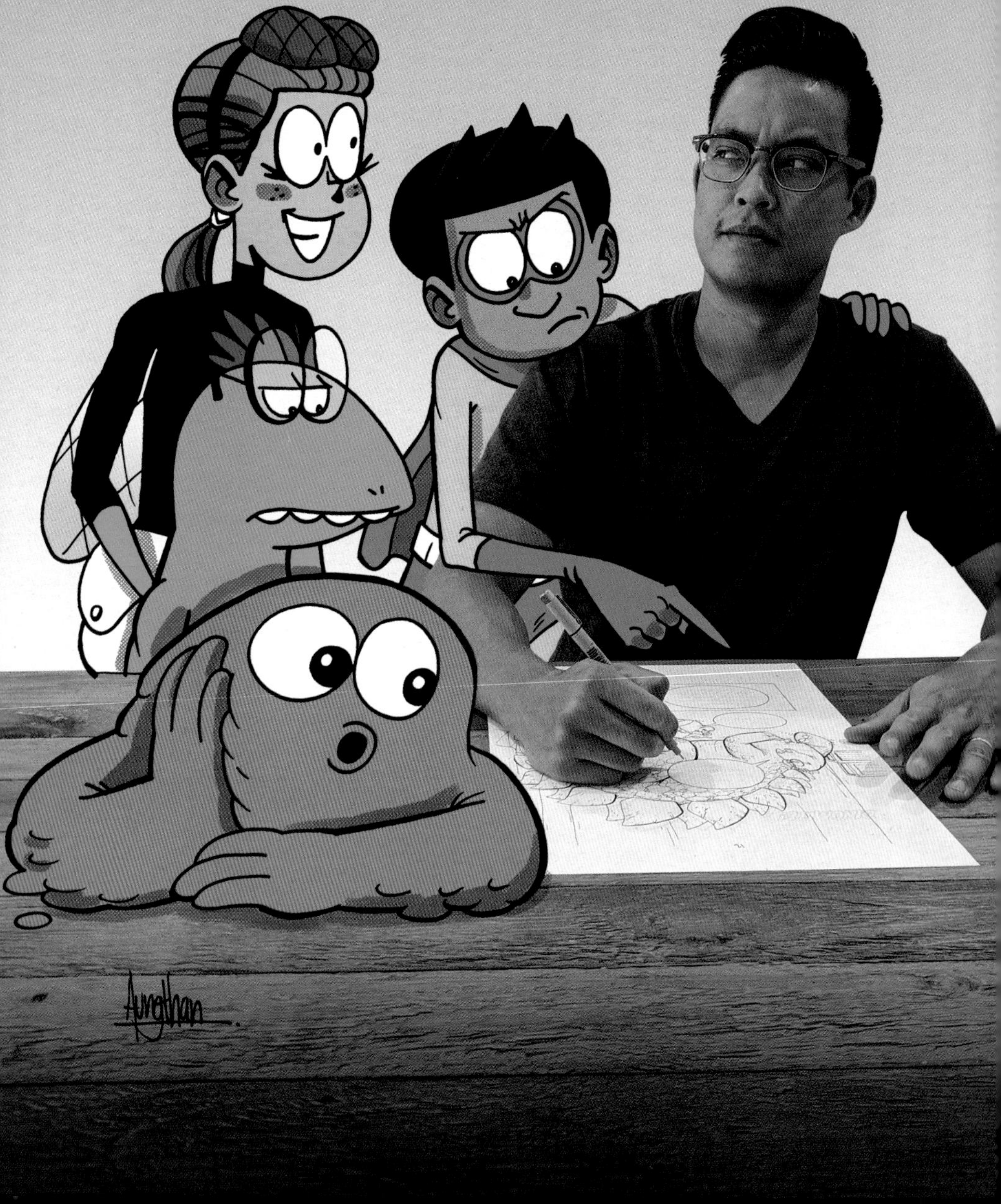

AungThan